**WELL, WHEN I GOT A HIT,
I RAN IT AGAIN. SAME THING
THE SECOND TIME."**

"Mandy . . ."

"It belongs to Captain Brass."

"Jim Brass?"

"He's the only Captain Brass I know. He was in the motel room. The fingerprint was on the doorknob to the bathroom. There was a partial on the nightstand that might be his, but there's not enough of it to get a positive match."

"You're right," Catherine said. "That is interesting. Or it might be, anyway. Do me a favor, Mandy. Let's keep this between us for now, okay?"

Mandy cocked her head, obviously surprised by the request. "Sure," she said. "No problem."

When she left, Catherine looked at her phone—still in her hand, but almost forgotten.

She should call Jim and ask him about the phone number and the fingerprints.

She should call Nick and tell him not to say anything about the number he'd found to anyone else.

Instead, she left the paperwork unfinished on her desk and hurried to her car. She wouldn't have minded if she'd never had to go back to the Rancho Center Motel, although she was convinced that was a pipe dream. But she hadn't anticipated going back quite so soon.

It was like waking up from a bad dream, then going back to sleep and finding herself stuck inside the same nightmare.

Original novels in the CSI series:

CSI: Crime Scene Investigation

CSI: Miami

CSI: NY

CSI:
CRIME SCENE INVESTIGATION™

BRASS IN POCKET
a novel

Jeff Mariotte

Based on the hit CBS series "CSI: Crime Scene Investigation" produced by CBS PRODUCTIONS, a business unit of CBS Broadcasting Inc.

Executive Producers: Jerry Bruckheimer, Carol Mendelsohn, Anthony E. Zuiker, Ann Donahue, Naren Shankar, Cynthia Chvatal, William Petersen, Jonathan Littman

Series created by: Anthony E. Zuiker

POCKET STAR BOOKS
New York   London   Toronto   Sydney

Pocket Star Books
A Division of Simon & Schuster, Inc.
1230 Avenue of the Americas
New York, NY 10020

This book is a work of fiction. Names, characters, places, and incidents either are products of the author's imagination or are used fictitiously. Any resemblance to actual events or locales or persons, living or dead, is entirely coincidental.

First Pocket Star Books paperback edition September 2009

POCKET STAR BOOKS and colophon are registered trademarks of Simon & Schuster, Inc.

For information about special discounts for bulk purchases, please contact Simon & Schuster Special Sales at 1-866-506-1949 or business@simonandschuster.com.

The Simon & Schuster Speakers Bureau can bring authors to your live event. For more information or to book an event contact the Simon & Schuster Speakers Bureau at 1-866-248-3049 or visit our website at www.simonspeakers.com.

Cover design by David Stevenson

Manufactured in the United States of America

10 9 8 7 6 5 4 3 2 1

ISBN 978-1-4165-4517-0

This novel and its author owe enormous debts to Anthony Zuiker, William Petersen, Marg Helgenberger, and the rest of the brilliant CSI cast, crew, writers, and producers, Maryann and Corinne, Howard and Katie and Ed, and Dr. D. P. Lyle, MD.

1

THE BULLETPROOF WINDOW was his first clue.

It shouldn't have been, but Brent McCurdy was beat. He had driven most of the way from Denver, snatching a couple of quick naps while his wife Charlene took her turn behind the wheel. They only had a week's vacation, and they wanted to spend that week in Las Vegas, playing slots and craps, watching shows and having fun . . . not staring at the highway between Vegas and Des Moines. So they powered through, Des Moines to Denver in one stretch and there to Vegas in the next, and by the time they reached the Rancho Center Motel at eight-forty that Friday night, Brent was stick-a-fork-in-it done.

A VACANCY sign burned in pink neon, like the legs of a flamingo set afire from within, but the motel office was dark, the door locked. Brent pressed his hands to the glass and stared inside. The place had a threadbare carpet with so many cigarette burns they looked like part of the pattern, and a scarred Formica counter with a big analog clock on the wall behind it. Had there been anyone inside, that person would have looked out and seen a man who was barely describable, of average height and average weight, with the slightest paunch swelling his dark blue polo shirt. His hair was brown, not long but not exceedingly short. His eyes were brown and unremarkable. In the eleventh grade, Brent's history teacher had recommended that he consider a career in the FBI, because he was a person who could blend in. He had decided against it, and now he managed a chain sporting goods store back in Iowa, and sometimes—but only rarely—regretted that decision.

Brent noticed a window built into the wall, almost like a drive-up window in a fast food joint, that could be accessed from behind the counter. He left the door and walked over to that window, finding thick, bulletproof plastic, scratched and fogged with age, with a little slot at the bottom to shove money or a credit card under and a small metal grate to speak through. A faint light glowed through the window, coming from a hallway he could barely make out. Looking through the Plexiglas was like trying to see through a blizzard. He'd had that experience a few times, which was why he had scheduled his vacation days for summertime. Driving in whiteout conditions didn't make for a relaxing beginning or end of a trip.

Finding the window tipped him off to the various signals that hadn't registered at first. Those had been, in fact, broken liquor bottles crunching under his feet as he walked from his parking place. Those had been used condoms and an empty syringe mixed in with greasy burger wrappers and lipstick-stained cigarette butts up against the curb. And those women he had barely noticed, coming out of a room at the end of the building? Well, back home he didn't see a lot of women in sparkly, low-cut spandex tops and skirts so short they could almost have qualified as belts, swaying with practiced near steadiness on four-inch heels, but that didn't mean he had never seen hookers before. Once in a while on the streets of Des Moines, but on TV, mostly. He had pay cable, after all. He should have known at a glance what they were.

He looked back toward his Ford Escape, a vehicle that had never before seemed so aptly named. Charlene and the kids were still inside, waiting, every bit as tired as he was, if not more so. They just wanted to get checked in and put their heads down on comfortable pillows. Brent had yet to inspect the pillows so he couldn't have testified to their comfort, but there was a young guy emerging into the hot July night from a room five doors down from that bulletproof window, and he wore an expression of such rapturous bliss that Brent guessed he was either high or he had just gone through a profound religious experience.

The Rancho Center Motel didn't seem to lend itself to the latter.

He should have done more thorough online research. The location had been convenient to both the Strip and Fremont Street, and the price was definitely right. But this joint was no family motel.

The pool, surrounded by a chain-link fence out in the middle of the parking lot, didn't even have water in it.

He could tell by a shadow on an inside wall that someone was coming down the interior hallway, toward the bulletproof window. Brent didn't want to have a face-to-face conversation with anyone who worked here. He didn't even care about getting his deposit back. He could call and cancel the reservation later, and he would only lose one night's rent. All he wanted was to flee this dump and find another room somewhere in the city—a room at a place in which he wouldn't feel that his life and the lives of his family members were in danger at every moment.

He turned away from the oncoming shadow and hurried to the Escape. When he opened the door, the dome light came on and Charlene blinked at him and raised a hand to her cheek. "Is everything okay, honey?"

"Nothing's okay," he said. "We're going somewhere else."

"Somewhere else? You mean a different motel? Why?"

"Because this place is awful," he said. Brent Junior and Carnie were sitting up in back, sleepy-eyed but awake, so he didn't want to go into a lot of detail. There was no sense terrifying the kids on their first night in Las Vegas.

"But I wanna go to bed!" Carnie cried. She was only four and hadn't been looking forward to the trip anyway, except for the promise of a swimming pool at the motel. She shook a stuffed lion at him with animal ferocity. "I'm tired!"

"We're all tired, Carnie." Brent closed his door and clicked his seat belt into place. "We'll find a better place. It won't take long."

"But we have reservations here," Charlene said. "What if there's a convention in town or something and we can't find another place?"

"There's always a convention in Las Vegas, Charlene, but there are something like a million hotel rooms in the city. I read that somewhere." He was probably exaggerating, but there were a lot of them. He had read the precise number, but if he was any good with numbers he probably wouldn't be making his living with bats and balls and racquets and shoes. "We'll drive around all night if we have to, but we're not staying here."

"Aren't most of them more expensive than this one? That's what you said, right? This one was a bargain?"

He put the vehicle in reverse and backed out of the space. "So we'll skip the shows, or cut back on meals. I don't care. This place—"

Brent Junior had been about to register an objection of his own, his six-year-old whine already gathering steam, when a loud bang sounded from behind them and silenced the boy. Brent thought it was the sound of a door being slammed. He shoved the SUV into drive and stepped on the gas. The engine's growl nearly drowned out screams from the motel. But then he heard shouting and a sharp report, louder than the first bang, and saw a bright spark near the pool that must have been a muzzle flash.

"Somebody's shooting!" he shouted. "Call nine-one-one!"

Charlene was already pawing her phone from her purse as the vehicle surged from the parking lot, cutting the angle wrong and bouncing off the curb with two wheels. Brent didn't care.

He just wanted to get gone, while he still could.

"Catherine's in charge."

Those had been Gil Grissom's last words before leaving the lab for the airport. He was flying off to Washington, D.C., where he would be a featured speaker at a symposium on forensic entomology, after which he would testify before a congressional committee about the necessity of public financing for small city crime labs. As it was, most rural, small town, and small city police forces sent their caseloads to the big city labs, which were already backed up with their own big city crime. The additional workload slowed everything down, a vicious circle that left felonies unsolved and criminals on the streets. Gil would be more comfortable talking about the insects that frequented dead bodies, but his testimony before Congress would be sincere and convincing, and Catherine Willows couldn't help feeling a tickle of associational pride at the knowledge that her boss was helping to make a difference on a national level.

She also didn't mind being in charge. She had kind of enjoyed it, in fact, when she had temporarily been swing shift supervisor. If she rather than Gil had been the actual supervisor, the lab would be a different place, but primarily in small, cosmetic ways. Gil ran it well and she had few real complaints about his leadership. Still, she was an ambitious woman with ideas of her own and the drive to want to put them into action. But if Gil hadn't been out of town, she might not have had to go to the Rancho Center Motel, which was just the kind of hole that made her want to burn her clothes and scrub her skin down with steel wool when she was finished. On this hot night, with the overloaded window air conditioners dripping onto the sidewalk, the building itself seemed to be sweating. The parking lot held a peculiar reek all its own. And she hadn't even reached the DB yet.

That was still waiting for her inside Room 119. The door from the parking lot was open. Catherine and Nick Stokes had to pass under yellow crime scene tape and sign a log sheet to get to it . . . a far cry from the more exclusive spots around town, where the crowd control ropes were crushed velvet and the bouncers didn't wear uniforms and badges.

"Take a deep breath, Nicky," she said outside the door. "Bad as it is out here, it'll be much worse in there."

Nick raised an eyebrow and twitched his lips, the closest thing to a smile he could muster at the moment. He knew the score. Catherine didn't think the reminder would offend him, but she had to watch herself. She was nobody's mom but Lindsey's, and Lindsey didn't work at the Las Vegas Police Department's crime lab.

The motel room looked pretty much as she had

expected it to. She had been here before—this wasn't the joint's first homicide—and this wasn't the kind of place that spent a lot of money on regular re-models. A bed sat in the middle of the room, with a nightstand made of some woodlike substance next to it. A small dresser stood against the opposite wall, near the smashed-in door. Lying in the rubble, just inside, was the small black handheld battering ram, like the kind police used for hard entries, that had al-most certainly done the smashing. There was a TV chained to a rack in one corner, six feet off the floor, and its remote was chained to the nightstand. The carpeting was of a mixture of colors chosen primarily for its ability to disguise vomit stains, and in the event of a fire would probably immediately turn into a poisonous gas. The walls were painted white, but on top of the paint was what looked like a year's worth of dust, giving it a flat gray appearance.

The foulest motel room's many sins faded in sig-nificance, however, when there was a body inside, and this one was no exception.

Assistant coroner David Phillips had already ar-rived. When Catherine entered the room, he looked up from the body, blinking behind his glasses. "Vic-tim's been dead less than thirty minutes," he said by way of greeting. "Obviously there's no rigor present yet. He took two bullets. First one through the left trapezius muscle; the second entered through the lower lip and exited through the top of the skull." He tilted his head toward the ceiling, and Catherine saw the knot of blood, brains, and hair pasted there.

"Hello to you, too," Catherine said.

"Oh, yeah, hi, Catherine. Nick."

"Hey," Nick said.

"So I'm guessing that's our COD?" Catherine asked. "The head shot, anyway?"

"That's my initial determination," David said. "Vic is a thirty-six-year-old male. Wallet in his back jeans pocket, with a Nevada DL identifying him as—"

"Deke Freeson," Catherine said. She had walked around the body far enough to see his face. What was left of it, anyway. In life it had been reasonably handsome—not as square-jawed as Nick Stokes, maybe, but with a good firm chin, full lips, a nose that jutted forward like it meant business but not so far it rounded the corner before the rest of him. Deke's eyes were his best feature, a brilliant blue that people remembered and remarked on long after even the most cursory meeting with him. She found herself oddly pleased that the bullet had missed them. His hair was sandy and spiked. She had, on more than one occasion, seen him out on the town with some showgirl or other. Had he ever asked, she might have dated him herself.

"Yeah, that's Deke," Nick said.

"You both know him?" David asked. He seemed surprised.

"Everybody in Vegas knows Deke," Nick said.

"I don't."

"You run with the wrong crowd," Catherine said. "Or maybe it's the right one, I don't know. He was a private detective. Strictly low budget, but he's a decent guy and a good investigator."

"He was on the job, years ago," Nick added. "Ex-military, too. I think he was a Gulf War vet."

"Well, there's a photocopied PI license in the wallet too, which I was about to tell you. I guess that comes as no surprise, though."

"Not at all," Catherine said. She hadn't known Deke Freeson well, but like Nick had said, everybody in Las Vegas knew him. Every cop, at least. Every dead body was sad, but the sorrow sliced with a sharper edge when the victim was someone you knew.

"There's a gun here," David said. "Close to his right hand. I think he was holding it when he fell."

"Desert Eagle?" Nick asked. "Fifty caliber? Brushed chrome?"

"That's right."

"Deke did love his firepower," Catherine said. "You found a license for that too, right?"

"Yeah. Maybe it would be easier if you tell me what you don't know about this guy, and then I can try to fill in the blanks."

"That should be obvious," Catherine said.

"Obvious how?"

"What we don't know," she said, "is who killed him."

2

AFTER THE PHOTOGRAPHS were taken and David Phillips had completed his preliminary examination, what was left of Deke Freeson was taken away. Catherine and Nick were not so lucky.

Their task was to process the room, which naturally required them to remain inside it. The smell was horrific, blood and urine and sweat competing for dominance with less immediately identifiable stenches. The room contained more fluids than Catherine cared to think about. Her first pass through, she focused on semen; the blood was more or less apparent, and by locating and identifying semen, she would be less likely to stand or sit in it or to accidentally place a hand in it. Her hands were gloved in multiple layers of latex, so she could peel off any that became contaminated. But still . . . she had her limits of tolerance, and the Rancho Center Motel room seemed determined to test them all.

She started with a handheld UV light, under

which semen would often fluoresce. Holding the light, she moved in a careful pattern, sweeping the room to find each incidence. As expected, she found multiple specimens, none of them particularly fresh (and several, to her dismay, apparently having survived multiple launderings of the sheets and bedspread). Each spot had to be swabbed, and the swabs treated with alpha-naphthyl phosphate and Brentamine Fast Blue. More often than not, the swabs turned purple almost immediately, indicating positive results. All the spots were dry, which made collecting and bagging them easier, but given the sheer number of them in the room, it was still a long process. Each would have to be analyzed back at the lab, where DNA analysis would help determine who had been in the room. Given the age of the stains, she suspected they wouldn't factor into the investigation, but until she knew for certain when Deke Freeson had arrived at the room, and what he was doing there, she couldn't afford to discount any potential leads.

Nick, meanwhile, had been taking a more global approach. After collecting bullets from the ceiling and headboard, he rummaged through drawers and the closet and the single suitcase and purse found in the room. "The purse belongs to Antoinette O'Brady of Las Vegas," he announced. "There's a wallet and cell phone still inside. Plenty of cash. She's fifty-six years old." He showed Catherine the driver's license picture. Antoinette O'Brady looked young for her age and wore her long blond hair and makeup in ways that made her look like she was trying to come across as younger still.

"If she lives in town, what's she doing staying in a dump like this?" Catherine asked.

"And where is she now? Maybe she's the shooter, not a motel guest. The room was registered to Freeson. He checked in yesterday."

"Which doesn't necessarily mean that one or both of them weren't here before that, either staying with someone else or registered under a different name. I doubt this place is too picky about checking ID. We'll have to look for any connections between them," Catherine said. "What about that suitcase?"

"I'm pretty sure it's not Deke's," Nick said. "Clothing and toiletries are consistent with the woman's height and weight, based on her license."

"How old is the license?"

"Less than a year old."

"Most people shave a few pounds off when they get a new license," Catherine said. "But if it's that recent, chances are it's in the ballpark. And I've never heard of anyone bringing a suitcase on a hit."

"Even if they did, they wouldn't unpack their toiletries in the bathroom," Nick observed. "It looks like she expected to stay for a while. Few days, anyway."

"A few days in this room might be enough to make me start shooting people too," Catherine said. She had finished with fluids, and used tweezers to lift a hair from the carpet and drop it into a small plastic envelope. Like the semen and blood, it would go to the lab for analysis. Chances were good it would have nothing to do with Deke Freeson or

Antoinette O'Brady, but it had to be done. "What else do we have?"

"Well, blood," Nick said.

"Obviously there's no shortage of that."

"That's for sure." He pointed at the bed. "High-velocity spatter here and on the headboard. More on the ceiling. Consistent with the two shots David described. I think the shooter came in the door—"

"Using the battering ram," Catherine interrupted.

"—right. Smashed in the door, dropped the ram, and fired the first shot. It hit Freeson just below the collarbone. Freeson was standing in front of the bed—there's backspatter on the floor in front of his position—when the shooter came in and fired. Blood sprayed his feet and the floor there. Some-one—presumably the shooter, since the transfer pattern doesn't match the shoes Freeson was wear-ing—stepped in it. The print is a sneaker print. Con-verse. And there's a void in the blood spatter on the bed."

"I noticed that too. So Deke was trying to shield someone—maybe Antoinette O'Brady—who was on the bed when he got shot. She was hit by blood spatter."

"Do you think Deke got off a shot?"

"Either that or just the sight of that big Desert Eagle made the shooter hesitate," Nick said. "The difference in the angle between the two shots indi-cates a delay of at least a second or two—first shot from a bit of a distance, the second closer, and at an upward angle."

"But if he did fire, where's his round? And a witness said someone fired from near the pool. What's up with that?"

"That's right. I'll have a look around out there."

"I'll be here," Catherine said. "Probably still collecting hairs."

Nick walked out to the pool area, stopping every few feet to look back toward the open door of the room. As long as there were no tall vehicles parked in front of the room, someone could have fired from around the pool. But why would they? And if there was someone else in the doorway, would they take the shot, knowing they might hit their partner or accomplice? He supposed the first shot could have been fired from there . . . but it didn't make sense to shoot at a closed door, and they hadn't found any sign of a bullet or bullet hole in the wreckage of the door. And no one would ram in the door and then run to the pool to shoot.

The pool smelled almost as bad as the room. Nick let himself in through an unlocked gate in the tall chain-link fence and walked around the concrete basin. At least a foot of trash coated the bottom, maybe more. He wondered if the motel had quit paying their Dumpster fees and intended to just use the pool instead.

He swept his flashlight's beam around but didn't spot any shell casings on the concrete surrounding the pool, or any other sign that someone had fired a weapon. He hoped he wouldn't have to go wading in the collected trash. But as he let his eye drift over the scene, taking in the fence and the view back toward the motel building, he saw that one corner of the fence, where it connected to an upright and a top rail on the side nearest the building, had been broken loose.

He circled back around the pool to take a closer look. The fence was broken so cleanly that it might have been clipped. But there was a crease in the top rail, the steel slightly blackened.

Nick stood in front of it and looked toward the room. Right on line.

He was starting to think the witness had been wrong. *The guy didn't see a muzzle flash,* he realized with sudden certainty, *he saw a spark.* Nick could confirm his hunch with laser beams, since the distance was too great for trajectory rods, but it looked like a bullet fired at a slight upward angle from near the bed in Room 119 would gain just enough elevation to hit the top rail right where the fence was broken. The witness reported that he was already trying to leave, that the first loud noise—no doubt the battering ram taking down the door—had frightened him. Looking through a rearview as he was trying to get the hell out of there, in the dark, even a small spark might have seemed like a bright flash.

If the round had glanced off the rail, then it had to have gone somewhere.

Unfortunately, the most likely place was down in the pool. The bullet would have been slowed, redirected by the rail, and fallen in. He shone a flashlight along the wall and spotted what looked like a fresh chip in the pool wall, but the momentum had been slowed enough that the bullet hadn't become embedded there.

Nick would have to go wading after all. And in something far worse than stagnant pool water.

"Deke Freeson did take a shot," Nick said when he came back into the room. "But his shot missed. It flew out the open door and struck a steel rail by the pool, causing a spark, which our witness saw and confused for a muzzle flash."

"He's from Iowa," Catherine said, knowing even as she spoke that it didn't explain anything. "Anyway, it didn't slow the shooter for long. He took another step or two into the room, and at closer range, shot Deke in the face."

"Both of those rounds I collected were nine millimeter," Nick said. "And the one I found by the pool was fifty caliber. Deke's trusty Desert Eagle."

"So did the shooter snatch Antoinette O'Brady?" Catherine asked. She stretched, working out the kinks that set in from too much close examination of evidence.

"I don't think so." Nick beckoned her into the bathroom. She suppressed a shudder as she walked in, imagining what a close examination of the room's every surface might reveal. "Look," he said. "The bathroom window's open. There's blood transfer on the window frame. We know whoever was on the bed behind Freeson was covered in his blood. And not only is his car not in the parking lot, but there are no cars in the lot that were not identified as belonging to a guest or motel staff. I think Antoinette O'Brady got out the window and took Freeson's car."

"So we need to post a Be on the Lookout."

"Already done."

She was impressed. While she had been examining bodily fluids, Nick had been busy too. "I found some hairs and fibers," she said. "At a guess, I'd say the hairs came from five or six different people. I have short and dark, long and blond, short and bleached, and a couple of fragments that are hard to make out with the naked eye but look to be more of a light brown. Various fibers, mostly cotton or acrylic, I think. It looks like there are some used tissues in the wastebasket by the sink, but I haven't collected those yet. Friction ridge impressions—lots of smudges but a couple of good clear ones, including some palm prints on the headboard."

"In the blood?"

"Under it. Oh, and look at this."

"What?"

She pointed to a spot near the door. "Bits of oily black soil on the carpet. It's fresh."

"Any guesses?"

"It could be a lot of things," she said. "I'd rather find out for sure than make assumptions now."

"You're the boss."

"For the moment, anyway."

"I live in the moment," Nick said with a grin.

Catherine appreciated the gesture. Nick knew Gil Grissom was his real boss, and he looked up to Gil. In his early days at the crime lab, he had practically hero-worshipped the man. But Gil was gone, and chain of command meant he reported to her.

Catherine's crime lab family had been shrinking lately—as had her real family these past few years, for that matter. Professionally, she had lost Sara

Sidle, who had quit the lab and left town, and War-rick Brown, to a killer's bullets. In civilian life, her father and her ex-husband had both been mur-dered, and her daughter Lindsey was rapidly be-coming a young woman who would need her mother less and less as each day passed.

Maybe the years were changing Catherine too, drawing out her maternal instincts and making her want to shelter people, to clutch those she cared about close to her. The urge not to be abandoned anymore was growing.

"Let's wrap this up and get out of here," she said. "The sooner we get this stuff to the lab, the better I'll like it."

"You and me both, Catherine." Nick took a plastic evidence bag and a pair of tweezers from his field kit and started collecting the black soil she had pointed out. "You and me both."

3

THE DRIVE TO THE Desert View Airport in North Las Vegas would have been an incredible pain at rush hour, since the city's population boom had overwhelmed its highway system, but at quarter after nine at night it wasn't so bad. Greg Sanders drove one of the lab's Yukon SUVs, with Riley Adams riding shotgun. Catherine and Nick were stuck at the Rancho Center Motel, a fleabag that Greg was not at all sorry to miss out on.

From the brief report he'd been given, he wasn't too certain why they were bothering with this trip. The real reason they had gone was that Catherine had told them to, and when Catherine was in charge they obviously went where she said. What he wasn't entirely sure of was whether or not a crime had been committed at the airport. And determining that wasn't the job of the crime lab—that was right there in the name. They investigated crime scenes, after the LVPD made the determination that there had, in fact, been a crime.

Apparently somebody was convinced, though, because they were rolling. Desert View was a small airfield, with a combination tower and administrative office building, some work sheds, an assortment of hangars, and a single runway lit by a series of low blue lights. Most of the buildings were of corrugated steel, but the tower/office complex was stucco or adobe, painted a pale green color. A uniformed cop met the Yukon at the entrance and directed them to the runway. "This is kind of cool, isn't it?" Greg said. "Driving on a runway where only airplanes get to go."

"And service vehicles, and random pickup trucks," Riley reminded him. "Just be sure you move before the next seven-forty-seven lands, Greg."

"Seven-forty-sevens land—" Greg began. Which was just what she wanted. When she replaced Sara, it took him weeks to get used to her quirky sense of humor. Even now, when he was concentrating on something else—driving on a runway, for instance—she could catch him off guard. It wasn't like he didn't have a sense of humor. He'd been class clown for most of his school years, and liked to think he continued the tradition at the crime lab. But hers was—well, it was different. It seemed to come from dark, unexpected places inside her, and she had such a wry, deadpan delivery that it was almost always surprising.

The runway was paved, but just barely. After the pavement ran out, there was nothing but scrubby desert leading up into the hills. The lights of Las

Vegas glowed to the south, turning the night sky a sparkling gray color that always reminded him of frost riming the black paint of the rented Volvo wagon his Nana and Papa Olaf had used when he visited Norway with them as a child. Flaccid air socks showed how still the night air was. *A breeze would be nice,* Greg thought. It would cool down eventually—and fairly rapidly, once all the city's concrete and steel and the hard desert floor released the day's heat—but for the moment, *sweltering* was the word that came to mind.

Two more uniformed cops flanked a small private plane. "There we go," he said, happy to change the subject from imaginary 747s. "That looks like our goal."

"It does indeed," Riley said. "Assuming our goal is a Piper Malibu Mirage, and those unis aren't just admiring it."

"They have their backs to it," Greg pointed out.

"Could be a cultural variation. You can never tell with cops."

"You do know your planes," Greg said, ignoring her other comments. That was, he had learned, the best way to deal with her. "Assuming you're right and you didn't just make that up."

"My mother wanted one of those," Riley said. Both of her parents were psychiatrists, Greg knew. Which meant a private plane that could cost a million bucks or so wasn't necessarily out of reach for them. "She had brochures, catalogs, DVDs. But my father thought they were dangerous."

"Did she know how to fly?"

"No."

"Then he might have been right." He braked the SUV a dozen feet away from the plane. The uniformed officers started toward them. "And depending on what we find here, we might decide he definitely was."

"Oh, there's no question about that. She isn't even a very good driver. If she got behind the controls of an airplane, I would go into an underground bunker until it was safe."

As they introduced themselves to the uniformed officers and signed the security log, a couple of people hiked out from the shadows, apparently coming from the tower or a nearby hangar. One was a woman, tall and lean as a fencepost, with sandy blond hair tied back in a ponytail. She wore a blue workshirt open over a red T-shirt, grease-stained blue jeans, and black work boots. The man with her was equally slender. His hair was short and dark, graying at the temples but mostly hidden under a ball cap bearing the Garmin logo. He wiped his hands on his jeans and then offered his right to Greg. "Stan Johnston," he said. His grip was crushing, his eyes deeply creased around the edges and terribly sad. "I can't say it's a pleasure, but thanks for coming, Detective."

"We're not detectives, Mr. Johnston. We're with the Las Vegas Crime Lab. I'm Greg Sanders, this is Riley Adams." Stan Johnston looked confused. "There has been a crime committed, right?" Greg asked.

"I'm Patti Van Dyke," the woman said in a throaty voice that made Greg think of whiskey and cigarettes. Neither of which seemed especially suited to aviation, but maybe she, like Riley's mother, remained earthbound. "Would it help if we told you what happened?"

Greg caught Riley's glance. There was a smile lurking just behind her lips, but she was professional enough to hold it back. "That would help a lot," she said.

"Well, that there Piper belongs to Jesse Dunwood," Patti said.

"Where is Mr. Dunwood now?" Greg asked. "Is he here?"

"Well, he's inside it."

"He's—"

"We figured there was no point in calling a bus," one of the unis said. "Coroner's on the way but I guess they're a little backed up tonight."

Every night, Greg thought. Las Vegas's murder rate, like its traffic, had swollen along with its population. "The coroner?"

"Maybe you'd better take a look, sir."

Greg and Riley walked toward the front of the aircraft until they could see inside through a side window.

The victim—Jesse Dunwood, according to the woman—was alone, sitting in the pilot's chair on the left side of the plane. He was a middle-aged white man, a little on the meaty side, with neatly cropped reddish-brown hair. His head was tilted back against his seat, his mouth hanging open, blue eyes wide and glassy. There was a slight flush to his skin, or else he might have been recently sunburned, but over a deep brown tan. He wore what looked like an expensive silk shirt, designer jeans, and loafers.

"That man is definitely dead," Riley said.

"No sign of foul play, though," Greg said. "That we can see from here, at least."

"Could be natural causes," Riley said. "Heart attack, stroke, something like that. But he's dead, no getting around that."

"Why don't you finish telling us what happened, Ms. Van Dyke?" Greg asked.

"Well, Stan here was in the tower, not me. I mean, I was up there part of the time, but not the whole time. I'm more of a grease monkey."

He had been hoping to hear the whole story from a single witness, but he had to take what he could get. "Okay, Mr. Johnston then. What happened?"

"Jesse went up for a sunset flight," Stan said. "He likes to do that, or else night flights. Looks at the lights of Las Vegas—city's a lot prettier at night than during the day, he always says."

"Can't argue with that," Riley said.

"Sometimes he takes a lady up there, to show it off," Stan continued.

"The same one?" Greg asked. "Or a different one each time?"

"Oh, different ones mostly," Patti said. "Sometimes two or three at a time. The airplane has four seats."

Other people, also airport employees from the looks of them, started to gather around. After Greg had the general outline down, he would have to separate them, because the detectives would want to interview them individually, without letting their versions of the story be shaped by what they had heard.

"Okay," Greg said, trying to steer the conversation back to basics. "So he went for a flight. When was that?"

Stan looked at his watch. "Wheels up about seven-fifteen," he said. "Landed just over an hour later, eight-twenty, eight-twenty-five or so. I can get you the exact times in the tower."

"We'll need that," Riley assured him.

"Then what happened?" Greg prodded.

"Then, nothing. He brought her in for a beautiful landing, as smooth as butter. The airplane taxied, slowed, and stopped. Jesse's been flying all his life—he used to be a fighter pilot in the Air Force. He could handle an aircraft like nobody's business."

"But then he never got out of the plane," Patti said. "That's when I thought maybe something was wrong. I went up to the tower and told Stan, 'Hey, you think something's wrong with Jesse? He's just sitting there on the runway.'"

"There sure enough was something wrong," one of the newcomers said. He was dressed in a janitor's gray coveralls, and although he looked short, Greg realized it was because his spine was bent almost in half and his left leg was enclosed in a steel brace. Straightened out, he would have been just over six feet tall. His hair was wispy and gray and his face was all edges and angles, with more than a day's stubble covering cheeks and chin, except where a puckered scar ran from the edge of his mouth to his right eye, like a fat white earthworm had settled onto his cheek to take a nap.

"Who are you?" Riley asked him.

"I'm Benny. Benny Kracsinski."

"Benny's a night janitor," a tall, heavyset African-American man said. He wore a striped dark blue jumpsuit that didn't quite hide the grease stains. Greg noted that his fingernails were extremely short, either bitten or seriously pared back. His shaved head gleamed in the light.

"Look, we'll get statements from all of you," Greg said. "But I'd like to do it one at a time. Is there someplace that the rest of you could wait while we talk to Mr. Johnston here?"

"Sure," Patti Van Dyke said. She pointed toward the tower. "The office is right over there, we got chairs and stuff."

Greg gestured to one of the uniformed cops. "Officer, can you escort these folks over there, and keep them separated once they get there?"

"Gotcha," the cop said.

"Before you go, though, let me know who you others are. I want to be able to keep your names straight."

"I'm Jamal Easton," the big man said, rubbing the palm of his hand across his head. "Anything I can do to help, just let me know."

The last person to identify herself was another Caucasian woman, small, dark, and taut, with a ready grin and an open manner. "Tonya Gravesend," she said. "I hope you find out what happened to Jesse. We all liked him."

"Amen," Jamal said. "We're like a little family here, we all get along."

"Strange family, then," Riley said.

"Someone will talk to each of you soon," Greg told them. "In the meantime, don't talk about this among yourselves, please."

"Don't want us to fix our stories, do you?" the janitor asked. *Kracsinski*, Greg remembered. *Benny.* "Makes sense, I guess."

"Please, just . . . go with the officer."

"This way," the uni said. Benny, Jamal, and Tonya followed. Riley had to twitch her head toward the others to get Patti to take the hint and go along.

"Now, Mr. Johnston, please continue," Greg said when the rest were out of earshot.

"There's not much more to tell," Stan said. "Like I told you before, Jesse landed, then his aircraft just sat there on the runway. Patti came up and we talked about it. There wasn't likely to be any more traffic in or out tonight, but still, we were getting worried, and you never know when someone might need to make an emergency landing. I called him on the radio, you know, a few times, but he never answered me. I told him I needed the runway cleared, even though I didn't really. Finally I sent Jamal over to check on him."

"Jamal works for the airport?"

"He's a mechanic. Private, but he mostly works here. And like he said, we all know each other and look out for each other."

"That's wonderful," Riley said. Greg couldn't tell if she meant it or not.

"Well, soon as Jamal got to the airplane, he called us over. Jesse, he was just like you see him there. Dead, no question about that."

"And no one had approached the plane?" Riley asked. "Until Jamal did?"

"Not a soul. It's mostly quiet around here this time of night. We're busiest on weekends, and on weekdays it's the mornings. A few people are like Jesse, enjoy night flying, but for the most part we're used for tourist flights over the Grand Canyon or short business trips, you know? That's all daytime stuff."

Headlights speared through the night. "Coroner's here," Riley announced.

"It's about time," Greg said. "Can you open the airplane, Mr. Johnston?"

"Is it okay to?"

"You mean legally? Yes, it's fine. Just get it open and then stand back, and don't touch anything you don't have to."

"Got it."

While he opened the cockpit, Riley moved close to Greg. "If he was murdered," she said in a low tone, "then we've got the ultimate locked-room mystery going here. Because not only was the victim alone in the room, but the room was five thousand feet in the air."

"Gives a new meaning to the mile-high club," Greg answered. "And not nearly as much fun as the old one."

4

"THIS REMINDS ME OF THE time in high school when we put a pig in the girls' locker room," Greg said as he and Riley retrieved their field kits from the Yukon.

"A pig?" Riley asked.

"There were some farms on the outskirts of Santa Gabriel. We paid a farmer a hundred bucks for one of his old pigs one night, and took him to school in the back of a pickup truck one of the guys had. We opened the locker room door and led him in. Then we bolted the door from the inside, climbed up on the lockers, and went out through the ceiling panels. When the coach opened up the gym in the morning, he had to get a custodian to cut through the bolt with an acetylene torch, which of course freaked out the pig even more than spending the night alone in a locker room had."

"This was you and those zany kids from Chess Club?" She had heard stories about Greg's younger days, not all of them directly from Greg.

"Hey, I had other friends."

"Sure you did, Greg."

Once Jesse Dunwood's body had been removed, they started to process the airplane like they would a car or any other vehicle. First they photographed it from a variety of angles, inside and out, then they inspected it with alternative light sources in hopes of pinpointing fingerprints, fluids, or fibers.

It was during this process that Riley found the tube. "Greg," she said. "Take a look at this."

Greg had been in the back, on his hands and knees examining the passenger area. When Riley spoke, he turned around, put his hands on the seat backs, and leaned forward. Riley trained her ALS inside the air vent above the instrument panel, moving it slowly back and forth so he could see what had caught her attention. "You see that?"

"There's something in there."

"Not just something," she said. "I think it's a hose or a tube of some kind."

Greg moved up front for a closer look. "You could be right. What do you think it's connected to?"

"I'm not sure," she said. "But it doesn't belong there. You can see the sides of the ventilation tube, and it's not part of that." If she had already found the murder weapon, maybe this night would be easier than she had feared. She wasn't used to Gil Grissom being out of town, and since Warrick Brown hadn't been replaced yet, Gil's absence left the night shift crew especially shorthanded. "We've got to find the other end."

Greg stuck his head out of the plane and called to the uniformed cop remaining outside, whose name, they had learned, was Morston. "Can you get Jamal Easton back out here? He's an airplane mechanic, and I think we can use him."

"No problem," the cop said. He hurried off toward the airport office.

Riley and Greg continued their routine while they waited for the mechanic, collecting fibers and fingerprints and whatever else turned up. The airplane appeared to have been maintained regularly, cleaned thoroughly inside and out, but there was a trash receptacle on board with some cough drop and gum wrappers inside it. The wadded-up chewing gum, like everything else they found, was collected in evidence bags.

The uniformed officer returned shortly with Jamal Easton. Riley showed him the hose she had found, through the vent. "Can you find the other end of this thing?" she asked. She already had a hunch where it might lead, but her expertise at identifying aircraft—familiar ones, anyway—didn't extend to tearing them apart. "Without touching anything you don't absolutely have to."

"I can do that," Jamal said. He gestured toward her gloved hands. "You need me to put on some gloves or something?"

His hands were huge, the kind that could palm a basketball. She suspected latex gloves might just split if he tried to put them on. But Greg took a pair from his kit and handed them over, and Jamal's hands reminded her of the resilience of that particular petroleum product.

Gloved up, Jamal opened the canopy. "I'll try to be careful," he said. Riley watched closely and made mental notes of any place he touched, in case she needed to explain why evidence had been smudged or otherwise obscured. Hands at his sides, Jamal peered at the engine, moving his head around to get different angles on it. Several times he asked for flashlights to be beamed inside, pointing to what he needed to have illuminated. "There you go," he said after a few minutes.

"What is it?" Riley asked.

"Light," he said. Riley pointed her mini Maglite where he directed. "That thing right there?" he said. "Thing that looks like a muffler? That's the engine exhaust collector."

"What's that?"

"The muffler."

He hadn't cracked a smile. She was beginning to like this guy. "And that thing sticking into it—"

"Through a crudely punched hole. That's right. That's the end of your tube."

"Carbon monoxide," Greg said at her shoulder. She hadn't even noticed that he'd gotten out of the plane.

"Looks that way. Postmortem hypostasis will be easy enough to read when they get the victim's clothes off at the morgue," Riley said. "Could this really blow enough carbon monoxide into the cockpit to kill him, though? It's only coming in one of the vents, so there's other ventilation at work."

Her question had been intended rhetorically, but Jamal Easton jumped in with both feet. "That depends on how the airplane is flown," he said. "In Jesse's case, I'd have to say yes, it could."

"How it's flown?" Greg asked. "What do you mean by that?"

Jamal took a deep breath and let his weight rest against the side of the plane, making himself comfortable. He gave every indication of having addressed this general topic more than once, and at considerable length.

"You folks ever heard of the great LOP/ROP debate?" he asked. Riley supposed they showed him blank faces, because he continued without much of a pause. "LOP means 'lean of peak.' ROP means 'rich of peak.' It describes two different flying techniques, and if you were to go into the airport office where everybody is waiting around and ask the people there about their preferences, I guarantee you'd start an argument that'll last until dawn. If not longer. I strongly urge you not to do so, because frankly I'm sick to death of it. Stan and Patti are both LOP folks, while Tonya and Benny are ROP types. To me, it all comes down to the individual aircraft and its pilot. Jesse knew what he was doing, no two ways about that, so I respected his decision."

"Even the janitor has a viewpoint on this?" Greg asked.

"It's hard to find any airport rat who doesn't."

"What does this have to do with the victim?" Riley asked. She was starting to fear that the man's explanation would last until dawn anyway, even without the argument.

"Jesse Dunwood flew ROP. He was devout about it."

"What does it all mean?" Greg asked. "You kind of lost me."

"Sorry." Jamal straightened up, and the airplane shifted without his weight against it. He moved his gaze between Greg and Riley and blew out a faint sigh, reminding her of a college professor addressing a pair of substandard students. "They're adjustments the pilot can make in the engine's exhaust gas temperature. We call that EGT. As you lean the mixture, adding more air and less fuel, your EGT gets higher. Keep leaning and it drops again, so that midpoint, just before it drops when it's running as hot as it'll get, is the *lean* of peak. *Rich* of peak means that the pilot likes to keep the fuel-to-air mixture on the *rich* side. Heavy on fuel, lighter on air. The increased fuel flow keeps the EGT down, but it obviously burns more fuel. On the flip side, the LOP folks claim that they have the smarts and the instrumentation to risk running a little hotter, knowing they're not going to erode their exhaust manifolds or set their engines on fire, and they'll save fuel in the bargain. As you might imagine, when fuel prices shoot up but air is still free, LOP gets more popular, and when fuel prices come down, you might see a little increase in ROP."

"I think I get the gist of it, but I'm not clear on how it ties in," Greg admitted. Riley knew that was hard for him to say—he was a brilliant guy, and he was usually the first to admit it. "Can you bring this back around to carbon monoxide?"

"Sorry," Jamal said. "I guess we all get carried away when we go there, even me. Like I said, Jesse

Dunwood is a serious ROP guy. A richer fuel mixture is going to generate much more carbon monoxide than a middle-of-the-road mixture or a lean of peak mix. A *lot* more. If he had been flying LOP, there might not have been enough of it blowing his way from the muffler to do any damage, given the other ventilation. But as it is, he was blasting almost pure carbon monoxide right into his face throughout his flight. The surprise isn't that he died, it's that he managed to complete the flight and bring the aircraft down for a landing *before* he died, instead of plunging it down in a residential neighborhood or into one of those high-rises on the Strip."

"That is a plus," Riley said. "Thanks, I think we get it now. If you could go back to the office and wait—without discussing this with the others, or starting the LOP versus ROP wars going—we'd appreciate it."

"Glad I could help," Jamal said. "Don't worry, I wouldn't dare bring that old chestnut up tonight. I will miss old Jesse, though." He nodded his big head and ambled off toward the building.

"Good work, Riley," Greg said. "I think we have a cause of death *and* a murder weapon now."

"Carbon monoxide poisoning and a rigged muffler."

"Exactly."

Officer Morston strode across the tarmac toward them, as energetic as if his shift had been just beginning. He was a tall, burly guy with a dark complexion and a preternaturally cheerful mood, especially for a patrol officer on the graveyard shift.

"So all we have left to do," Greg continued, "is to figure out who did the rigging."

"Which means we're really just getting started."

Greg gestured to the uniform. "Officer Morston, we've got a lot more work to do on this airplane. I need to have it towed into its hangar, and I'm going to need you to make sure no one disturbs it until that happens."

"Got it," Officer Morston said. "Anything else?"

"No, I think that'll be plenty," Greg said. "We'll dig into it as soon as it's safe inside."

Greg was reaching for his phone to call for a tow when they heard Catherine's voice over his radio.

Catherine, Riley thought.

Every time it looked like their shift might get a little easier. . . .

5

CATHERINE RADIOED GREG because she had known him longer than she had Riley. Gil might have been more systematic, would maybe have called Riley because he had called Greg the last time. Or perhaps he still would have chosen Greg simply because he had seniority over Riley. Catherine didn't pretend there was anything to her decision but familiarity, though—she chose Greg because he had been part of her lab family longer than Riley. In the long run, it didn't make much difference, and as she got to know Riley better, she was sure that would change.

"What's up?" Greg asked.

"How's it going out there?"

"We're making some progress. This is definitely a homicide. Someone rigged the victim's airplane muffler to fill his cockpit with carbon monoxide. We still have to process the plane, because that's our crime scene. But it'll be a big job."

"Is it secure?" Catherine asked.

"It will be in a little while. We're going to park it in a hangar here. There's a uniform who's going to stay with it until it's safely inside, and then we'll work it."

"Tell the uni to stay with it a while longer, Greg. I need you to go somewhere else."

"Really? Where?" She thought she heard a sigh in his voice. She could hardly blame him, but she couldn't go out on another call herself yet. She had brought all the collected evidence—the hairs, fibers, lifted fingerprints, and so on—from the motel room scene back to the lab to get its analysis started. Because there was a dead body in the room and a woman missing—the address shown on Antoinette O'Brady's driver's license didn't exist, and the document itself was now in the Questioned Documents unit to determine if it was real or not—that case had priority, and she intended to stay on it until the woman was found.

"Northeast side," she said. She read the address off the report she had received.

"That's way out there," Greg said.

"Murder knows no bounds."

"So it's another homicide?"

"I don't actually know yet. There's a new casino under construction out there. Pretty far from the Strip, but I guess the theory is that people will go just about anywhere to throw away their money. And as bad as traffic's getting in the city, maybe they've got a point. With all the new housing developments out that way, there might be plenty of people who would gamble more if they didn't have to drive into town." The casinos relied more on visitors than locals for their business, but plenty of visitors became locals once they'd had a taste of the city, and there were even plenty of natives who enjoyed a game of poker or a night at the slots. Gambling addicts tended to congregate in areas with casinos, and Las Vegas had more than its fair share.

"I suppose. But if we don't know it's a homicide . . ."

"That's what you need to determine. You did a good job with the airport scene, right? Confirmed that pretty quickly."

"Yeah." Definitely a sigh that time. "Is this the same sort of thing, then?"

"Not exactly." Catherine glanced at the report again. "This new casino is called the Empire. You'll spot the signs when you get close, I'm sure. Anyway, they just broke ground today, after years of wrangling and environmental impact reports and the like. There's an archeologist on board to make sure the construction doesn't disturb any archeological sites, and sure enough, today she found bones."

"Old bones on the first day? That's good job security. Look, I know there's no statute of limitations on murder, but—"

"I didn't say they were old, Greg. Nor did I say the bones were human."

"Catherine . . . I hope you're not pulling me off a real homicide to go look at some animal bones, because—"

"Have faith, Greg. I'm not going to tell you what to expect when you get there, because I want you to have an open mind. Just . . . the clock's ticking on this one. The casino owners are going to want to move full steam ahead, and they've already been held up by a day because of—because of what the archeologist found. So get out there and make a determination before they decide to plow forward anyway and contaminate the scene."

"As soon as we can get this airplane secured, Catherine, we're on the way."

"Good," she said. "Let me know what you find out."

Catherine wanted to get back to the layout room, where she and Nick had put some of the objects they had taken from the motel, but before she could leave her desk, her cell phone rang. The ring tone meant that it was Lindsey calling. Part of her wanted to ignore it, because this was showing every sign of being an extremely busy shift . . . oh, what the hell. The case would still be there five minutes from now. Lindsey was her only child, and Catherine tried to balance work and family as well as she could. She picked up the phone. "Hi, Lindsey," she said.

"Mom." Lindsey got the one word out, then a sob burst from her, and Catherine felt it in her stomach, twisting her from the inside.

"What's wrong, Lindsey? Are you in trouble? Are you hurt?"

"N-no," Lindsey managed after several seconds. "It's nothing like that."

"What's the matter, then?"

"I . . . you know my friend Sondra, right?"

She had met Sondra a few times, more than she had most of Lindsey's friends. Short, blond hair with the tips dyed black, just this side of pudgy. She had a sweet smile, but a grating laugh. "Yes, I know her. What about her?"

"I was . . . I was at this club tonight?"

"Which one?"

"Don't worry, it was a twenty-one and under place. No booze, no fake IDs."

"Okay," Catherine said. She guessed her message about fake IDs had gotten through. She also guessed it wouldn't last for long, and until Lindsey was twenty-one, it would be a continuing issue. "So you were at the club. What happened?"

"I was, you know, listening to the music, hanging with my friends, dancing a little. And then I saw Sondra, but she didn't see me. She hadn't come with us. She was in one of the booths, stretched out on the pillows, and she was practically doing it with this guy. They had their tongues so far down each other's throats I thought they would both choke."

"Well, that's tacky, but why does it have you so upset, honey?"

"Mom, Sondra is like practically engaged to Jayden!"

Right. Jayden. Six three, acne-ravaged skin, tattoos, dyed-black hair left long on one side, buzz-shaved on the other. Catherine thought that style was decades out of date, not that it had ever been attractive. But she still saw people with Mohawks around from time to time, so there was just no telling about fashion. Jayden always wore black, right down to the studded leather bracelets on his wrists and the beads on either end of the bar he kept through his left eyebrow. She remembered him, and the way Sondra had cozied up to him when she and Lindsey had run into them at the mall. "Practically engaged?"

"They're planning to get married next year," Lindsey said. "You might not think much of them, Mom, but they're like my most stable friends. They both have good jobs, and Jayden is in college. He's going to be an investment banker."

Not looking like that, Catherine thought. But one of the first things a mother learned was when to keep her mouth shut, and she did so now.

"Anyway, I . . . well, you know, I don't have a lot of experience with a solid family life. But I thought Sondra and Jayden could really pull it off, you know. They've been together for years. They've never broken up. They have like a five-year plan, getting married, getting their degrees, making some money, having a kid. The whole deal. And then tonight I saw Sondra getting busy with this guy at the club, a guy I've never seen before, one of those scummy-looking older guys with a silk shirt open to his navel . . . it just about made me sick."

Catherine still hadn't figured out exactly what she was supposed to do about it. Sondra was seventeen, so even if they'd had sex, the guy couldn't be charged with statutory rape. "Did he hurt her?"

"I don't know. I don't think so. Mom, that's not the point!"

"Forgive me for being dense, Lindsey, but I'm a little distracted here tonight. What exactly is the point, then?"

"The point is, what do you think I should do?"

"Have you talked to her about it? Maybe she and Jayden broke up."

"I saw Jayden this afternoon, and he said everything was fine. I don't know what to say to Sondra, though. We just left the club so she wouldn't see us."

"Well, you can pretend you didn't see her—"

"Mom, she's my *friend*!" Catherine had to move the phone away from her ear in self-defense. Daughters could hit just the right tone to make their mothers feel both stupid and useless. It had to be in the genetic coding, because Catherine could remember using it on her own mother, but never in Lindsey's presence.

She felt like she had to respond to the issue if not to the tone. "Can't you just tell her what you saw and find out what's going on?"

"I don't know if I can do that. I mean, not without it turning into some whole huge deal. But I can't just pretend it didn't happen, either. I don't know what to say to her, and I can't spend the rest of my life avoiding her."

Although she really needed to get back to work, Catherine was heartened that Lindsey had actually called her for relationship advice. Usually she preferred to keep her private life at a far remove from her mother. She honestly didn't know what advice to offer, though, beyond the two suggestions that Lindsey had just shot down. "I'll think about it," she said. "If I have any brilliant insights, I'll call you."

"Please! As soon as you can!" Lindsey said. "'Bye!"

Just like that, she was gone. Catherine didn't expect any brilliant insights to strike her, but she would do what she could. When the job wasn't taking precedence, that was.

Which it nearly always did.

6

PATTI VAN DYKE DROVE the blue tractor that towed Jesse Dunwood's plane into its usual hangar. After confirming that Officer Morston could stay with the plane and that Detective Grayson Williams had arrived to take statements from the various airport employees, Greg and Riley drove across the north edge of the city to the construction site for the new Empire Hotel and Casino.

As Catherine had suggested, there were signs galore flanking the project, some of them showing artist's renditions of a massive structure that looked vaguely like a high-rise version of the Roman Colosseum.

"Nice," Greg said. "I thought we had moved beyond that whole theme casino thing. You think they'll run gladiatorial games?"

"If people can place bets on the gladiators? They'll make a fortune."

"You're probably right."

As at the airport, when Greg approached the site he kept an eye out for a police officer or telltale yellow crime scene tape. He saw the former, a uniformed cop who was waiting just outside a tall, closed gate. She approached the driver's window with a friendly smile. "You're with the lab?" she said. The name VILLANUEVA barely fit on her name tag.

"That's right. I'm CSI Sanders and this is CSI Adams."

"I was told to expect you. I hope this isn't a waste of all our time."

"That makes three of us," Riley said. "I don't imagine it would thrill the taxpayers, either."

"Probably not," Officer Villanueva replied. "I'll get the gate open, then you can follow me down the graded road for about an eighth of a mile. The last little bit you'll have to cover on foot."

She did as she said, opening the gate, then closing it behind the SUV. Inside the fence, the only illumination came from moonlight and a little bit of spillover from floodlights showing off the signs on the far side of the fence. Officer Villanueva covered the distance at a brisk jog. "Bet she runs marathons," Riley said. "She has that runner's look about her. Lean and hungry."

Riley, Greg noted, was plenty lean herself. He wondered who the first guy in the lab to ask her out would be, then realized it had no doubt already happened. The fact that he hadn't yet heard about it was the only surprise. His money was on Hodges. Greg parked where Villanueva indicated, beside some piles of recently overturned earth. He and

Riley got their field kits and flashlights from the back of the SUV. "It's this way," the officer said.

"Did you talk to the archeologist who made the find?" Riley asked her as they threaded between mounds of moonlit dirt.

"Not me, no. She was gone when I got here. I took over from another officer who had some paperwork to take care of. It's been pretty quiet here since I came on. But at least it's starting to cool off, right?"

It was, Greg realized. Not time to break out the jackets yet, but he was no longer sweating. Villanueva stopped and pointed down at a shallow depression in the earth. Greg and Riley passed her, shining their lights into the depression. The white of bone was unmistakable.

A lot of bone. The depression held mounds of bones, layers of them filling the space. The archeologist had clearly dug them out but then left them more or less as she found them, not wanting to disturb the scene more than she already had.

"Was there ever a butcher shop here?" Riley asked. "Or a ranch that might have used this area to slaughter livestock?"

"Not that I've ever seen, and I'm a native," Officer Villanueva said. "My folks and I used to ride dirt bikes out here. It's always been open desert. Housing projects have been moving in on it, but there's never been anything here besides cactus and sand."

"How long has the property been fenced off?" Greg asked.

"Just for a couple of days. It's been surveyed and

marked, with those plastic tags tied to stakes and plants and such, for months, but the construction company didn't put up fencing until they were ready to start digging."

"Well, someone's been coming in here and leaving this stuff," Greg said. "You don't get this sort of concentration by accident."

"According to what I was told, the archeologist said she looked everything over and determined that they're all animal bones," Officer Villanueva said. "Dogs, cats, mice, hamsters, pigs. The newest is a sheep." She pointed, and Greg turned his light on a mostly intact sheep carcass. "No human remains at all."

"That's good," Greg said. "Because if there were human ones in there, she would have been seriously trashing our crime scene."

"It's still a crime," Riley said. Her voice was tight, and when Greg glanced over he saw that she was so tense that veins stood out on her neck like ropes. "I mean, sometimes I like animals more than people. I'd love to know who put these bones here."

"I don't know if finding out is a big priority tonight, since we're a little shorthanded and we have actual dead humans to deal with," Greg said, attempting to steer the conversation back to the business at hand. Riley was getting emotional about the crime scene. He had been one of the first CSIs at a horrific scene where dead fighting dogs had been dumped, but those bodies had been fresher than these, their fur still intact in most cases. And there had been a woman's body close by, which had redirected his focus. Still, he didn't like the idea of animal bones piled up out here in the middle of the desert any more than Riley did. "But we're here, so I guess it can't hurt to look around a bit."

"One more thing," Officer Villanueva said. She toed a coffee can, its opening covered by a tight-fitting plastic top. "The archeologist found these in among the bones. That's when she decided to call the police."

Greg put his kit down, took out a pair of latex gloves, and tugged them on over his hands. Covered up, he opened the coffee can and looked inside. As soon as he shook it, he knew what it contained, and a quick peek confirmed his guess.

He wished the archeologist had left them where she'd found them instead of picking them up. It would be hard to get a conviction based on such a compromised crime scene, if it came to that. He might have to interview the archeologist, and he would definitely want to know if she had taken pictures of the scene before she poked around in the bones.

"Bullets," he said. "Looks like forty-fives, mostly, but a couple of twenty-twos as well. Eight of them."

"A hunter wouldn't shoot animals and then bury them," Riley said. "And a hunter wouldn't shoot dogs and cats and hamsters and sheep, either."

"This was no hunter," Greg agreed. "Get some photos, Riley. Officer, can I get to that sheep without walking on the other bones?"

The depression was a little more than eight feet across, and almost three deep. Officer Villanueva led him around to the far side while Riley circled the pit snapping pictures, her flash strobing the night.

There, most of its bulk hidden from the front by the pile of bones, white against white, was the corpse of a recently killed sheep, its wool painted in spots with dried blood that resembled rust stains. While he looked it over, Riley put the camera away and beamed her light down into the pit.

"Greg?" Riley had sunk to her knees by the edge of the depression. She had gloved up too, and she held a bone in the air, lighting it with her flashlight. "I've got tool marks here. They look like knife marks to me. Cuts are deep enough to scrape bone."

"Great," Greg said. "Does this mean we've got a sicko who likes to kill animals? Because that *is* a crime."

He went toward the sheep, his gut churning unpleasantly with every step. He didn't expect to like what he found.

The sheep had been dead for a week or so, Greg speculated, but no more than that. Its flesh was loose and just starting to cave in under the coils of wool. Further investigation could reveal precisely how long it had been dead—that was the sort of thing Grissom was good at; he could look at the insects crawling around on and inside it and pinpoint a time of death within hours, under most circumstances. Greg had yet to amass the experience to do that.

"I have a dog skull here with a bullet hole in it," Riley announced. "Execution-style, back of the head."

Greg didn't answer. The sheep appeared to be the biggest animal in the pit by a wide margin. The smell of its decomposing flesh and filthy, bloody wool was cloying, almost gagging him, and he found himself breathing through his mouth. The wool twitched with activity. Maggots, probably. He tried not to think about those as he reached for it. The animal was on its side, legs toward him, head curled in toward its chest, where most of the blood was gathered.

He had a bad feeling about that.

"It's a ewe," he said.

"It's a you?" Riley echoed. "What do you mean, it's a me?"

"E-w-e. A female . . . never mind." Why was he such easy prey for her? Because he didn't expect such a pretty woman to be such a smart-ass? Not like he hadn't known plenty of pretty smart-asses in his life. Humor was how Riley dealt with tense situations, though, and if he had to be the target this time, so be it. But he couldn't allow it to distract him. *Focus, Greg. Look at the throat.* He took a handful of wool and tilted the head back. It moved easily. *Too easy.*

When he exposed the neck, he knew why.

An opening gaped there, like a black-rimmed smile, the flesh curling away from the gap.

Greg made a choking noise and released it.

Someone had slit the ewe's throat.

That didn't happen in nature. Not that way. Not that clean a cut.

A knife had made that slice.

Bullets, knives, cut marks. Animals of varying sizes and descriptions, all killed and then left here.

What kind of person would do something like this?

From the look on Riley's face, her jaw tight and trembling, her lips almost vanished in a thin white line, her eyes gleaming in the reflected glow of her flashlight, he knew he wouldn't want to be that person if she found him.

But he couldn't help hoping that she did find him.

7

NICK STOKES HAD OBTAINED a warrant to search Deke Freeson's office. There wasn't, as it turned out, much of anyone to object to such a search. Freeson had once been married and had a son, but he and his wife had been divorced for years, and she and their son had both died during Hurricane Katrina, when they were trapped in an apartment building that collapsed on them.

From what little Nick knew about Freeson's private life, tragedy seemed to buzz around him the way flies did around feces. Nick was surprised the man could still get dates, particularly from some of the beautiful women he had been seen with, considering his lady friends had a history of developing terrible diseases, running into immovable objects while driving fast cars, or otherwise becoming former lady friends in various, usually painful ways. He had been the subject of an investigation once, when someone had noticed that very pattern—Nick remembered that Jim Brass had handled the case, in fact—but it had turned out that Deke Freeson was simply a very unlucky guy.

Or, to be more precise, any woman who spent too much time with him was unlucky. Brass had told Nick once that he thought Freeson just attracted women on a downward spiral. He moved through Las Vegas's underbelly, and the people he met were rarely without serious problems. Freeson himself never seemed to suffer, except perhaps emotionally or psychically. He was healthy, had all his original body parts, and no more scars than the average guy. He had made it through the Gulf War and a career on the LVPD after that conflict, and then years as a private investigator, without once getting shot or stabbed or run over.

Until he had the misfortune to go to a room at the Rancho Center Motel. *That place should be razed,* Nick thought, *and the ground salted where it had stood.* An exorcism might not be out of order. Its continued existence was a blight on the city of Las Vegas, and didn't say much for humanity in general.

Freeson's office was small, a single room upstairs over a coffee shop on Charleston, with two desks and some filing cabinets crammed into it. It didn't even have a bathroom of its own, but shared one with several other office suites. The little room smelled like sweat and mildew. Freeson had a part-time assistant named Camille Blaise who had come over and opened the office for Nick. She was waiting in the hallway now, reading over the warrant Nick had handed her.

When she wasn't around, Freeson used a voicemail system provided by the phone company, for which Nick knew he'd have to get the luds. Before he sent her into the hall, he'd had Blaise show him which desk was Freeson's and give him Freeson's computer password. There was a flat-screen monitor on the desk. Nick reached under the desk and turned on the computer. Once booted up, he scanned the files, but it looked like he used it mostly for e-mail and web browsing. That was a lot of what PIs did these days, hitting the online databases instead of doing old-fashioned footwork. It was no doubt quicker and more efficient, but Nick thought it eliminated some of the perceived glamour of the profession. It made a PI into just another keyboard jockey, like an accountant or a programmer.

According to Camille Blaise, Freeson kept all of his records on paper, not on the hard drive. He stuffed his receivables and payables in file folders, except for the most recent ones—piles of credit card receipts and bills were tossed without organization of any kind into a desk drawer. Nick briefly wondered what exactly Camille did for him. She looked like the kind of assistant someone hired at a strip club after a few too many margaritas. Freeson had a week-at-a-glance calendar in his top desk drawer where he jotted notes and appointments—coded ones, it appeared, in most cases, but Nick didn't see any notes written in a female hand. Nick guessed Freeson met clients downstairs in the coffee shop rather than letting them into his office, which would hardly inspire confidence, whether or not his assistant was around.

Like Catherine, Nick had heard that Freeson was

a pretty good detective. Which meant he didn't keep
his place this way because he couldn't afford anything better. Nick's interpretation was that he just
didn't care about the trappings—the nice office, the
presentable staff, the latest high-tech gadget or accounting system. Deke Freeson wanted to focus on
the work, on solving his clients' problems, and anything that didn't contribute directly to that wasn't
important to him. Nick couldn't fault that. He liked
his work area more organized, but if he had chosen
to be a private detective, he figured he'd be much
the same way about an office—he wouldn't care if it
was impressive to clients, he would just want it to
be functional so he could do the work.

Urgency gnawed at him. Psychoanalyzing the
dead man wasn't his job. Finding the possibly live
woman who was missing—that was his job now,
and he had to give up trying to figure out Freeson
and keep looking for Antoinette O'Brady. He rifled
through the filing cabinets but couldn't find any
files with the name *O'Brady* on them, Antoinette or
otherwise. He looked through the calendar entries,
trying to find an entry that he could decipher as her
name or initials. No luck.

He went to the door, opened it. Camille was sitting on the floor, still studying the warrant as if it
contained every fact she would ever need to know.
"Ms. Blaise, can you come in here please?" he
asked.

She snapped her gum and nodded.

She looked nineteen or twenty. Dark eyes
popped out of her pale, skinny face, framed by limp,

dark brown hair. She wore too much mascara, smudged by tears that might well have been the genuine article, and her lipstick was a bright red that made Nick think of Hollywood starlets from eras gone by. He didn't know if the clothes she was wearing were typical work clothes or not, but her white cotton tank top was almost too loose to confine her small breasts, and her pants, clinging desperately to skinny hips, could have been torn off by a strong wind. When she moved, there was a liquid quality to her motion, as if she had been poured rather than grown.

"Yeah?"

"I need some information about Deke."

"Yeah?"

No wonder she's part time, Nick thought. *If she worked full time she'd drive anyone crazy.* "I can't really make heads or tails of his filing system."

"You and me both."

"So you didn't do any of his filing?"

"He never wanted me to touch that stuff. Or his, you know, money stuff."

"You mean like accounting?"

"Right, that."

"What exactly did you do for him?"

"Exactly?" She held Nick's gaze, but there was the slightest lowering of her eyelids. She probably thought it made her look sexy. Maybe it worked on some men.

"Of a professional nature, I mean."

"Oh, that." She pressed a fingertip to the corner of her mouth, as if there was an on-off button hidden there. "I answered his phone. I handled his correspondence—you know, dumping his junk mail, prioritizing the important stuff. He was teaching me to use some of the online databases so I could help with public records searches and things like that. And if he needed a map or a book or something like that, I would get those for him."

Nick had to admit he was surprised by her answer. "What if I wanted to know what cases he was working on now? How could I find out?"

"He keeps his files in the cabinets, alphabetically. He's good at that. Kept, whatever."

"Is there any chronological cross-reference? I couldn't find the name I was looking for in there."

"What is it? Maybe I did a records search or something on it."

"Antoinette O'Brady."

She shook her head, causing her hair to flap into her face. "Nope. I've never heard of her."

"Not as someone associated with some other case?"

"I just said no."

"Okay. How about this—have you ever heard of the Rancho Center Motel?"

Camille swallowed. "That's where he . . . where you said he ate it."

"That's right. In a room registered in his name. Do you have any idea why he would get a room there?"

"As far as I know the only reasons to go there are to catch something, from dirty needles or diseased hookers."

"So you have heard of the place."

"Heard of, yes. Deke never said anything about going there, though. I would have made him wear a body condom."

"Would he have told you if he was?"

"Like I said, not if he was going there to catch something."

"We don't think that was the case." Nick searched for some other angle of questioning that might shed more light on Freeson's relationship to the missing Antoinette. "Do you know his e-mail password?"

"Hell, no. And he doesn't know mine."

"Did he write down notes? If he was talking on the phone or something? Any kind of pad, or—"

"Ooh, yeah," Camille interrupted. "There's a notepad somewhere. One of those deals with a spiral binding on top."

"I didn't see it on his desk."

"He left it all over the place. One of my jobs was to find wherever it was and put it back on his desk." She started searching through the drawers of her own desk, which Nick had already glanced in— mostly empty, but she had a phone book, a manicure set, and a plastic container with something frightening beginning to grow inside it shoved into them.

Then she turned over a stack of newspapers on the one visitor's chair, and shoved them off onto the floor. The small notepad had been tucked beneath them. "Here it is!" Camille declared. She handed it to Nick, who flipped through the pages quickly, watching for Antoinette O'Brady's name or initials, or any reference to the Rancho Center. Something in this office had to connect Freeson with Antoinette, and he meant to find it.

On the second to last used page of the notepad, a phone number had been scribbled down, but with no name attached. Nick was about to flip the page, but something about that number struck him. He stopped, stared at it. Definitely familiar. He turned the page, saw nothing of interest on the next one, and turned back.

And realized whose number it was.

To confirm it, he checked his own cell phone's contact list.

Bingo.

He pushed a button and the phone started to ring.

"This is Supervisor Willows," Catherine said. She had been back at her desk, working on seemingly endless amounts of paperwork as she waited for results from Trace, when her cell phone rang once more. She grabbed it up hoping for an update from Lindsey, but the ring tone was wrong and the name *Nick Stokes* showed on the screen.

"Hey, Catherine."

"Nick, did you find anything at Deke's office?"

"I don't know yet. Maybe. You know where Brass is tonight?"

"He's off duty, so no, I have no idea. Why?"

"I found his cell number written on a pad in Deke Freeson's office," Nick said. "On the next to the last page that had any writing on it. He doesn't seem to believe in dating anything except his actual case notes—oh, and bills. But his assistant says he used this notebook all the time, to record phone conversations and that sort of thing. So I'm guessing he called Brass in the last few days, or had a call from him."

"That's a little coincidental, maybe, but not necessarily anything more than that. A lot of PIs have occasion to call cops from time to time. And we already know that Deke knew Brass."

"Because Brass investigated him?"

"They probably knew each other even before that. They were on the force at the same time. Don't read too much into it, Nick, that's all I'm saying. I'll give Brass a courtesy call, tell him what's up, and see what he says."

"Sounds good."

"Did you find anything on Antoinette O'Brady?"

"Not a damned thing. It's like she doesn't exist. Freeson's assistant has never heard of her, either."

"That's what I was afraid of. Keep looking, Nick. I don't think a woman who doesn't exist needs clothes and toothpaste and makeup."

She had just hung up and was still holding the phone, thinking about the endless forms requiring her attention, when there was a soft knock on her door. She looked up to see Mandy Webster standing there, her stance awkward, with a hesitant half smile on her face. Dark bangs fell across her brow, almost obscuring her right eye. "What is it, Mandy?"

"I've got results on some of those impressions lifted at the motel," Mandy said. "Interesting ones, maybe."

"What'd you get?"

"Well, some of them belong to Deke Freeson."

"Which makes sense," Catherine said. "Since we know he was in the room."

"Yeah, no big shocker there. But another one—well, when I got a hit, I ran it again. Same thing the second time."

"Mandy . . ."

"It belongs to Captain Brass."

"Jim Brass?"

"He's the only Captain Brass I know. He was in the motel room. The fingerprint was on the doorknob to the bathroom. There was a partial on the nightstand that might be his, but there's not enough of it to get a positive match."

"You're right," Catherine said. "That is interesting. Or it might be, anyway. Do me a favor, Mandy. Let's keep this between us for now, okay?"

Mandy cocked her head, obviously surprised by the request. "Sure," she said. "No problem."

When she left, Catherine looked at her phone—still in her hand, but almost forgotten.

She should call Jim and ask him about the phone number and the fingerprints.

She should call Nick and tell him not to say anything about the number he'd found to anyone else.

Instead, she left the paperwork unfinished on her desk and hurried to her car. She wouldn't have minded if she'd never had to go back to the Rancho Center Motel, although she was convinced that was a pipe dream. But she hadn't anticipated going back quite so soon.

It was like waking up from a bad dream, then going back to sleep and finding herself stuck inside the same nightmare.

8

"YOU EVER HEAR OF A man named Jim Brass?" Nick asked. He had sent Camille Blaise back into the hallway while he called Catherine, then retrieved her. She seemed relieved to be let back into the office.

"Umm, let me see. Nope."

"You don't like being in the hall?"

"It's, like, boring out there. And kinda scary. These guys have some kind of office down the hall, just past the bathrooms, and they get some freaks through here."

"What kind of freaks?"

"Like homeless guys, I guess. I know I shouldn't be afraid of them. But I think they look at me and see someone who they could carry around in their pocket. If they have pockets."

"How old are you, Ms. Blaise?"

"I'm twenty." She pressed her arms flat against her sides and stuck out her chest, as if standing for inspection. "Three days ago, in fact. You need to see my license?"

"That shouldn't be necessary. Do you live alone, with parents, or what?"

"What does this have to do with anything?"

"I'm just trying to get a clearer picture of Deke's life."

"I live alone. My parents are back in New Haven."

"Been in Vegas long?"

"Couple years. Okay, four years, I guess."

"How did you meet Deke?"

"Can I sit?"

"Sure."

She took her own chair, rolling it in behind her desk. Suddenly she looked more professional, her mood more serious, even her posture toned down somehow. "I like being an assistant, you know?"

"Compared to what?"

"When I met him I was . . . well, I was a runaway. I hitched a ride to Vegas, and when I got here I fell in with some bad people. Deke was working a case and he saw me getting beat up by . . . by this guy."

By your pimp, Nick mentally filled in. He kept his mouth shut.

"He broke it up," she went on. "Broke the guy's arm and jaw, in fact. He took me out for breakfast and by the end of it he offered me a job. Even though I was a mess, with black eyes and blood and snot coming out my nose and lips split open, he thought I had something to offer."

"I see."

Camille shook her head again. "No, you don't. You don't see anything except what your cop eyes want to see. He never touched me like you're thinking, in a, you know, sexual way. Never once. He saw that I could be a help to him and he paid me to do work that would help. He gave me as many hours as he could afford. I got my own place and I've stayed straight and out of trouble. For *him*."

She had read him right, and Nick was sorry for that. He didn't like seeing kids abused, and he hated pimps with a fiery passion. He'd even had a short affair with a prostitute named Kristy Hopkins, until her pimp had murdered her. The fact that Nick had been blamed for the murder had nothing to do with his disdain for their kind—it was a pure, raw anger at bottom-feeders who preyed on the weak and made their living off the labor of others. But he had made an assumption about Camille—a series of them—and he regretted having done so.

"I'm sorry, Ms. Blaise," he said. "Honestly. I know this is hard on you."

"And it's going to get harder." She sniffed. "I don't know what I'm gonna do now. I mean, he can't even write me a letter of recommendation, can he?"

"I guess not."

"Or answer phone calls about my references."

"I can write you a letter, Camille."

A surprised smile lit her face. "You would do that for me?"

"I'd have to be honest. Say I don't know you that well, but in the course of my investigation I learned what you had done for Freeson."

"Better than a poke in the eye with a burning hot

rod, right?" The smile vanished, replaced by a side-long look of distrust. "What would you want for it?"

"Nothing. I just want you to get another job you like. Here in Las Vegas or back in New Haven, either one. Or someplace else entirely, if you'd rather. I wouldn't blame you if you wanted to move, after this."

"Vegas, baby," she said with a grin. "I'm staying put."

He couldn't deny being glad to hear that. It wasn't that he was interested in her, romantically or sexually. She was definitely not his type, and too young even if she had been. But he wanted to know that the dirty side of Las Vegas didn't have to spit out all the people it chewed up—that there were some who could look it in the eye and survive it, whole and relatively undamaged. He had begun to think Camille Blaise might be one of those.

"One more thing, before I let you go. Can you think of anyone, recently or not, who might have had a grudge against Deke? I've been thinking it's all got something to do with this Antoinette O'Brady, but maybe I'm way off base. Maybe she went on the run because she had witnessed Deke's murder and she's afraid, and Deke was the shooter's only target all along."

Camille smiled again, not with the wattage displayed last time, but with real satisfaction. "There was this one guy. Penfold . . . Will Penfold, that's it."

"Good. Thank you. What's his beef with Freeson?"

"He hired us. He doesn't have a lot of money—he drives a beer truck, for God's sake, for Copper Blade

Beer and Beverage. But he had this idea that he thought would make him, like, a billion dollars. He had this partner he went in on it with, and then he thought the partner was selling him out, meeting with big companies and trying to sell the idea out from under him. He hired us to find out if the partner was really doing what he thought."

"What was his great idea?"

"Beer-flavored underwear."

Nick felt his jaw falling open. "You're kidding me."

Another shake of the head, another flurry of hair. "Nope."

"Was the partner cheating him?"

"Trying to. Only it turns out nobody was that interested."

"Imagine that."

"But Will didn't believe Deke. I mean, when he said there were no buyers for the idea. He thought Deke had been bought off by the partner, and they were splitting the millions that rightfully should have been his. He punched Deke, right in the throat." She pointed to the visitor's chair. "Came up out of that chair and just laid into him, right in front of me. I was screaming and thought I'd have to call the cops. But Deke just took a couple of punches, then grabbed this guy Penfold, held his arms down, and told him to get the hell out and not come back. Penfold left, and on his way out he said if he found out Deke was in bed with his partner, he would kill him."

"He wasn't, though," Nick said. "In bed. Figuratively."

"Or any other way. But maybe Penfold doesn't

believe that. He might still think there's a million bucks calling his name."

"For beer-flavored underwear. I'll check Will Penfold out, Camille. Thanks."

"Thank *you*."

"For what?"

"For explaining why you asked the question you did. For not assuming I'm some idiot just because I'm young and cuddlesome."

"I didn't say you were cuddlesome. I don't think I've ever used that word before."

"You don't need to. I already know I am. But you know what? It turns out that somebody can be adorable and not stupid at the same time. Go figure."

"Yeah, go figure," Nick said.

Twenty-five minutes after getting Mandy's news, on top of Nick's, Catherine was back at the Rancho Center Motel, looking at the sign-in log kept by the uniformed officer posted outside the room until she released it. Her signature was on it, as were Nick's and David's. Various other cops, uniformed and detectives, had been in. The guys who had picked up the body for the coroner's office had signed it.

Jim Brass, though, had not signed the sheet.

The easiest explanation—that Brass had heard the original call, been in the neighborhood, stopped by and seen Deke's body before she got there—was the one she had been very much hoping would turn out to be correct.

But that wasn't the case.

If Brass hadn't been here since the police had first

shown up, that meant he had been here before that. Most likely while Deke Freeson was still alive.

Now she had a dead private investigator who Brass had known, a missing woman, a police-style battering ram left at the scene, and Brass's finger-prints in the room.

Maybe Brass had a good explanation for it all.

Catherine devoutly hoped that he did.

9

RILEY HAD ALREADY photographed the bone pit from every possible angle except underneath the bones looking up. Now she focused on individual bones, photographing the ones on which she had found unnatural nicks, cuts, and scrapes. In her profession, these were considered "tool marks" until the actual "tools" that had caused them were identified, but she knew that they were really knife marks. The attacker would have had to strike hard and deep to leave these marks in the bones—strikes that, to her, indicated explosive fury.

Fury directed toward innocent animals.

Riley had grown up knowing that people's mental states came in every condition—calm, disturbed, disoriented, brimming with contentment or quivering with confusion or roiling with rage. Her parents dealt with it by studying the workings of the mind and trying to help people achieve some sort of balance.

Riley's response to this knowledge had been different. People had to want help to seek out psychiatric care—or they had to be forced into it by the courts. In the latter case, it was often too late to do much to help their victims. That became Riley's goal: helping them—even belatedly—by working to identify and apprehend the perpetrators before whatever disconnected wires they had in their brains caused them to injure or kill again, and by giving voice to the dead by interpreting the clues left by the circumstances of their deaths.

People were never responsible for their own murders, in her mind. But they could bear some of the blame, on occasion, through bad choices they made, the sorts of people they chose to be around, the acts they committed that might drive others to that final, extreme action. Animals, though, rarely made such poor choices, and when they were antagonistic toward people, it was never malicious. They were slaughtered for food and hunted for sport. However she felt about those two activities, this pit was evidence of something else—pure cruelty toward creatures who had done nothing to deserve it and who, in most cases, could not fight back.

While she photographed cut bones and bullet holes, Greg was busily collecting specimens of animal hair, soil samples, and tiny bits of vegetation found inside the pit. One never knew where the smallest clue might lead, so they took specimens of everything.

"Riley?"

"Yeah?"

"Come here for a second."

Riley carefully set down the bullet-scarred skull she was about to take a picture of and made her way around the pit. Greg had gone back to the sheep, and he was holding its head up, shining his light at the animal's throat. "Something just occurred to me," he said. "Look at these wounds."

She had already looked once. Which, really, was more than enough. "Is there something new?"

"Look closely. Around the edges."

She forced herself to move in for a more careful examination. You couldn't be squeamish in this business, but she had to fight back a wave of revulsion. "Okay." She thought she saw what he was talking about—he had tipped her off by saying *wounds*, plural, instead of *wound*. "There are smaller, more shallow cuts around the periphery of the big cut."

"They show hesitation," Greg pointed out. "As if the cutter was taking practice cuts before making the final, more confident slice. Building up his courage, maybe."

"But he had already killed all these other animals."

"Nothing this big, though. It's still a step up, from a dog or cat to an animal this size. I'm betting we'll find that the smallest animals came first, and the larger ones are more recent."

"A size progression," Riley said.

"Exactly."

"You're thinking something, Greg. I can see it in your eyes."

"I'm thinking that these are *all* just practice. The progression worries me."

She had to ask, even though she was afraid she knew the answer. She had been starting to think the same thing. "Worries you because . . . ?"

"Because people who do this sort of thing often don't stop with animals."

"They move on to people," she said.

"That's right. Whoever did this is seriously disturbed. I'm afraid we might be looking at the early stages of a serial killer in the making. The use of guns and knives bothers me, too, instead of one or the other. It's like he's trying to figure out what he's most comfortable with. I can't find any bullet holes in the sheep, so maybe he's settled on knives. And another thing—now that the hotel construction has begun, he has to know his burial pit will be found, or already has been. What sort of response might that trigger? I think we should check for any recent unsolved homicides with knives or guns, and see if there are any factors in common with these killings."

"You think he's already taken that next step?"

"No way to tell, but if he hasn't, I want to find him before he does. And if he has, I want to find him before he does it again. Once you've done a sheep, a human being is pretty much the next size up."

"I just have a few more photos to get. Are you about done?"

"Just about," Greg said. "Let's finish this and get out of here. I want to get the ME's van out here to pick up this sheep—I think it'll bear a closer examination."

"Doc Robbins will love having a murdered sheep on his table," Riley said.

"Believe me," Greg said, specifically remembering a gut-shot deer wearing a cocktail dress, "he's had a lot worse."

Nick had just arrived back at the lab and was on his way to Catherine's office when David Hodges waylaid him. Lean, with short graying hair and an almost pathological desire to please those to whom he reported, Hodges was hard to like, but also hard to seriously dislike. Nick tolerated him and tried to maintain a positive attitude about him, as he did with most people, but Hodges could get on his nerves. For sure he grated on Grissom sometimes, but Gil respected his scientific ability and occasional insight, if not his personality. Nick could do no less.

"Nick," Hodges said. "Busy night."

"They always are, Dave."

"You manage to get through them, though, and usually with a smile on your face. A person's got to admire that."

"I guess so." Nick nodded to the file folder Hodges carried. "You got something for me?"

"Oh, right." Hodges shook his head briskly, as if he had completely forgotten why he had interrupted Nick. "That oily residue you brought in? From the motel scene."

"What about it?"

Hodges flipped open the folder and glanced inside. "It's mostly diethylene glycol monomethyl ether."

The compound sounded familiar to Nick, but he couldn't place it. "What's that?" he asked with a shake of his head.

"It's the major component of brake fluid."

"Brake fluid."

"Someone walked into that room with brake fluid on his shoes."

"The first officers on the scene didn't secure the parking lot—which, frankly, was pretty disgusting. Not as bad as the room, but bad. So we didn't take specimens of the various fluids found there. I guess I could go back over, see if I can find any brake fluid."

Hodges shrugged. "Not my idea of a good time, necessarily, but whatever you have to do. I'll keep working on this and try to narrow it down further."

"Thanks, Dave."

Hodges was already turning around, heading back to his lab. "It's what I live for!"

Seeing Hodges reminded Nick that he still needed results from Wendy Simms, upon whom Hodges had a long-standing crush. Instead of continuing on to Catherine's office, Nick decided to detour past Wendy's workstation. She was bent over a comparison microscope when he entered. "Hey, Wendy," he said.

"Nick, hi." She flashed a quick smile, brushed dark brown hair off her cheek.

"What's new in blood?"

"Blood in general, or particular blood?"

"Blood from the Rancho Center Motel."

"Oh, that blood." She consulted a printout on the countertop. "Sounds like that scene was quite the mess."

"It was."

"But the thing is, although there was a lot of blood, all the samples belonged to the same person."

"Deke Freeson?"

"I'm still waiting for confirmation on that," Wendy said. "But if that was your gunshot victim, then I'm betting yes."

"So all the samples we brought in were identical?"

"Right."

"Including the blood on the bathroom window frame?"

"All of it."

"Okay. I guess that clears that up."

"Hope so, Nick."

Nick walked away, finally headed for Catherine's office.

No blood but Freeson's was good news. As good as could be hoped for, in any case. It meant that whatever had happened to Antoinette O'Brady, at least she hadn't been injured—to the point of bleeding—in the motel room. The blood transfer on the window frame had probably come from the spatter she had picked up by being on the bed, behind Deke Freeson when he was shot. And probably prone, or crouched low, since the shot had been a through-and-through but had not hit her. The whole scenario was starting to come together in his head.

He needed to run it by Catherine.

But before he did that he needed a few minutes, to see if he could work the last bugs out.

Once again, he delayed that particular visit.

10

"THIS IS GRISSOM."

"Gil, it's Catherine. I'm sorry to bother you so late."

"I'm not on East Coast time yet anyway, Catherine. I've been going over my presentation. Is everything okay out there?"

Catherine had to think about that one. Ordinarily it would have been a simple question with a yes or no answer, but not this time. She spooled a lock of red hair around her index finger. "Not exactly, no."

"What's going on?"

She glanced at the door to make sure no one might overhear. This time of night, her office was essentially private, and would be until the day shift came on. But she had left the door open, to send the message to her team that she was always accessible. Gil had offered to let her use his office while he was away, but he would only be gone for a few days, and his peculiar set of hobbies—collections of insects, reptiles, and other creatures, jarred and bagged, everywhere you looked—made that room less than welcoming to just about anyone but him. It was bad enough that he had given her his beloved irradiated fetal pig, which she felt compelled to keep around so as not to hurt his feelings, but she didn't want to pass the nights surrounded by his other prizes. "It's . . . well, it's a little complicated, Gil. It's about Brass."

"Jim Brass?"

"That's the one."

"What about him?"

"Well, we had a crime scene tonight, at the Rancho Center Motel. A homicide."

"That's hardly surprising," Gil said. "The place is a dump."

"And then some. Deke Freeson was shot. The PI?"

"I know him. He's a bit of a hard-luck case."

"Who Brass investigated once."

"Right, but it went nowhere."

"That's what I understand. Anyway, Brass's fingerprints were in the motel room, in multiple places. I'm still waiting for hair and fiber analysis to see if there's anything else linking him to the scene."

"He is a detective, Catherine."

"He's off duty tonight, and he didn't sign the motel log."

"Okay . . . that is a little strange. So your presumption is that he was there before the homicide?

Or after, but for some reason he didn't sign in. If he knew the victim was Freeson, he might have been upset, distracted. Is there anything else?"

"Nick went to Freeson's office and looked around there. Brass's cell phone number was written on a notepad sometime within the last few days. We're still waiting on the phone records to see when, or if, they talked."

"That's a more concrete connection, but it's still not definitive. Any more?"

"That's everything I know so far, Gil. I guess I just have a weird feeling about it."

"Did you ask Jim about it?"

"I called and left him a message. He hasn't returned my call yet."

"Okay."

"Does the name Antoinette O'Brady mean anything to you? She's a local woman, fifty-six years old, according to her driver's license. I'm thinking the name is probably an alias, but whoever she is, she was in the room at some point. She went out a window, with some of Deke's blood on her, and she's missing now."

"She doesn't sound familiar."

Someone passed by in the hallway, and Catherine waited until the footsteps had faded into the distance. "I know I'm fishing here. But since I haven't been able to ask him directly . . ."

"I know how you feel, Catherine. You know Jim. You like him. We all do. You don't want to think he's mixed up in anything. But you're a CSI. We can't prejudge the situation; we have to let the facts fall where they fall. The evidence will tell you what to think."

"I know, Gil."

"Of course you do. Keep working it. Keep it as quiet as you can, and don't make your mind up about anything. Brass deserves a presumption of innocence, just like anyone else. But depending on where the evidence leads you, he doesn't get any special dispensation from the facts."

"Got it. I guess I just wanted to hear someone say it who wasn't me."

"I understand."

"Thanks, Gil. And I hope your presentation goes well."

"It will if I can ever get any sleep. Keep me posted if there are any new developments."

"I'll do that." She sat there holding the phone in her hands. Gil hadn't told her anything she hadn't been telling herself. Coming from him, however, it carried a different weight. She might have been trying to convince herself of something, one way or another, but not Gil. He liked Brass as much as the rest of them did, but if Brass was mixed up in murder and the evidence proved it, Gil would be the first to admit that Brass had to go down.

She hoped desperately that was not the case. She had lost too many friends and loved ones lately. She couldn't bear to lose Jim Brass too. Certainly not that way.

If she had to make the call, though, she would make it. Nobody got away with murder, not if she had anything to say about it.

Not even a close friend. Maybe *especially* not a

close friend. That would make the betrayal all the worse.

"Catherine?"

Nick's appearance at the doorway startled her. She had been inside her own head, not registering his footsteps in the hall or his tapping on the door, until his voice broke the spell. "Nicky, come on in."

"Have you talked to Brass yet?"

"Not yet," she said. "I'm still waiting for him to call me back."

"I've been doing some thinking."

"That's what you get paid for."

"I thought I got paid for carrying heavy stuff and spending a lot of time on my hands and knees looking at stains," he said with a grin. "But what I've been thinking is, I believe our initial reconstruction at the scene was probably pretty close. I think Deke Freeson *was* in the room with Antoinette O'Brady. Not sure yet if they were there *with* each other, if you get what I'm saying, or if she was a client or what."

"I get what you're saying."

"Someone broke in the door with that battering ram. Maybe two someones, given all the trace we found."

"Then again, who knows how well those rooms are cleaned? I'm surprised we didn't find more than we did. Like the missing contents of Al Capone's safe, maybe."

"Yeah, I didn't get the sense that cleanliness was a huge priority there. Anyhow, he or she or they came in, dropped the battering ram, and fired a gun. Deke was hit but returned fire, and he missed. His assailant moved in closer, point-blank range so he wouldn't miss with the second shot, and fired again. Antoinette was behind Deke on the bed, crouched down low enough to not get hit. She got spattered with his blood, then ran and got away out the window. She probably took Deke's car. The assailant gave chase, which is why when the cops got there, barely five minutes later—"

"Which is a great response time for that neighborhood," Catherine interrupted.

"Someone deserves a commendation. Point is, by the time they got there, all the vehicles in the parking lot could be accounted for among the guests. So either the attacker was a motel guest, which is unlikely, or he or they took off after Antoinette. Who escaped, by the way, covered in blood and without her purse, wallet, phone, or ID."

"Which should make it difficult for her to hide out anywhere. I wish we had something more than a phony driver's license to go on."

"We know it's a fake?"

"I'm pretty sure. Most fifty-six-year-old women keep more in their wallets than a driver's license and a Visa card, which was also issued recently. Her cell phone's brand-new, too, hasn't even been used. Prepaid, purchased in a convenience store probably, without a contract. Credit cards, library card, supermarket reward card, various business cards . . . she didn't have any of that. It makes me think she was trying out a new identity, and maybe had just started working on it."

"She could be out there on her own, then. Exposed and vulnerable."

"If she was the target, and not a bystander," Catherine said.

"Can we afford to think otherwise?"

"Not really. Deke's already dead. But as far as we know, *she's* still alive, so we've got to find her."

"Well, I'm heading back over to that rat hole to see if there's brake fluid in the parking lot."

"I'd be surprised if there's any kind of fluid that's not in that parking lot, Nick."

"Yeah, that's pretty much how I feel about it. But someone went into that room with brake fluid on his shoes, and it wasn't Freeson."

"Okay, check it out. Maybe it does mean something, or maybe someone just spilled brake fluid in the parking lot and Antoinette O'Brady walked in it. Or one of the cops." *Or Jim Brass,* she thought but didn't say. No point in stressing his involvement.

When Nick had left again, Catherine turned over the scenario in her head. In the craziness of the night so far, she had almost forgotten about the battering ram. It was the same kind LVPD officers used, which meant that Brass might have had access to it. It had gone into the fingerprint lab, so Catherine headed down there.

She found Mandy removing an orange ceramic table lamp from the cyanoacrylate fuming chamber. The same stuff that was found in superglue, it turned out, not only adhered well, but was perfect for revealing friction ridge impressions. The chamber looked like a phone booth, and the lamp was suspended from pulleys in the center of it. There were smaller chambers, but none that would accommodate such a tall—and hideously ugly—lamp. "Is that from the motel?" she asked.

"Yeah," Mandy said. "It was next to the bed. Nick figured that people in a strange room reach in for the switch before they really know where it is, so they might touch any part of the lamp."

"Get anything off it?"

"Just smudges. Lots of them. I don't think the thing's been cleaned for a year."

"What about that battering ram?" Catherine asked. "Anything on there?"

"No. Smudges again. I'd guess whoever touched it last wore gloves, since you couldn't really use it without gripping the handle, and that was wiped pretty clean. It probably spends most of its time riding around in the trunk of a car."

"Can I see it?"

"Of course." Mandy pointed at it. "I haven't had a chance to get it to evidence storage yet."

"It's been a busy night," Catherine said.

"When isn't it?"

"Right." Catherine studied the battering ram, a cylinder of black steel about two inches in diameter and eighteen inches long, with a handle in the middle and various labels beneath that. Short and heavy enough to punch through most doors, it could be used with one hand, leaving the other free to hold a weapon. Overkill for that motel's doors, probably, but the attacker might not have known what he would be dealing with until he got there. It definitely looked like the ones she'd seen LVPD officers using for forcible entries.

She looked more closely at the labels until she found a serial number at the bottom of one. "Mandy, I need a piece of paper," she said. "And a pen."

Mandy put them both next to the battering ram. Catherine wrote down the serial number.

If it was police issue, she would find out who it had belonged to. And that person would have a hell of a lot of explaining to do.

11

THE SERIAL NUMBER CATHERINE found on the battering ram traced back to a patrol car used by two LVPD cops—partners named Lee Wolfson and Garland Tuva. Catherine could have confronted them alone, but there were two of them, and in her experience cops in pairs didn't always want to acknowledge the professional seniority of a slightly built woman, no matter how tough she really was. Sometimes cops by themselves didn't want to, either, but when they had someone to show off for, it was worse. Anyway, she wanted a witness with her. She wasn't ready to accuse them yet of anything untoward, but she needed to find out how their battering ram had wound up at the scene of a homicide.

Nick had already left to look for brake fluid at the motel, but Greg and Riley had just come in from the Empire Hotel and Casino's construction site, so she grabbed Greg.

Catherine found out from dispatch that Officers

Wolfson and Tuva were on shift, and arranged to meet them outside a twenty-four-hour coffee shop on Sahara. Through the restaurant's windows, she could see a couple of people punching coins into slot machines, and a few others drooping over coffee or lemonade or slices of pie. The interior decor was basic fifties bland, updated only with a fresh coat of dark yellow paint once every decade or so. The outside was midcentury modern, of interest to architecture students studying that era, but coming across only as dated to Catherine.

The squad car was parked out in front. As Catherine and Greg approached it, two uniformed cops emerged from the restaurant. The smaller of the two—blond, mustached, and wiry—carried a Styrofoam cup with a plastic lid, steam slipping from the opening. The other one must have been six five and three hundred pounds, with olive skin and dark hair and eyes. A Pacific Islander, Catherine guessed, Samoan or Hawaiian maybe.

"You the CSIs?" the small one asked.

"That's right," Catherine said. "I'm Supervisor Willows. This is CSI Sanders."

"Lee Wolfson," the smaller one said. He grinned at her in a way that she guessed was the one he used when trying to pick up women in bars. Maybe there were even some who went for his smile. Catherine wouldn't have been one of them. "And Garland Tuva. You can call him Tiny."

Brilliantly original nickname, she thought. She knew better than to employ sarcasm, though, at least until she had a better sense of these two. "I'll just call him Officer Tuva."

Wolfson shrugged and the grin vanished. "Suit yourself. What can we do for you, Supervisor Willows?"

"I'd like to know the whereabouts of the hand-held battering ram assigned to your vehicle."

"So would we," Tuva said.

"You got a line on it?" Wolfson asked. "I thought you CSIs would be busy working on more important crimes, but if you think you have something, let's hear it."

"What are you talking about?" Catherine asked.

"Our battering ram. Isn't that what you're here about? It was stolen from the trunk. What was it, Tiny, two days ago?"

"Yup, that's right," Tuva said.

"We reported it," Wolfson said. "You wouldn't believe the paperwork. Outrageous. So, if you found it . . ."

"We found it, all right," Catherine said. "At a homicide scene. It was used to open a door."

"That's what they're good at," Wolfson said. "Oh boy, so you weren't just looking for the ram?"

"No."

"Oh well. Whatever works. When can we get it back?"

"It's evidence in a homicide," Catherine reminded him. "It could be a while."

"We already have a replacement, so I guess it's not urgent," Wolfson said. "I just figured if we could turn it back in, maybe our lieutenant would be happy. It takes a lot to make her happy. That battering ram might just do the job."

Tuva laughed at that. His teeth were very white

and very large. Catherine chose to ignore the re-
mark, because to follow up on it might mean filing a
sexual harassment claim against the cops. Wolfson
had been skating on thin ice, but he hadn't quite
broken through yet. Talk about paperwork. . . .

On the way back to the crime lab, Catherine was
silent, trying to work through in her head the possible ramifications the conversation had raised. Maybe
the battering ram really had been stolen from the vehicle's trunk, although it would take a pretty bold
thief to break into a squad car's trunk and carry it
away. Or maybe Wolfson and Tuva had left it behind
someplace, and then reported it stolen when they realized their error? Maybe they had given the ram
away, or sold it, and ditto. What she didn't want to
think, but had to consider, was that they had been
actively involved in Deke Freeson's murder. Even
the scenario that they had given it away or sold it
implicated them as accessories before the fact. But
she had probed with a few more questions and
quickly decided that without more to go on, she
would get nowhere with them. If she came up with
additional evidence linking them to the motel, then
she could charge them. They would lawyer up and
the force would close ranks around them, at least
until it was definitively shown that they had partici-
pated in a homicide. Even then, some of their fellow
cops would support them. The thin blue line didn't
break easily when it was drawn around some of
their own.

"Catherine?" Greg asked, drawing her away from
her private reflection.

"Yes, Greg?"

"That bone pit you sent us to. At the Empire Casino construction site."

"Yeah, what about it?"

"It was pretty disturbing. There were lots of bones there, from a bunch of different animals. But they had been shot or stabbed and dumped there over what looks like a period of years. Except for one sheep, which has probably just been there for a few days, certainly not much more than a week, if that; everything else was picked completely clean. So there's a pretty big gap in time between the killing of that sheep and the rest of the animals."

"That is strange."

"Here's what gets to me, though. I think it all indicates a serial killer in training. There are premortem or perimortem practice cuts on the sheep's neck. There's a progression, I'm betting, between the times of death of the smaller animals, building up to larger and larger, and finally to the freshly killed sheep. And now this person's burial site has been violated. I don't think he's started killing people yet—and for the sake of argument, let's say it *is* a 'he' doing this—because I expect he would have dumped them in the same place, at least until the Empire construction site was fenced off. But I don't know that for a fact, and the shock of finding out that his site has been discovered might spur him to something more drastic."

"It's a long jump from sheep to people," Catherine pointed out.

"It is, except that's how many serial killers get

their start. Torturing animals, then killing them, then graduating to human victims."

Catherine nodded. She knew that, but had wanted to hear Greg verbalize it in case he had any other insights. "Right," she said.

"My first impulse was to want to pull files on recent unsolveds, to see if there are any matching patterns. It wouldn't hurt to do that, but I have this feeling that while he thought his site was secure, he was probably okay doing animals. He was still in practice mode with that sheep, getting closer to humans, but he hadn't made that leap yet. Now that it's compromised, though, all bets are off. Who knows what that's done to his precariously balanced mental state?"

"What do you think we should do now, Greg? Got any ideas?"

"Now I think we should watch out for disappearances—homeless people, streetwalkers . . . any easy victims. Kidnappings without ransom demands. No way to tell how this guy would pick human victims after preying on animals, but I would expect victims of opportunity would be the likeliest ones at first. I don't know if the discovery of his burial site will really push him over the edge, but then again, I think he was pretty close to the edge to begin with."

Catherine parked the Yukon in the lab garage and set the brake. "Okay," she said. "Disappearances, check. Brass is off tonight, but I'll call Sam Vega and make sure he keeps us in the loop."

"Thanks. It really is the strangest feeling, standing there, surrounded by all those bones, and just knowing the guy who put them there is itching to try his skills on people."

"You wouldn't be human if it didn't affect you," she said. "I'll make the call. In the meantime, you try to pinpoint how wide the time gap is between the sheep and the other animals. Maybe he's been out of town or something."

"That's a good idea, Catherine."

"I know it is." She smiled and opened her door. "I'm just full of 'em."

12

WENDY SIMMS CAUGHT Catherine on her way back
into the lab. "Catherine, I got the first results on
some of that semen from the motel room scene."

"Walk with me," Catherine said. Depending on
what those results were, she might not want them
broadcast to the whole lab. She desperately did not
want to hear about anything else connecting Brass
to that room. He still hadn't called her back or answered his radio.

"Okay," Wendy said. She fell in step with Catherine.

"What did you learn?"

"It's a little strange."

"Just what I need tonight. More strange."

"I could come back tomorrow night."

"Kidding," Catherine said.

"Me too."

They reached Catherine's office and went inside.
Catherine sat behind her desk. Her voicemail light

was flashing, but then again it usually was. "What've you got, Wendy?"

"Okay," Wendy said again. "There's a DNA match to a guy named Bart Gorecki. He's in the system because he did time in Folsom for aggravated assault."

That might have been the best news Catherine had heard all night. "Sounds promising. We need to find out how he knows Deke Freeson, and—"

"Here's the thing, though."

"What thing?"

"Bart Gorecki died in 2002. In Folsom."

"Oh."

"Yeah, that's how I felt."

"You're sure about that?"

"I'm positive, Catherine. I can bring you the file . . ."

"That's not necessary, Wendy. I believe you. Keep working on the rest of it, and we'll figure this out."

Wendy left the office. DNA wasn't foolproof, Catherine knew. It was one of the best tools the CSIs had ever had, but mistakes could be made, either through human error or technical problems.

But still, she hated to have a name in her grasp and then to lose it in the space of mere seconds.

She needed something else to go on, and she needed it fast.

David Hodges was immersed in a document showing the chemical compositions of different brands of brake fluid—who knew there were so many?—when the phone in his lab rang. It took three rings to snap him from his concentration and remind him that he had a phone in the lab—days went by between calls sometimes, although there were also nights it never seemed to let up. This had been one of the former, until now.

He crossed the room and snatched up the receiver. "Trace lab, this is Hodges."

"Hey, Hodges," a familiar, gravelly voice said. "This is Brass. How you doing?"

Brass? Calling me? "Captain Brass, this is a surprise. To what do I owe the honor?"

"Apparently there's an investigation going on around a homicide at the Rancho Center Motel."

"That would be correct, yes."

"I tried calling Catherine, but I guess she's a little busy. And I know you usually manage to stay tapped in to whatever's going on around there. I was hoping you could bring me up to speed."

"Oh, wow . . ." Hodges couldn't quite believe the captain was calling him for information. That implied a lot of trust. "You know, sir, I haven't really heard a lot about it yet. I know Catherine and Nick are on it, and Mandy's working on"—he was going to say "fingerprints," but decided that sounded too mundane—"friction ridge impressions, and Wendy's on fluids, epithelials, and hair. So far, all I've got is that someone stepped in brake fluid before walking into the room, and that there were a lot of cotton fibers, some silk ones, and tons of nylon, spandex, and the like in the room. Body glitter, too, somebody in there was a big fan of body glitter." Hookers, probably, they went in for that sort of thing. Or so he had heard. But he didn't intend to speculate for the captain. Just the facts.

After he was finished with the motel room's trace,

he had soil from an animal burial pit waiting for him. He was in no great hurry to get to that—dead animals were terrible and all, but a lesser priority than a dead man and a missing woman.

"So you don't know where things stand in general? No suspect identified, anything like that?"

Hodges wished he'd been able to get out of his lab more, or had been able to pry something out of Nick Stokes when they had last spoken. He didn't want to let the captain down, but he genuinely didn't know, and lying to him was out of the question. "I, uhh, I'll try to find out for you. You want me to call you back?"

"I'll check in with you when I have a chance. Thanks, Hodges." Brass ended the call abruptly.

It was kind of amazing, Hodges thought, that the captain would call *him*, and not somebody like Nick Stokes or Greg Sanders when he had been unable to get through to Catherine. Maybe he was higher up on the totem pole than he realized.

Not as high as he *should* be, of course. With Grissom out of town, they should have asked Hodges to run the lab. Not that there was anything wrong with Catherine's leadership, but she was more valuable out in the field. Hodges *had* been in the field, and he didn't much like it. The field could be filthy and frequently disgusting, and the extremes of weather were unpleasant. Only someone like Greg Sanders could actively seek to exchange the safety and comfort of the lab, with its climate-controlled sterility, for fieldwork. *Not for me,* Hodges thought. But putting him in charge of the lab? He would have the place running like the proverbial well-oiled machine in no time. His genius didn't just lie in science, but in organization as well.

And people skills.

Okay, maybe not so much the latter—at least, people didn't always seem to appreciate those skills the way they should.

But organization?

Pure genius.

Walking to the morgue, Riley couldn't help wondering about the sort of person who would make a career out of opening up dead people and looking inside. It seemed, on the surface, such a ghoulish practice. The human body, people said, was a beautiful thing, and in the abstract, she couldn't argue with that. But they were generally talking about the outside when they said that. The inside looked basically like a bunch of raw meat carried around in a bag of skin—and that was when the internal parts were healthy. When the organs were diseased or otherwise distressed, they stopped looking so much like meat. There wasn't much she could compare a heavy smoker's lungs to, or a big drinker's liver, or an ulcerated intestine. She stopped trying, because she was verging on the ghoulish now herself.

Doc Robbins was no ghoul. He was, in fact, one of the most centered people she knew. He had a life among the living—a family, hobbies, and interests. He was smart, educated, and well informed. He didn't seem to have an unhealthy fascination with death. Instead, he was abundantly alive, and one of the few people she came into contact with regularly who seemed to appreciate her sense of humor, and who could give it back in kind.

She had heard that Albert Robbins had grown up around medicine. His mother had been a nurse, and he had always intended to become a doctor. According to the stories she had heard, the accident that claimed his legs also reshuffled his priorities, causing him to direct his medical practice toward helping the less fortunate, until economic circumstances forced him to close his clinic's doors. After that he became a coroner, and eventually moved to Las Vegas as chief medical examiner.

A reasonable career path, all things considered. Still . . . she worked with dead bodies on a near-daily basis too, but she left them behind, or stayed put to investigate the scene while they were taken away. If this job had required her to stick her hands inside them as a regular practice, she would probably turn to teaching or selling insurance or carrying the mail.

The only career that might be worse was the one her parents had embraced—sticking their hands (metaphorically anyway) into the brains of live people. Psychiatrists, she thought sometimes, were the closest things she knew of to socially acceptable zombies, always on the prowl for more brains to consume.

She pushed open the door and stepped into the morgue. As always, the cold bit at her cheeks.

"Good evening, Riley," Doc Robbins said. He was, as usual, up to his elbows in gore. "Thanks for coming down."

"Is that Jesse Dunwood?"

"It is. Would you like a closer look?"

"I'm fine right here, thanks."

"It's really quite interesting. Have you ever seen the effects of carbon monoxide poisoning?"

"Only from the outside."

"It turns the blood and some internal organs a vivid red color. Really very attractive, almost cheerful. You might think of it the next time you get an ice cream sundae with a cherry on top."

"Does that mean the carbon monoxide poisoning is definitely our COD?"

"That's correct. To be more precise, the mechanism of Mr. Dunwood's death was asphyxiation. Carbon monoxide binds easily to hemoglobin, producing carboxyhemoglobin. Carboxyhemoglobin contains no usable oxygen, so it can't supply needed oxygen to the body's tissues. Mr. Dunwood's saturation level is sixty percent, which in any human will cause almost certain death by asphyxia. He stopped breathing, therefore he died."

"Got it," Riley said. The takeaway message was that the cause of death was asphyxiation, but the reason for that was the carbon monoxide pumped into the airplane's cockpit. So whoever had punctured the muffler and run the hose to the vent had, in fact, murdered Jesse Dunwood—giving Riley a third important piece of information. The manner of death. Homicide. Mechanism, cause, and manner—the building blocks she needed to begin making a case. "Thanks, Doc," she said, starting back through the doors.

"I hope I haven't put you off sundaes," he called.

Riley stopped in the doorway. "We should get one together sometime," she said. "Extra cherries."

"That sounds like fun."

She let the door swing closed.

Ice cream with a coroner.

Fun times, indeed.

13

"Catherine, it's Sam Vega."

"Hi, Sam," Catherine said. The detective wouldn't call her just to pass the time. She hoped he had good news for her, because she was more than ready to hear some. "What's going on?"

"You asked for a heads-up, so I'm giving you one. I don't know yet if this is anything, and it's way too early to tell if it's going to be. But we've had a report of a young woman missing from the Palermo."

So much for good news, but she couldn't deny that it was news. "Missing how long, Sam?"

"She hasn't been seen since seven-thirty."

"Tonight?" Catherine glanced at the clock. Just past midnight. Early still. Casinos didn't put up clocks because they didn't want people knowing just how long they had been throwing their money down, and it was easy to lose track of time.

"Yeah, tonight."

"What's the story?"

"Her name is Melinda Spence. Twenty-two years old. She's here from Hamilton, Ohio, for a family re-union. They're all staying at the Palermo, on one of those group-rate deals. She showed up for a buffet dinner, then said she was going to go play the quarter slots for a while before they all went to a ten o'clock show. Ten o'clock came and went, and she didn't make it to the meeting place. She's not answering her phone. Family members say she's just about the most reliable person on the face of the earth."

"Family members can be remarkably ignorant about one another," Catherine pointed out. She wouldn't have minded having slightly less personal experience with that truism. "Ignorant, blind, or both."

"True. That's why I'm saying I don't know what the deal is on this yet. She might have met someone and is getting busy in one of their rooms right now. She might have gone to another casino, isn't wearing a watch, whatever. It's early, by Vegas standards. And you know people sometimes act out of character here."

"Right."

"So maybe she's just ignoring her phone. It's been known to happen."

"Yes, it has." Lindsey had made a science of it. If Melinda Spence needed any excuses later, maybe Catherine could put the two of them in touch. Unless of course Lindsey ignored the phone when Catherine called her about it.

"But you said you wanted to know about any

disappearances or unsolveds that turned up. Her family's worried about her, and their worry feels like the real deal to me. I can't launch an investigation yet, until more time passes or we have some reason to suspect foul play, but I just wanted to tip you off."

"Okay, Sam, thanks. I'll drop in on the family and have a look around."

"Let me know if you find anything useful, Catherine. 'Bye."

She sat at her desk for another minute, pondering the situation. Sam was right: a young woman, in Las Vegas for maybe the first time, could get involved in all sorts of things that she might not want the rest of her family to know about. It didn't necessarily mean she was in any danger.

But her family was worried, and given Greg's theory about a would-be serial killer preparing to make the move to human victims, maybe it had reason to be. She couldn't discount the possibility, however remote. One missing woman was plenty for one night, and now it appeared that she might have two on her hands.

She called Greg into her office and described the situation as Sam had outlined it.

"I should get over to the Palermo," he said when she had finished. "And those bones should be moved up on the lab's priority list. They're the key to this whole thing."

Catherine had to admire his enthusiasm. "So far, they're still just animal bones, Greg, and we have plenty going on here tonight. Jesse Dunwood is a dead human being, and Antoinette O'Brady is a missing human being. Melinda Spence might also be missing, but we don't know that for certain. The other, more concrete issues have to take precedence."

"I know," he said bitterly. "Sometimes I want to clone myself so I can be everywhere at once."

"I know the feeling, Greg. Dunwood is your first case, and now we know it was a homicide. Get back out to that airport and finish processing that airplane."

"That could take hours, Catherine!"

"It'll take as long as it takes. Go with Riley and get it done."

He looked like he wanted to say something else, but he didn't.

He was smart enough to rein himself in when he needed to. He had made the right choice this time, because Catherine was in no mood to be second-guessed.

This was the boring part of the job.

Greg and Riley had already checked out the airplane and photographed it extensively. Officer Morston swore that no one had touched it in their absence.

Which meant it was time to go over the aircraft, inch by inch, looking for the minutest bits of possible evidence. Riley got a small handheld vacuum cleaner and started on the cockpit floor, picking up whatever dirt and fibers might have been dropped there. Those had probably mostly come from Dunwood himself, but the killer would have had to enter the cockpit to position the tube just right behind the vent. The Locard exchange principle said that any time a person comes into contact with another person, place, or object, there's an exchange of materials, each leaving some trace of the event on the other. Modern forensic science was largely based on that principle, and exceptions were rare indeed. So if the murderer had been inside the cockpit, there should be some sign of his or her presence there. Greg and Riley couldn't fathom any way to have placed the tube without entering the cockpit.

While Riley worked inside the plane, Greg landed the unenviable task of examining the engine, muffler, and tube. Taking apart an airplane was a dirty job, so it was possible that he would be able to find greasy fingerprints. In fact, he did, all over and around the muffler. He photographed these visible prints, known as *patent* prints, then lifted them with tape. Easy part done. Now he had to look for the *latent* impressions, ones that couldn't be seen with the naked eye. Even very clean hands left faint oily traces on surfaces they touched, and engine parts were ideal depositories for them.

"You're back," a voice called from the hangar door.

Greg turned around. Jamal Easton looked in at him, head gleaming in the hangar's overhead lights. "This is a secure area, Mr. Easton."

"I understand. I'm not coming in. I just wanted to see how your investigation's going."

"It's a laborious process." The vacuum cleaner was still humming inside the cockpit—Riley might not even be aware they had a visitor.

"I bet it is."

"Is there something I can do for you?"

Jamal shoved his hands deep into his hip pockets and swayed from heel to heel. He looked like a shy kid asking a girl to the movies. "I just thought maybe you should know something, in case it's important," he said. "Jesse Dunwood? I mean, I liked him, and he was a hell of a pilot. Always nice enough to me. Some folks look down on mechanics, but not Jesse. But here's what you should know. He was having a thing with Tonya Gravesend."

"A thing? You mean an affair?"

"That's right. It was hot and heavy for a while there. But he broke it off, a couple of weeks ago."

"Was he married?"

"Oh, no, not Jesse. He liked to play the field, always squiring some new babe around. That was a holdover from his jet jockey days, I think. Women go for pilots, and there's a certain type drawn to fighter pilots. Nobody could tie him down. I don't know why he broke up with Tonya, but she was stomping around here for days, slamming doors and shooting him the dick-eye every time she saw him. I overheard her talking on her cell phone to a friend, and Jesse's name came up in a derogatory way. A less charitable man might even say threatening. I got the feeling he was kind of a jerk to her."

"Did you tell all this to Detective Williams?"

"Oh yeah. I told him the whole deal."

"That's great, then." *Why are you bothering me with it?* he almost asked. But he had a feeling the man would tell him anyway. Some people just had to talk. That's what confessionals were for, but sometimes the nearest CSI would do just as well.

"I just figured, you know, you're investigating it too. So you ought to know."

"I'm a crime scene investigator, Mr. Easton. The detective is the one who's trying to find Mr. Dunwood's killer."

"Okay, understood," Jamal said, nodding his big head. "I just wanted everyone to be in the same loop."

"I appreciate that."

"I'll wish you a good night then, sir. You let me know if you need anything else."

"I'll do that." Jamal Easton wandered off into the darkness beyond the hangar, and Greg went back to work, wondering if Jamal had some unstated motive for telling him all that.

He started with an ultraviolet light, beaming it this way and that over the muffler. A couple of faint prints showed up, but nothing very clear beyond the patent prints he'd already found. Which meant getting out the dust. He picked a rich carbon black powder, to show up against the gray steel of the muffler. The wand he used was no brush at all, but a magnetic device that never actually touched the surface he was dusting. He concentrated his efforts around the hole that had been bored into the muffler, and on the black plastic tubing near the point of insertion, figuring that the killer would have had his hands all over them in those places.

He was playing loud music in his head, trying to drown out the hum of Riley's vacuum, when the drum part fell out of syncopation and he realized someone was knocking on the hangar door. He

looked over and saw Patti Van Dyke smiling hesi-
tantly at him.

"Please don't come in here," Greg said. Another
one? He shouldn't have let Morston go on a lunch
break, but he hadn't thought the officer would be
needed for a while.

"Okay, but can I talk to you a minute, though?
Can you come here?"

Greg put down his supplies and walked over toward her. She still wore an uneasy smile. It looked
like something she'd picked up at a discount store
that didn't quite fit on her face. "What is it,
ma'am?"

"If you don't hang around airports, you don't
know the kind of drama we got going on in a place
like this. Between pilots and ground crew and
couch rats, we got a TV soap opera going on seven
days a week. Even the TV soaps get weekends off,
but weekends are when ours get really juicy."

"Are you saying that you think one of the airport
people might have killed Jesse Dunwood?"

"All I'm saying is that some of them aren't too
sorry he's dead."

"I thought he was well liked."

"Well, in public that's what we all say. We don't
like to air our dirty laundry. But it's there just the
same."

"If there's something specific you know—"

Patti barely let him get the words out. "Jesse and
Jamal, they fought all the time."

It hadn't sounded that way just minutes ago,
when Jamal Easton was expressing his admiration
for Dunwood. "You mean they argued?"

"Well, usually. To put it mildly, I'd say. They got into real hollering matches sometimes. Ugly, vicious ones. Jesse made some racial comments about Jamal that we all thought were over the line, but he was a customer—one of the airport's best customers—so there wasn't much anybody felt like they could do about it. Then last week, or maybe, no, eight or ten days ago, I guess, they got into it for real."

"Physically?"

"That's what I'm saying. It started with shouting, then pushing. Finally they were all over each other and throwing punches. Jesse ended up knocking Jamal down. He kicked him a couple of times in the ribs, and said something like 'You're lucky I don't kill you right here.' He was kind of a bully, Jesse was. I had my hand on the phone, ready to call the cops if he tried to do anything more to Jamal. He backed off and we helped Jamal up, but he didn't ever go to the hospital or anything. The bad blood passed after that, but they were never going to be friendly again, you could just tell."

As he had with Jamal, Greg asked if she had told Detective Williams her story. She assured him that she had, in great detail. Hearing that, Greg talked her into leaving so he could finish his work.

The night was slipping away from him while he listened to airport gossip. He went back to the SUV to get a jacket, since the air was finally turning cool, and then returned to the airplane.

While he worked, almost on autopilot, Greg had to keep reminding himself not to let his mind drift to the animal bones at the Empire construction site and the missing woman from the Palermo. Catherine was right, after all—Jesse Dunwood had been murdered and deserved his full attention. He wouldn't do anybody any favors by letting his thoughts be scattered.

His fingerprint powder revealed more faint impressions, but just a few. He photographed and lifted these as well, then started in on the engine canopy, where anyone would have to touch it to open it. He hoped Jamal Easton's gloved hands hadn't obscured anything important when he went inside the canopy and found the rigged muffler. Detective Williams had made sure that fingerprints had been taken from all the airport personnel on duty tonight. As always, those people were told they were bring printed for purposes of elimination. Sometimes it was even true, but the hope was always that they would all be used for elimination except the one set that wasn't.

"Hey, pal," a scratchy voice called. Greg tried not to sigh audibly. *Oh my God, please give me a break tonight.* He turned and saw the disabled janitor, Benny Kracsinski, a few steps in from the doorway, leaning on a worn, chipped wooden cane. Hard for a janitor to get around with a cane, Greg guessed, since brooms and other cleaning tools often worked best with two hands.

"Stay right there," Greg said. Riley's vacuum was still running. How was it that she never heard these interruptions? "I'll come to you."

He did. Benny cocked his head, looking up at Greg with hooded eyes. His jaw was thick with silvery stubble. "I hope you find the bastard who did that to Jesse."

"I'm working on it," Greg said. The hint was utterly lost on Benny.

"Good, good. You find him, you put him away for a long time, okay?"

"That's the idea. Can I ask you—did you like Dunwood? A lot of people seem to have had some sort of difficulty with him."

"I got no problems with him myself. He was a rich guy, right? But he was always nice enough to those of us who aren't so lucky. He always gave me a present at Christmas, you know, a bottle of something or maybe some kind of gadget. Most pilots fly out of here don't know the cleaning staff exists, but Jesse, he paid attention to everyone."

"Was there anybody with a particular grudge against him, that you knew of?" Greg found himself asking, even though he knew the detective had covered this ground.

Benny considered this for a moment. His fingers rubbing his chin made a sandpaper sound. "Lately, I'd have to say Stan Johnston."

"The tower controller?"

"Yeah, Stan. He had borrowed some money from Jesse. I guess a lot of it, over the years. People don't pay any attention to a guy cleaning toilets or sweeping floors, so I heard stuff. Jesse had reached the point where he didn't think Stan ever meant to pay him back. He was trying to collect, even threatened to sue Stan. There were—well, let's just say there were some angry words tossed back and forth."

"I see," Greg said. "Did you tell all this to the detective?"

"Maybe not in quite such detail," Benny said.

"It would be a good idea to call him up and fill him in," Greg suggested. "I appreciate the tip, but you can't hold back when you're questioned."

"I understand. I ain't saying it was Stan who did it, mind you. I just thought you oughtta know."

"I get it, Mr. Kracsinski. Thanks again."

Benny touched his forehead in a casual salute, then hobbled off into the dark, his cane tapping the ground every few paces.

Greg waited until he was gone, then crossed the hangar and shut the door. He turned back toward the plane, thought better of it, and locked the door.

Now, he thought, *maybe I can get some work done.*

14

THE INTERVIEW ROOM WAS nobody's idea of a pleasant place to while away the hours. The walls and floor were all shades of gray and black; the table and chairs were gray. Nick supposed there were names for all the different shades—charcoal, slate, things like that—but at a certain point, gray was just gray, period. Everybody who walked in knew the big mirror on one wall was really a window, and anybody might be watching, unseen, from the other side. It was, to put it mildly, one of the most institutional-looking rooms Nick had ever spent time in. Even the designers of mental hospitals tried harder to lighten the mood.

Which was precisely the point. The room was meant to make suspects uncomfortable, to keep them unsettled. Like right now. Nick sat across from Will Penfold, who fidgeted and squirmed as if his chair had been set on fire. Penfold had deeply tanned skin, his left arm a veritable skin cancer petri

dish, thanks to what appeared to be a lifelong habit
of hanging it out the window as he drove his beer
truck. His hair was cropped short and tattoos spilled
from his neck and across his shoulders. He scratched
at his goatee from time to time, as if insects had settled there. He hadn't been charged with anything,
and he hadn't called, or asked for, an attorney. Nick
was happy to leave it that way, for now.

"I understand you hired Deke Freeson to do
some investigative work," Nick began.

"That's right. Biggest waste of money in my life."
He chuckled dryly. "And believe me, I've got a lot of
competition for that. I tried to stop payment on my
retainer check, but he'd already cashed it."

"I hear you," Nick said. "What was your problem
with him? If you don't mind me asking." It couldn't
hurt to act like Penfold's friend, to try to work gen-
tly through his natural defenses.

Penfold put his hands flat on the smooth tabletop
and pressed, as if trying to push the table legs
through the floor. "Unless I missed something,
when you hire a private detective, that guy is supposed to work *for* you, right?"

"That's generally the case," Nick said. "Is that not
what happened?"

"No-oo," Penfold said. He was clearly still angry
about his experience with Freeson. "That is not
what happened," he said, imitating Nick. *Maybe he's
lucky Freeson didn't shoot him, if this is his usual way of
relating to other people. Then again, maybe he's just a better shot than Freeson.*

"Tell me about it, then."

"Okay, whatever. I had this brilliant idea. Once in a lifetime brilliant, you feel me?"

Nick managed to hide his laugh with a forced cough. "This is the beer underpants idea?"

"Beer-flavored underwear," Penfold corrected. "For men or women, and not just underpants. Thongs, bras, boxers, briefs, everything."

"I . . . I guess I'm missing something. Why?"

"Who doesn't love beer, dawg? Right? And face facts—you know how much women love it when a guy rips their pants off with his teeth?"

Penfold paused. He really did expect an answer.

"I guess maybe I've heard that."

"Trust me, man. They do. Start 'em off like that and you really get 'em revved up."

"Okay."

"And plus while you're at it, maybe you'll give them some attention, right? They like that, too. And if everything tastes like beer, what dude's not gonna dive right in? It works the other way, too, because chicks like beer as much as some dudes do."

"And you know this because of your professional experience in the malt beverage industry."

"Because I drive a beer truck, yeah. You wouldn't believe how many chicks honk and wave. Some of 'em even flash me on the highway. They love the suds, bro."

"Okay, so you had this idea." Nick still didn't think much of the idea, even after the impassioned description of it. "Then what happened?"

"I drive a beer truck, dude. I don't know jack about product development and marketing and all that crap. But I know this guy, Abner Klein."

"And Abner knows about those things?"

"I thought he did. He's this screen printer, right, does apparel for some of the big casinos and other clients. I mean big national clients. You see a T-shirt or hoodie with the Lucky Dragon or the Romanov logo on it, Abner made that. So I figure, dude knows the apparel business. He'll know who to pitch the beer underwear idea to and how to go about it. Someone will buy it and then we'll both be set for life. Sweet, huh?"

"Sweet," Nick agreed. "So what happened?"

"What happened was that Abner screwed me."

"Screwed you how? Hey, you want a soda or something?"

"You got a brew?"

"I'll get you a soda. Hang tight." Nick let himself out of the interview room and went to fetch a bottled soda and a straw. Most people didn't use a straw for a bottle or a can, and as a beer connoisseur, he doubted that Penfold would. But he might be more likely to use one with a bottle than a can. If he did use the straw, he would leave DNA on it, which maybe could be matched to DNA found in the motel room. Even if he didn't, he might leave some on the bottle, and he would definitely leave fingerprints all over both the bottle and the table. Since Nick was trying to get his cooperation, acquiring prints and DNA surreptitiously might help advance his cause more than asking for them outright.

Returning to the gray-on-gray room, Nick set the bottle down on the table, just far enough away that Penfold had to rise up out of his seat and reach for it. Just to make him a little more off balance. He had been the guy's pal and all he got was an extended riff about beer underwear. Time to turn things up a notch. He had also carried in a field kit, which he put on the floor beside his own chair, where Penfold couldn't get a good look at it. "Let's get real here, Penfold," he said. "You went to this guy Abner because you didn't know squat about how to develop your idea. And Abner cheated you, right?"

"I thought he was cheating me, man." Penfold sat back down, took a sip through the straw, then left the bottle on the table and placed his hands in his lap. His whole demeanor was different now, his shoulders slumped, his gaze downcast. He moved his eyes to look up at Nick, but not his head. "I thought he was going to partner with me, but instead I heard back from a couple of buddies that he was taking the idea to apparel manufacturers and claiming it as his own. I had put up half the dough to get some prototypes made, and if he was ripping me off, I had to know."

"So you hired Freeson."

"That's right. He was supposed to find out if Abner was straight up or not."

"And then?"

"Then I heard from these same buddies that Freeson had probably gone into business with Abner. He kept not being able to find anything out, he said. He talked to some of the people Abner did, but he claimed Abner was making people sign those, whatever, nondisclosive agreements before he would tell them the idea, so without a court order they wouldn't talk to him. Seemed suspicious as hell to me."

"Nondisclosure," Nick said.

"What?"

"It's called a nondisclosure agreement, not nondisclosive. And it's a standard business practice."

"It is?"

"Absolutely. Freeson was telling you the truth."

"He was?"

"Sounds like it to me. The conversations Abner was having were legally proprietary. If people had described their conversations with Abner to Freeson, they would have been breaking binding legal contracts."

"No way."

"That's right. Did you ever just ask Abner?"

"My buddies told me he would just lie to me if he was really pulling something."

"Sounds like your buddies are idiots."

"Some of 'em, yeah."

"But you listened to them."

"Dawg, that's what bros are for. To have each other's backs."

"Right. Did these bros have any way of knowing that what they were claiming was true?"

"Just . . . you know, they're dudes who have been around. Maybe they were just telling me what they *thought* Abner was up to. But they said it like they knew."

"Right," Nick said again. "So they were guessing, and you believed them."

Penfold looked like someone had killed his dog. "You think Abner was on the up-and-up?"

"I don't see any reason not to."

"Even though he never brought in an offer?"

"I'd be more surprised to hear that he did get an offer."

"Really?"

"Really."

"That's harsh, dawg."

"Just being honest with you, Will." Nick opened his field kit, took out a color glossy, and dropped it on the table. Freeson could be recognized in the photo in spite of the hole in his face, but Nick was pretty sure the hole would make the biggest impression. He dropped it faceup on the table in front of Penfold. "You killed Deke Freeson for no reason."

Penfold grabbed the edge of the table in both hands, his eyes suddenly the size of small balloons. He turned away from the photograph. "*Killed?* No way, dude. No way."

"You didn't break into a motel room and shoot him, that what you're telling me?"

"Man . . . okay, fine. I tried to hit him once, at his office. I landed a punch and just about pissed myself. That girl, Camille, his secretary or whatever, she saw it happen. I thought I would die of shame."

"She thought you were pretty mad."

"I was. I was goddamned furious. But I couldn't even get in a decent shot. My fist hit his, I don't know, his shoulder or something. I felt it all the way up my arm. That night I had to drink myself to sleep. No way could I cap a guy."

"Where were you earlier tonight?"

"Making deliveries. I was in the truck until nine."

"Plenty of people see you?"

"People at every store I stopped at. Plus it's all in my log, and stored on the GPS in my truck."

"Okay. You don't mind if I swab your hands?"

"If you what who?"

"Swab your hands."

"Will it hurt?"

"Not a bit."

"What does it mean?"

Nick didn't think there was any harm in explaining. Penfold's story sounded pretty convincing. "I'm looking for something called gunshot residue," he said. "It usually dissipates in a couple of hours, or through hand washing, but sometimes traces of it hang around."

"How would I get it on me?"

"By shooting a gun."

Penfold smiled. "Swab away, boss. I haven't shot a gun in fifteen years."

Nick opened his kit and took out several pieces of filter paper. He brushed one over Penfold's right hand—he had used that one to grip the soda bottle, so Nick knew he was right-handed—then brushed his left hand with another, then swiped his arms and finally his shirt.

"That's it?" Penfold asked.

"Almost," Nick said. He put a couple of drops of diphenylamine on each piece of paper. They didn't change color.

"What's that mean?"

"Means nothing."

"What?"

"It means there's no gunshot residue on you. If it had turned blue, then I'd have to run some confirmatory tests to make sure it wasn't reading urine, tobacco, or certain other substances. But it didn't, so you're clean."

"I told you."

"Unless you washed it off and changed clothes."

"Dude, I told you, I didn't shoot nobody! I was making my rounds. Check my truck!"

"I will."

"Do I get to go home?"

"Soon," Nick said. "Just hang for a while. You can go after I've looked over your truck."

"Dude, my truck is at home! The *cops* drove me here!"

Nick closed his kit up. "Then I guess you'll have to hang for a little while longer."

15

AFTER BENNY KRACSINSKI left the hangar, Greg turned back to his work once again. Too many interruptions. He still had to lift some of the prints he had revealed with the dust, so he took the tape and captured them, pressing the tape down on a white backing card to preserve the impressions intact.

A few minutes later he heard a rapping at the door. *This is getting insane.* Greg suppressed a curse and looked over his shoulder. He couldn't not answer it—what if it was Williams, or Officer Morston with something important? He went to the door and unlocked it. Tonya Gravesend stood there, her hands stuffed into her pockets.

"You can't come in right now," he said, wondering where Officer Morston had gone for lunch. California, maybe, at this rate.

"Oh, I'm sorry." She shrugged. "Am I okay here?"

"Where you are is fine," he said. "Just stay right there." He really would have preferred her just about anywhere else—at her own home, or in the airport office, or thirty-five thousand feet in the air behind the controls of a jumbo jet. Or maybe lunching in California with Officer Morston. But Jamal Easton had suggested she be looked at for Dunwood's murder, so he figured it couldn't hurt to give her as much time as the others had taken. Maybe he would learn something helpful. "What can I do for you?"

"Oh," she said. "Oh . . . I just . . . I wanted to thank you for what you're doing here."

Greg gave a modest shrug. "It's our job."

"But someone's got to find out what happened to Jesse, and you two seem like the people who can do it."

"We'll do what we can. The detectives will figure things out, don't worry about that, and we'll provide the physical evidence they need to get a conviction."

"I sure hope so." She touched the inner corner of her right eye, like a bad actress faking tears. "I really do."

"You and Mr. Dunwood were . . . close?"

"Oh, close, yes. We were . . . well, let's just say we were close for a while. Very close."

"Close like close friends? Or lovers?"

"Oh, I'd say both. Both. Lovers and friends."

"But you said you were close for a while, which sounds like it means not anymore. Did something happen to end it?"

Tonya chewed on her lower lip. "You could put it that way. I guess what happened was that I found out that Jesse and I had different agendas. I wanted something that might last for a while, and he wanted changes of scenery. Constant changes of scenery."

"So you two broke up."

"Yes. Oh, we broke up, yes."

"You sound a little . . . angry? Bitter, maybe?"

"I can't deny that he pissed me off. Not so much the breaking up with me part, because I was expecting that all along. It was more the way he did it . . . or didn't do it, because he didn't really do anything. He just kind of assumed it was understood."

"I can see how that might upset you."

"Oh, I'm not the only one who gets upset with Jesse. Not by a country mile, no, sir. He's got a knack for upsetting people."

"Is there anyone in particular you're thinking of, Ms. Gravesend?"

"Oh, I don't . . . oh, okay. I guess it's all right to tell you."

"Of course it is."

"I found out we were done when he showed up with another woman for one of his night flights. When you're flying your own small plane, it's hard to . . . you know, join the mile-high club. But there are still things you can do. Things that can be done to you while you're flying, if you're a guy. Things that Jesse was particularly fond of. He brought this woman in a couple of weeks ago—"

"Do you know her name?"

"No idea. Slutty McBoobsome is what I called her. She was hot-looking, you know what I mean? Tons of long red hair, great figure. The kind of woman who doesn't mind showing off what she's got, and she's got plenty to show. Anyway, I saw them headed for the hangar and I stopped him to ask, you know, what's up. And he said we had some laughs, and now he was going to have some laughs with this new woman. What they didn't know was that her husband apparently didn't trust her very much. Didn't trust her for good reason, I guess. He was pretty sneaky about it, and when they landed, guess who was waiting?"

"The husband."

"The husband. Oh, you should have seen her face when she got out of the plane and saw him there. It was priceless."

"What happened?"

"What happened was that this guy—you could tell he works out and he had to be twenty or thirty years younger than Jesse—he laid Jesse out. Bam! One good punch put Jesse on the floor."

"Really?"

"Oh yes. I was so mad at him I didn't really even mind seeing it happen. Then, while Jesse was down, the guy leaned over him and lifted his head up by the hair and told him that if he ever saw Jesse sniffing around his wife again, he would kill him."

"He really said that?"

"Oh yes. He said that he would kill him."

"I meant 'sniffing around.'"

Tonya laughed. "Maybe he's the old-fashioned type. I tell you, it was something to see him drop Jesse like that."

"Do you think he really would have killed Jesse?"

"I don't know. He could have, that's what I

wanted to tell you. Because the guy was royally pissed off. Like he shouldn't have known all along that his wife was that kind of girl. But I guess maybe he did, and that's why he was following her."

"Did you tell all this to Detective Williams?" He should have asked that question first, and maybe saved himself ten minutes.

"No. I didn't like him. He was too . . . I don't know. Abrupt."

That didn't sound like the Grayson Williams he knew. "That's not how it's supposed to work, Ms. Gravesend."

She gave an exaggerated shrug. "Oh, bad me. Are you going to spank me now?"

"No, but I'll have a detective interview you again."

"There'll be no spanking during working hours," Riley said.

She had finally emerged from the cockpit and stood outside the airplane.

Tonya gave another shrug, a minimal one this time, and turned to leave. "I'll talk to whoever you need me to," she said.

"I appreciate that."

"That one likes to make trouble," Riley said, after Tonya was gone and the door was locked again.

"She does? Is that an insight from growing up with psychiatrists?"

"It's an insight from living my life in the real world. You should try it sometime." Before Greg could form a response, she asked, "Did you find anything in there? When you weren't busy chatting?"

"Plenty of impressions," Greg said. "We may find

that they're perfectly legitimate, but at least Mandy will earn another day's pay."

"Job security is never a bad thing. I've got a few from inside the cockpit, too."

"I thought you were vacuuming."

"I was. Then I wasn't. Do you hear the vacuum?"

"Now that you mention it, no. But I kept being interrupted. You didn't hear all those people come around? Half the airport staff, it seems like."

"I guess I must have missed them." She wore a wry grin.

"Or you chose to miss them."

"We'll never know."

Greg got a grip on the tube and yanked it free of the hole. It was black, its opening an eighth of an inch in diameter. "We'll have to figure out where this came from," he said. "It's polyethylene, not the softer rubber I would have used if for that purpose."

"It worked, though. So maybe you wouldn't be as successful a murderer as whoever rigged this."

"I think I'd be pretty good at it," Greg said. "I mean, if I wanted to be. You learn a lot in this job about what to do, and especially what not to do."

"Yeah. Like don't get caught. Can I see that?" She held out her hand, and he handed the end of the tube to her. She turned it around in her hands, looking at every side. "This looks like irrigation tubing. We should see if the airport has a drip irrigation system for the landscaping. And check out these faint marks around the cut end. This was cut with something that circled around the tube, and it was circled a few more times than necessary."

"It could have been a knife, just slicing around the outside instead of bearing down or sawing."

"Either way, we have tool marks. If we can find a suspect tool, we'll be able to match it up to these."

"That's a good catch," Greg said. "I guess if you can work without a lot of people distracting you, it's easier to notice things like that."

"I guess you're right." Riley coiled the tubing and put it into a big plastic bag. "Maybe you should try that sometime, too."

16

SEE," CATHERINE SAID, "the thing about DNA is that it's highly individualized."

"So I understand," Sam Vega said. They were in his unmarked car, heading for an address in west Las Vegas. "I do pay attention, Catherine."

"Sorry, I didn't mean to sound like an Intro to Forensics professor, Sam. What I'm trying to say is that everybody has their own distinctive DNA, as you know. Everybody's has lots of things in common, but enough different that nobody matches up exactly. Except . . ."

"There's an except?"

"Except identical twins."

"Really? They have the same DNA?"

She found herself wanting to explain, but holding her tongue. Sam was a smart cop, and he probably knew everything the average detective needed to know about DNA.

Except for the part about twins. But that wasn't

the kind of thing that even the experts thought about in every case. Generally speaking, when you found a DNA match for somebody, that was the person you were looking for. Nobody wanted to have to check in every case to see if that suspect had an identical twin.

The basic building blocks of all life were the four purine bases: adenine, cytosine, guanine, and thymine. Scientists, in a rare example of common sense, referred to them by their initials, A, C, G, and T. They could be combined in DNA strands by the billions, in any order whatsoever. Every human being had about six billion bases in his or her DNA. Because the combinations were so variable, nobody matched anybody else, and DNA typing was the most accurate and reliable way science had yet found to positively identify an individual.

Unless, of course, that individual was an identical twin.

"Same DNA," she said, leaving out the rest of it.

"But they don't have the same fingerprints. I arrested a pair of identical twins once. Prostitutes. They had a wild scam going, confusing their johns and stealing them blind. You could not tell them apart. But their fingerprints were different."

"That's right, identical twins have the same DNA but still have different fingerprints. We're not quite sure why."

"The world is a strange place."

"If it wasn't, we wouldn't need so many cops."

"That's an excellent point."

"So this guy we're going to see . . ."

"His name is Cliff Gorecki. He's the twin brother

of a man named Bart Gorecki, who died in prison in California, several years ago. Because he was in prison, and DNA evidence was used in his trial, a semen sample we collected at the Rancho Center Motel matched his DNA. But it couldn't have been his, because while that motel doesn't do its laundry that often or that well, the chance of a sample from pre-2002 turning up on a bedspread today is exceedingly slim."

"Slimmer than the chance that he had a twin brother."

"Statistically, I'm not positive. But I checked the twin angle before I tried to date the semen."

Sam smiled. "I don't blame you."

"Since Cliff lives here in Las Vegas, it seems far more likely that it's his deposit at the motel, not his brother's. Cliff has a record, too, although not one as colorful as his late brother's. He pleaded guilty to a B&E a few years ago, and he's had a couple of misdemeanor convictions, but nothing where DNA came into it. Since he was in the same room where Deke Freeson was murdered, we'd like to find out what he was doing there, and when he was doing it."

"I have a pretty good idea what he was doing," Sam said.

"And with who," Catherine added. "That might be important, too."

"Well, we're here. Let's find out." He parked in front of a two-story apartment building. All the rooms faced onto the street, with a walkway running in front of the doors on the second floor and a staircase at each end. VISTA MONTANA was spelled out in wrought-iron script on a brick wall. Catherine couldn't see any mountains, but then again it was dark.

They went up one staircase and Sam rang the doorbell of Apartment 11. He waited a couple minutes, then rang it again.

"Some people," he muttered.

"It *is* late."

"We're awake. Why aren't they?"

"If we start comparing civilians' lives to ours, Sam, none of us is going to come out well."

He had his finger on the buzzer again when the door opened. A man stood inside, wearing boxer shorts with cartoon characters on them. His legs, arms, and chest were covered with a thick mat of curly black hair that crept up his neck, as if he had waded up to his chin in glue and then barbershop clippings. "What the hell?" he asked.

"Cliff Gorecki?" Sam asked.

"Yeah, who the hell are you?"

Sam and Catherine showed him their badges. "Detective Sam Vega, and this is Supervisor Catherine Willows of the crime lab. We'd like to ask you some questions."

"Do you have any idea what time it is?"

"Do you have any idea how many people ask us that?"

"I'm not surprised, if you go around knocking on people's doors at all hours. Don't you have any common decency?"

Catherine wanted to make a crack about how anyone with common decency would cover up the fur on his body, but professionalism won out. "We're sorry to disturb you at this hour," she said. She sniffed the air coming from the apartment, which carried a faint odor of leftover Chinese food. Suddenly, she was hungry. "We wouldn't if it wasn't important."

A sleepy female voice called out from inside the apartment. "Who is it, baby?"

"It's nothing," he said over his shoulder. "Don't worry about it." He glared at Catherine and Sam. "Now you woke up my wife, too. Good job."

"Mr. Gorecki," Catherine said, "when were you most recently at the Rancho Center Motel?"

Gorecki looked at the ground for a second, then snapped his head back up. "Never heard of it."

"That's not very convincing, sir," Sam said. "You'll have to do better than that."

"I mean, I drive by it sometimes, I guess. But I've never stayed there or been inside."

"My understanding is that more people take rooms by the hour than actually stay there," Catherine said. "Are you saying if I look through their check-in records and credit card receipts, I won't find your name?"

He stepped outside the door and pulled it behind him, apparently more concerned about keeping something quiet than his lack of clothing. He spoke in a low voice. "Look, I got nothing to hide from you people. But my wife . . . she might not understand."

"I'm not your wife, so why don't you try me?"

"A man's got needs, right?"

"As do we all," Catherine said.

"I love Lori, but you can't always get everything you want from one woman. So sometimes . . . okay, hell, I admit it. I pick up a girl from time to time. Just for a little variety. And that motel is a handy place to take 'em. Not expensive, nobody asks any questions or looks too closely at you. Like you said, you can get a room by the hour there."

"Now we're getting somewhere," Sam said. "When were you there last?"

Gorecki looked skyward this time. "I guess it was . . . four days ago?" he said. "In the afternoon."

"Are you sure about that? Nothing more recent?"

"It's not something I do so often I can't keep track."

"Can anyone corroborate that story?" Sam asked.

"I paid with a debit card," Gorecki said. "So like you said, you can check their records."

"But you weren't alone, right?" Catherine asked. "There was a witness."

"Yeah." He hesitated. Sam jutted his chin at Gorecki and he went on. "But I don't know how you'd find . . . well, her, I guess."

"You guess?"

He leaned toward them and lowered his voice even more. "Look, she calls herself Sugar Bear—that's all I know about her. She's big, tall. I picked her up over on Main, we went to the motel, did what we did, and I dropped her off again. End of story. I don't have her cell number or anything."

"Oh, don't worry about that. Every cop in Las Vegas knows Sugar Bear," Sam said. "We know how to find her."

"You do?"

"Mr. Gorecki, even in Las Vegas there aren't many two hundred and seventy–pound transvestite hookers working the streets. I'm sure we can get our hands on her if we need to."

Gorecki immediately went crimson. Catherine thought his skin even glowed through the thick fur coat, but that might have been an illusion.

"We're not judging you here, Mr. Gorecki," said Catherine, "but we'd appreciate some honesty. You weren't at the motel today or tonight?"

"No. Hell no. I was with my wife and some buddies, playing cards."

"We'll need a list of their names and a way to reach them."

"No problem." He ducked back inside, returned with an envelope and a pen, and scrawled four names and phone numbers onto it. "Here you go."

"Thank you," Catherine said. "By the way, do you know someone named Antoinette O'Brady?"

Gorecki picked at some of the fur thatching his belly. "Doesn't sound familiar."

"How about Deke Freeson?" Sam asked.

"Nope."

"Okay, fine," Catherine said. "Thanks for your co-operation."

"And don't go anywhere," Sam said. "In case we need to talk to you again."

Gorecki pushed the door open again and started through it. "I got nowhere to go and no money to get me there. You don't got to worry about me."

"Stay out of trouble," Sam said. "And if I were you, I'd keep away from Sugar Bear for a while."

"Sugar Bear?" A petite woman had silently walked up behind Gorecki, barefoot, wearing only a short silky nightgown that left almost nothing to the imagination. Her hair was dark brown and loose, her eyes tired. She was too young and not blond enough to be Antoinette O'Brady. "What about Sugar Bear?"

Here it comes, Catherine thought. "Let's go, Sam. I think he's in enough trouble without us here."

"It's nothing, baby. Go back to bed."

"You bastard," she said. Gorecki started to close the door, but her voice came through anyway. "You know I hate it when you see her without me."

The door shut, muffling their voices. Catherine and Sam started down the stairs. "Wow," Sam said.

"Wow what?"

"People can really fool you."

"We wouldn't be people if we didn't," Catherine said. "I think that's what we're best at."

17

MOST NIGHTS, GIL GRISSOM seemed to juggle three or four cases at once without breaking a sweat. So why, Catherine wondered, did handling the logistics of everything seem so complicated? Go here, go there, send this CSI to that scene and another one to this scene. Keep the lab techs busy, coordinate with the detectives, prepare reports for the undersheriff. Piece of cake, Catherine would have thought, except that it wasn't. She had felt one step behind all night long. Everyone seemed to have their hands more than full, too much going on, herself included.

She was worried about Jim Brass, worried about Antoinette O'Brady, and now worried about Melinda Spence. She made time for a quick call to Lindsey, just to reassure herself that some things were well in her world, but got her daughter's voicemail. Finally sleeping, she told herself, the crisis over Sondra and Jayden already settled. She would answer if she wasn't asleep, as she should be at this time of night.

Still, the call that was meant to put Catherine at ease only made her more uptight because she hadn't been able to hear Lindsey's voice. She knew she had less to worry about than a lot of other parents—Lindsey was smart and careful, and had so far resisted a lot of the temptations to which young people often succumbed.

That didn't mean Catherine didn't worry.

Archie Johnson knocked twice, and Catherine waved him into the office. Every visitor felt like another interruption, one more thing preventing her from getting something else done, even though she understood that every person in the lab was working just as hard as she was, and had a contribution to make. Instead of sitting down, he stood behind the guest chair with his hands on the back. He seemed to tower over the desk, and his upswept black hair added at least an extra inch to his height.

"Mandy got an AFIS hit off some fingerprints from the motel," Archie said. "Surprisingly, Antoinette O'Brady really is Antoinette O'Brady."

"Mystery solved. Now we can all go home."

"Mystery just beginning," Archie countered. "She was in the system because of some minor run-ins with the law in the 1970s and '80s, back east. Petty theft, drunk and disorderly, that kind of thing. Running with the wrong crowd, it sounds like. But that old record didn't give us much information that might help anybody find her now. Mandy's still running more prints, so I did a little poking around."

"Which is what you do so well."

"One of my many talents, yes. And I did find out some interesting tidbits."

"Such as?"

"Such as while her name used to be Antoinette O'Brady, for the last twenty-four years she has officially been Antoinette Blago. That driver's license she was carrying is a phony, but the state of Nevada has issued one under the Blago name."

"Blago—that sounds familiar," Catherine said. On another night she would have latched right on to it, but tonight the name was just one of too many things swimming around her.

"Think wise guys," Archie said. "She's married to Emil Blago."

The name clicked everything into place. "Ohh. He's a *serious* wise guy."

"The kind who built Vegas. At least, according to Greg."

"Greg is fascinated by our city's criminal history, isn't he?"

"It's a compelling topic. And even though he's only been in town a few years, Blago seems determined to live up to the archetype."

"This certainly puts a different spin on Antoinette's disappearance. And Deke Freeson's murder."

"One more thing." Archie pulled a piece of paper from the pocket of his lab coat. "I actually printed this for you, because . . . well, because high school pictures are funny."

"High school?" Catherine reached for the paper. On it were printed two strips of black-and-white photos from a decades-old high school yearbook.

"Grover Cleveland High School, Newark, New Jersey, 1970. Antoinette O'Brady's in the top row, second from the left."

The girl in the picture had long, straight blond hair held down by a leather headband wrapped across her forehead. She wore heavy eye shadow and smirked at the camera with her eyes half-shut. She seemed to be saying she knew her whole life was a joke—the photographer, the school, and all the rest of it—and she had more important places to be. Looking at her, Catherine could see a resemblance, across the years, to the driver's license picture of Antoinette O'Brady. "She looks like a troublemaker. The same person?"

"It's definitely the same person," Archie said. "I ran FR on it and the two pictures are a positive match."

Catherine did a quick facial recognition analysis of her own, holding the two pictures side by side. The lab's facial recognition software would study and compare eighty different nodal points—the depth of the eye sockets, the distance between the eyes, the shape of the cheekbones, and so on—to determine if two faces were the same. She came up with the exact result Archie's software had: Antoinette O'Brady was indeed Antoinette O'Brady. "That's good to know," she said.

"Now look at the bottom row, center," Archie said. "Same school, same class."

Catherine scanned the other row. Boston, Boynton, Brass . . .

"Brass?" she asked. She already knew the answer. *Brass, James,* the caption said. And sure enough, from inside a beefy young man, Jim's direct eyes glared at her. His mouth hadn't changed much either, the lips thin, the corners curled in a grin amused at all the world's foibles. His dark hair was longer than she would have expected, appearing to shoot off in every direction at once, like a box of fireworks with a flare thrown into the middle, barely contained by the frame of the photograph. He wore a light turtleneck, and the chains of a medallion were visible draped across his collarbones. "Wow," Catherine said. "I'd never have believed it. I guess this is before he volunteered for Vietnam."

"If you had hair like that, you'd want to get out of the country, too. That's why I had to print it out. We can blackmail the captain for whatever we need."

The meaning of the two rows of pictures sank in, delayed by the unexpected appearance of the young Jim Brass. "Wait, you're saying that Jim Brass went to high school with Antoinette O'Brady? And she's married to Emil Blago?"

Archie gave her a smile. "That's what I'm saying. I told you it was interesting."

Catherine sent Archie away, and prepared for another late-night visit, this time to see Emil Blago. She wanted to know what he knew about his wife's disappearance. Antoinette could have come home and they'd been looking for her for no reason. She was barely out of her office when Nick Stokes caught up to her, walking quickly. "You going somewhere, Catherine?" he asked.

She looked up and down the hall to make sure

they were alone. "I'm going to see a mobster named Emil Blago." She briefly described Archie's findings.

"I've got to see that picture of Brass," Nick said.

"Oh, don't worry, everyone's going to see it."

"That's good. Don't rush off yet, though."

"What is it?"

"Couple things. Number one, I believe Will Penfold is clean. I've confirmed that he was making rounds in his beer truck when Freeson was killed, just like he says."

"Okay, strike one. What's number two?"

"Hodges came through."

"In what way?"

"He identified the type of brake fluid you found on the carpet at the Rancho Center Motel. It's a unique high-performance blend, only used in auto racing. Even if you could buy it at a store, you wouldn't, because the stuff costs about twenty times what ordinary brake fluid costs."

"Okay. And that tells us what, exactly?"

Nick suppressed a grin, but she could see it creasing the skin around his eyes. "According to the manufacturer, there's only one racing team in Las Vegas that uses it. They're called Supra Racing, and they're headquartered near the Clark County Raceway. I did a quick public records search and found out that they're owned by a company called Supra, Inc."

"Never heard of them."

"Supra, Inc. owns a bunch of businesses in the city. Apartment buildings, a couple of restaurants, some commercial and industrial real estate, among other things. And it's a known front for one Emil Blago."

The news hit Catherine with the force of a slap. Sometimes things just fell into place. "You don't say."

"I do say."

"Okay, this changes things. Thanks, Nicky. I need to . . . to take a minute to process this."

"Glad I could make your night even more complicated," he said.

"At least I can do the same for you. Riley's just back from the airport—take her and get out to Supra Racing, see what you can find out there."

Catherine returned to her office. The whole night felt like a cleverly constructed trap, one roadblock after another thrown in front of her every time she tried to escape.

What she wanted to do more than anything was to track down Jim Brass and ask him what the hell he was mixed up in. But she couldn't risk that. Now she *hoped* he didn't return her earlier calls, because she didn't know what she would be able to say.

Things had gotten too problematic too fast. The deeper Brass sank into this whole mess, the more she couldn't risk tipping him off that she was onto it until she knew enough to mean something. If Brass had committed a crime, if he had to be charged, she didn't want to force her hand too soon.

And if he hadn't done anything wrong, why hadn't he been in touch? Why not make sure his coworkers knew what was going on so they could help?

She would have sworn that Brass was no criminal. But he was no idiot, either. The more little bits and pieces of Deke Freeson's last night she learned about, the more it seemed that he was behaving like one or the other.

Maybe even both at once.

And that wasn't like the Jim Brass that she knew, not in the slightest. . . .

18

Supra Racing was housed in a big stand-alone pink stucco building. One side jutted toward the street and appeared to house offices, while the other, recessed with a big paved area in front, had four garage-style doors side by side with porthole-type windows about five feet from the ground. Nick guessed that was the shop. A couple of vehicles sat on the pavement, including a van decorated with Supra Racing decals.

Nick and Riley parked next to the van. Lights blazed inside the front office, so they went to the front door. It was stainless steel and glass and looked in on an empty reception area. It was also locked. Nick banged on it a couple of times, then Riley softly tapped a key against the glass, making a much sharper sound.

A minute passed before a big, dark bruiser swarmed into view through an interior doorway. His hair was short and spiked, and tattoos scrolled

up both suntanned arms, a snake on one side and a
dragon on the other. Nick supposed they might well
meet in the middle somewhere, under his stained
red T-shirt. "We're closed!" the man shouted.

Nick and Riley held their badges to the glass.
"Nothing lasts forever," Riley said. "You're open
again."

The guy shrugged, said something to a person in
the other room, and unlocked the door. "What?"

"What do you mean, what?" Nick walked in past
the guy, Riley following. Behind a waist-high
counter were a couple of desks. A glass-fronted display case held trophies, and the walls were covered
with racing posters and framed photos of the racing
team in action and enjoying victory celebrations. A
faint scent of marijuana hung in the air. "Maybe
we're racing fans."

"Then you can watch on TV," the big guy said. He
scratched his ribs, or where his ribs should be, although layers of fat and muscle buried them.

Another man came into the reception area, this
one Hispanic, short but muscular, with broad shoulders and tattoos of his own. His arms and chest
strained his polo shirt to its breaking point. "What's
goin' on?"

"They're cops," the big man said.

"Actually, we're crime scene investigators," Riley
corrected. Nick wouldn't have minded letting these
two thugs think they were regular cops for a few
minutes longer. On the other hand, they might not
understand the difference. A lot of people—especially people living on the wrong side of the law—
never saw beyond the badge and gun.

"You got a warrant?" the shorter one asked.

"Easy," Nick said, holding out his hands. "Slow down. We haven't even said anything to you yet. We're not here to search the joint. We just have a couple of questions. Is Mr. Blago here?"

"Never heard of him."

"Come on, anybody who reads the sports page knows Emil Blago owns Supra Racing."

"Maybe I only read the funnies." The short one seemed like the spokesman—the big guy stood back now, watching. His expression never changed. Nick couldn't tell if he was smiling or tasting some bad fish he'd had for dinner.

"There's no reason to get all defensive," Riley said. "We just wanted to talk to him if he's here. If not, no biggie. Do you know if his wife has been around lately? What's her name, Antoinette?"

The two men shared a glance. "You keep tabs on *your* boss's wife?" the short one asked.

"He's not married," Nick said. He might have been by now, if Sara Sidle hadn't left town.

"Lemme tell you, if he was, you wouldn't. You'd keep your eyes on the ground and your nose outta their business."

"You're probably right. We didn't mean anything by it—we just wanted to talk to her and figured if she was here that would make it easy."

"She's not. Why would she be, this time of night?"

"I see what you're saying," Riley said. "Nobody here but you two, right? And you don't know anything about anything?"

The big man finally spoke again. "That's about the size of it."

"Maybe we'll just come back during regular business hours," Riley said. "Maybe with some detectives along too, just for fun. And maybe a few drug-sniffing dogs. Does that work for you?"

"Whatever you gotta do, lady."

"Hold on," Nick said. His cell phone was letting him know he had a message. He flipped it open and found a text and photo, sent over by Wendy Simms. She had gotten a DNA hit off some of the hairs found in the motel room. They belonged to a man named Victor Whendt, who, according to the brief message, had a number of violent crimes on his sheet. The picture showed a white man with short brown hair, a broad face, and thick features, his small, deep-set eyes staring into the camera with undisguised contempt. *Works 4 Blago*, she had written.

"You want to text your girlfriend, do it somewhere else," the short man said. "We got stuff to do."

"I bet you do," Nick said. He closed the phone and walked over to the wall with the most framed photographs hanging on it. Ignoring the glares of the two men, he studied them. He didn't see Victor Whendt until the fourth picture, in which Victor was spraying champagne on a winning driver and a couple of women who looked like strippers. "Hey, that's Vic Whendt, isn't it?" he asked. "He works with you guys, right?"

"Sometimes," the big man said.

"You want to see our personnel records?" the short one asked. "Come back with a warrant."

"I'm not asking for his Social Security number,"

Nick said. "I just was surprised to see him there. You know Vic?"

The short man glared at him, but didn't speak. That was answer enough for Nick. They both knew Victor Whendt. "Never mind," Nick said. "Let's go."

"Have a good night, boys," Riley said on the way out. "Don't break any laws."

The big guy locked the door behind them and stood there watching until they were back in the department SUV.

"What was that about?" Riley asked. "Who's Vic Whendt?"

"He works for Supra Racing," Nick said. "But he seems to have other outside interests, too. He was in the motel room where Deke Freeson was murdered. And from which Antoinette Blago disappeared."

"Interesting," Riley said. "I guess Supra is worth taking a closer look at."

"Probably. But during business hours seems to make more sense—I don't think these guys could tie their own shoes, much less manage a criminal enterprise."

"Or a racing team?"

"Definitely not a racing team."

Catherine knew she shouldn't go to Victor Whendt's house without a detective along. It was unprofessional. It wasn't safe. She would pitch a fit if one of her CSIs had made the same decision without consulting anyone.

But involving the LVPD might mean answering questions about the case that she wasn't comfort-

able talking about yet. If Whendt was home, he
might bring the conversation around to Brass. She
wasn't ready to reveal her concerns about Brass to
anyone outside of her immediate circle, and certainly not to any of the detectives on duty tonight.
Since finding out what she had about the connection between Brass and Antoinette O'Brady, she was
sorry that she had taken Sam Vega to Cliff Gorecki's
place, because he would want to keep tabs on the
investigation's progress.

So she took two uniformed cops, who wouldn't
expect to be kept in the loop, to Whendt's condo
near Decatur and Washington. She assigned one to
watch the back and the other to cover her from in
front, making sure the officer would stand back far
enough that he wouldn't overhear any conversation.

There was nothing especially glitzy about Whendt's
complex. It had been built sometime in the last
decade and looked like about a million others in Las
Vegas, with light brown stucco walls and red tile roofs.
The desert landscaping incorporated palm trees, not
native to the region, on the theory, she supposed, that
one desert was pretty much like another. Outside the
buildings were carports, most of their spaces full this
time of night, but the one labeled "1219," matching
Whendt's unit, was empty. One of the four units had
lights on inside, but not 1219 itself, which was an upstairs condo with a wide balcony facing out toward a
pool. Moonlight sparkled on the water. She heard the
steady hum of an air conditioner, the strident chirrup
of crickets, and the sound of her own heels clacking
on the sidewalk. Someone had been outside smoking

a cigar, but not for a while; the fragrance was an after-thought on the still night air.

Catherine rang the doorbell of 1219, standing on a mat emblazoned with pictures of daisies. The word *welcome* didn't appear on the mat, and considering the time of night, she doubted that it would be applied to her in person, either.

The second time she pushed the illuminated button, the door opened abruptly while her finger was still on it. The person opening it wasn't Vic Whendt, though, but a slender young woman with red hair and a deep tan, wearing a black tank top that showed off most of her stomach and low-rise cotton pajama bottoms. She wrinkled her forehead and studied the badge Catherine showed her.

"It's kinda late," she said.

"I know it is," Catherine said. "I'm sorry about the hour. I'm looking for Victor Whendt, is he here?"

The woman shook her head. "I'm Mrs. Whendt."

She didn't offer a first name. Instead, she showed Catherine her left hand. A gold ring gleamed there, the metal still buffed to a high polish. It encompassed a rock easily four times the size of the one Eddie had bought Catherine, so many years ago. Not that diamonds were a girl's best friend in any but the most romantic of fantasies, or really meant a lot to Catherine. Still, a woman remembered these things.

"How long?"

"Seven weeks," Mrs. Whendt said. Still new enough to make it fresh and exciting.

"Where's your husband?"

Mrs. Whendt shrugged, a motion that seemed to involve her entire body and not just her shoulders. She was willowy and toned, with a pretty, perky face anchored by deep brown eyes. Catherine could see what the attraction was, for Vic, at least. She had yet to find out what Mrs. Whendt saw in a husband who would let her live in such a bland condo while spending what must have been several months' worth of mortgage payments on the ring. "He's out. Working, probably. He works some funky hours."

"Doing what?"

"He doesn't say, and I don't ask. He works for a racing team, that's all I know. And we get some awesome seats at the track. But it's noisy as all hell there, and it really doesn't smell great."

Catherine sniffed the air wafting from inside, catching the scents of a pine-scented cleanser and maybe a peach-flavored candle. "Something like that's important to you?"

Mrs. Whendt touched the tip of her tiny nose. The gesture was so cute Catherine almost couldn't stand it. "Vic says I have a nose like a bloodhound."

"Does he smoke cigars?"

"Never! God, no. Our downstairs neighbor does, but his wife won't let him smoke them in the house. He has to do it outside. I don't blame her, except that I wouldn't let him back in as long as he had that smell clinging to him."

"When did you see Vic last?"

Another shrug, but this one was slightly less animated. "Lunchtime, I guess. He had a tuna sandwich. I made a roast for dinner, and rolls, but he couldn't make it home."

"Does that happen often, Mrs. Whendt? That he doesn't come home when you expect him to?"

"Sometimes. Like I said, funky hours. He doesn't always know when the team's going to need him to do something."

"Do you know Emil Blago?"

Mrs. Whendt's forehead wrinkled again. Catherine had known puppies that weren't as cute. "What's this all about, anyway?"

"It's about a police matter. If you don't know anything about his business, then maybe it doesn't concern you. But if you do . . ."

"I told you I don't. I'm not really into cars anyway. All I know is they have a shower at the shop, so he doesn't have to come home smelling like grease. And they pay him pretty well. He said he was probably in for a bonus this week."

"Did he say for what?"

"Am I not making sense to you? I don't know. He doesn't tell me about his work. Sometimes he talks about the other guys on the team, but he doesn't tell me what they do. Changing carburetors or whatever . . . I wouldn't even understand what he was talking about. The only thing I know about cars is how to drive one, and I'm not so great at that, either."

"Okay," Catherine said. This was looking like a dead end. If she could bottle Mrs. Whendt's adorableness, she could retire from the lab, but otherwise she wasn't making any headway here. "Do you know when he'll be home?"

"All I know is, whenever he is, it won't be too soon for me!"

Catherine was afraid the new Mrs. Whendt would start jumping for joy at the mere prospect of his return. She thanked the young woman, and left her to steep in her own cuteness.

If Vic Whendt had actually killed Deke Freeson and went away for it, his next roommate wouldn't be nearly so appealing.

19

NICK AND RILEY HAD traveled less than a block from Supra Racing when a dark blue Mustang with racing stripes turned a corner and came toward them. Nick barely glanced its way until it passed beneath a streetlight, illuminating the driver for an instant. The man was talking on a cell phone, holding the wheel with his left hand and wearing a worried expression. He had short hair, deep eyes, and blunt features, and it took a second for them to register.

"That's him!" Nick shouted.

"Him who?" Riley asked.

Nick was already pulling the Yukon into a screeching U-turn. "Vic Whendt!"

"The guy in the pictures?"

"Yeah. The guy in the motel room with Deke Freeson." His voice was tight. He muscled the SUV back into the lane. The Mustang was already accelerating, tearing past Supra Racing and continuing down the same road.

"I hope he's not one of the team's drivers," Riley said.

"Didn't look like it in the pictures on the wall." He didn't know for sure, though. He had never heard of the guy, but that didn't mean he hadn't had some racing experience, only that he wasn't Mario Andretti or Jeff Gordon.

Nick put his foot down on the gas and the Yukon bolted forward. Up ahead, approaching an intersection, the Mustang's brake lights flashed briefly. "Oh boy," Nick muttered. The Mustang cut left, already accelerating halfway through the turn. "Hang on, Riley."

"Did you think I haven't been?"

Nick hit the lights and the siren. He couldn't outrun the Mustang, so if Whendt knew how to drive at all, Nick had to hope the obvious accoutrements of law enforcement would persuade him to stop.

Riley grabbed the microphone and called for backup, giving their position and a description of Whendt's car. They had his license plate number. They would catch up to the car, sooner or later, but if it wasn't sooner, there was no guarantee that Whendt would still be in it when they did.

At the corner, Nick braked just enough to slow their forward momentum and slid into the turn. The SUV's rear end started to fishtail, but he leaned on the accelerator and the vehicle straightened.

He heard sirens in the distance, but the chase had already ended. Whendt had boxed himself in. Ahead of him was a railroad track, its gate down, a long freight train lumbering past. Red lights flashed, out of sync with the lights the crime lab's Yukon threw on the surrounding buildings and bounced off the Mustang's rear window.

Nick cut the siren but left the lights going. Vic Whendt was already opening his door.

"Cancel the backup," Nick said. "Doesn't look like we'll need it." Nick drew his weapon, stepped out of the Yukon, and aimed at Whendt's door. "On the ground, now!" he shouted. "Facedown, hands above your head!"

"It's cool!" Whendt called. He assumed the prone position so quickly Nick was sure he had done it before. With Riley covering Whendt, Nick handcuffed him, searched him, and then hoisted him to his feet.

Whendt was clean. No weapons, no drugs. His keys were still in the Mustang's ignition. Nick fished Whendt's wallet from his back pocket. It held a couple hundred dollars in cash, some credit cards, a driver's license, and other assorted plastic. He wore a yellow cotton short-sleeved shirt open over a clean white T-shirt, expensive jeans, and leather loafers. Nick had been hoping for bloodstains, but there weren't any to be seen. He smelled of cologne, not gunpowder.

"Mind telling me what this is all about?" Whendt asked once he was on his feet.

"You should know. You're the one who rabbited."

"Of course I did. I was driving to work and you took one look at me, then flipped a U-ey and started chasing me. Scared the hell out of me."

"With lights and siren going," Nick said.

"Not at first. First you just came after me. I

freaked. When someone starts chasing you down on a city street in the middle of the night, it's nerve-wracking. You didn't hit your siren until after I made the turn, and when you did, I stopped."

"You stopped because there was a train in your way."

"Dude, I work around the corner, I know there's a train track here. I just panicked because you looked like a stranger trying to heist me or something."

"Nick." Riley gave him a beckoning nod.

"Don't move an inch," Nick warned Whendt, and then stepped aside so Riley could address him out of the suspect's earshot. He kept his gaze fixed on Whendt and his hand on his weapon, just in case.

"Nick, he does have a point," Riley said. "He was around the corner before you hit the siren. He did stop at the train tracks, but look where he stopped."

Nick glanced at the Mustang. She was right. Whendt had pulled out of the traffic lanes and parked on the right shoulder, where a law-abiding citizen would stop for a police car.

"I guess so. But he works for Emil Blago. And he *was* in that motel room."

"We don't know when or why. And you already might know this, but he's innocent until proven guilty."

Nick released a sigh. The adrenaline rush from the brief chase would take a while to wear off, but he couldn't deny the validity of Riley's argument. "Okay, okay, fine. I know. I'll dial it down a few notches."

"Good idea," she said.

They returned to Whendt, and Nick unlocked the handcuffs. "Sorry, sir, honest mistake," he said. "Thing is, we did go to Supra looking for you, so when we saw you and you ran . . . well, you can see how it looked."

"Looking for me?" Whendt seemed genuinely surprised. Nick had been sure he was on the phone to the guys at the Supra office, being told that the police were looking for him. But that was a supposition, not a fact. And CSIs had to deal in facts. "What for?"

"Do you know someone named Deke Freeson?"

Whendt pressed two fingertips into his left temple, as if suffering a sudden headache. "Doesn't sound familiar."

"You sure about that? Think before you answer."

"I hear a lot of names. Maybe I heard that one once, and maybe not. It's not somebody I know personally, though. He in the racing business?"

Nick ignored the question. "You were in a room at the Rancho Center Motel recently. Your boss's wife was in the same room."

"My boss isn't even married. His name is Frank—"

"I'm talking about Emil Blago."

"Who?"

"The owner of Supra Racing."

Whendt cracked a smile. "Oh, him, yeah. I've heard of him. He hardly ever comes around, though. Apparently he owns a lot of businesses in town. He's a busy guy with lots on his plate besides us."

"So I've heard. You know his wife?"

"Annette, something like that? Seen her a couple times. She's kind of hot, for an old lady."

"So what were you doing in that motel room?"

"What does anybody do in a motel room? Sleeping."

"That's all?"

"Mostly all," Whendt said with a shrug. "I was in a bar not far away. This is, I guess, last Thursday night. Met a woman. We had some drinks, had some laughs. When we were ready to leave, neither of us was in any condition to drive, and we wanted the fun to continue. So we walked over to the motel and got a room."

"So if I go over their registrations, I'll find your name there?"

He considered the question before answering. "No, I guess not. She paid for the room."

"What's her name?"

He took even longer with this one. "Janey, Janet, Janice . . . something like that."

"Last name?"

Another shrug. "No clue."

"Nice. You get her phone number? E-mail?"

"It was a bar hookup, man, that's all. And a late one at that."

"And it's just a big coincidence that Blago's wife was in that same room tonight?"

"I guess it is. Pretty sure there was only one woman in there when I was there, and she wasn't nearly as old as Mrs. Blago."

Nick caught Riley's eye. "Do you mind if we swab your hands and shirt?" she asked. She had gone back to the Yukon for her field kit.

"What for?"

"Gunshot residue," she said.

"First you think I'm taking my boss's wife to a motel, and now you think I shot someone? What the hell is going on here?"

"It's a yes or no question, Mr. Whendt," Nick said. "And if the answer is no, we just might have to hold you while we get a warrant."

"On what grounds?"

"You did run from us."

"And I explained why I did that."

"It'll only take a second," Riley said.

"Whatever," Whendt said. "If it gives you a thrill, do it."

That's not what it's about, Nick wanted to say. *Putting away bad guys is where we get the thrills, and if you are a bad guy . . .*

So far, however, Whendt hadn't given them anything to go on. "Where were you earlier this evening?" Nick asked while Riley broke out the swabs. "About eight-forty-five?"

Whendt glanced at the expensive watch on his wrist. "I would have been having dinner, I guess. I think we were wrapping up right around then?"

"Where?"

"A friend's house."

"But there were other people there, who can vouch for you?"

Whendt stood there as Riley swabbed his hands and wrists and the front of his shirt. "Seven of them. That enough? You need sworn affidavits?"

"We'll look into it." If Whendt was involved in Blago's criminal enterprises, in addition to being employed by his racing company, it wouldn't be hard for him to round up seven people to provide him an alibi.

"Negative," Riley said, having tested her swabs. Nick knew if they took Whendt in, they could check further—raid his closet for other clothes he might have worn earlier, look in his hair for traces of gunshot residue invisible to the naked eye but not to a scanning electron microscope. He hadn't given them cause to make an arrest, though, and he'd had the right answer to every question. His attitude had been combative, but his actions compliant.

The fact that Antoinette Blago had been in the same room might be sheer coincidence.

Grissom said there was no such thing as coincidence. But the connections between events could be tenuous, even invisible until something else revealed them, so Nick wasn't sure exactly what the difference was. Grissom would assume a link between Whendt's presence in the motel room and Antoinette's, and so did Nick. But he couldn't yet prove it.

"Okay," he said at last. "You can go. We might need to talk to you again, though."

"I'll be looking forward to it," Whendt said, his voice thick with sarcasm. "This was the highlight of my day, guys."

Emil Blago's estate was on the northwest side, off Summerlin Parkway in Country Club Hills. A tall, whitewashed wall surrounded it. Through an ornate wrought-iron gate, Catherine could see a veritable tropical jungle, with carefully positioned spotlights beaming up the trunks of towering palms, banana trees, and other plants utterly out of place in the desert landscape. The entire southwestern United States was suffering an extended drought, and Blago must have been using a small city's worth of water just to keep his garden lush. That alone should have been reason enough to arrest him. The house itself was invisible from the gate, which was probably the reason for the foliage. Crime bosses never wanted to make things easy for their enemies.

The gate, of course, was locked. There had been a guard on duty at the entrance to the development, and she half-expected to find another one here, but she didn't see any. There was an intercom mounted on the wall beside the gate, and a couple of cameras, one high up on either side so they could cover the whole area.

She pushed the intercom button. A male voice responded almost immediately. "Can I help you?"

Catherine showed her badge to the cameras. "Las Vegas Crime Lab," she said. "I need to talk to Emil Blago."

"I'm sorry," the voice said. "Mr. Blago doesn't care to be disturbed at this hour. I'm Paul, Mr. Blago's estate manager. Is there anything I can do for you?"

"I'm here on police business. So Mr. Blago can—"

"Have you a warrant?"

"Excuse me?"

"Have you a warrant for Mr. Blago's arrest? Or to enter the premises?"

"No," Catherine said. "I haven't a warrant."

"I have strict instructions not to disturb Mr. Blago before eight o'clock in the morning," Paul the estate manager said. "So unless you have a warrant, I'm going to have to ask you to leave."

"Did I mention that this is a police investigation?"

"Mr. Blago is always happy to cooperate with law enforcement," Paul said. "So if you'd like to call Mr. Blago's attorney after eight A.M., we can arrange for a visit to the house, or you can meet Mr. Blago at his attorney's office and he'll answer all your questions."

Catherine was stuck. She could always shoot the lock, but that would probably just get the city sued and her in trouble. Paul was right—without a warrant, she couldn't compel him to open up and let her in. "How about Mrs. Blago?" she tried. "Is she home?"

"I'm afraid I'm not at liberty to divulge that information."

"Come on, Paul, help me out here. I'm not asking anything complicated. Is she there or isn't she?"

"You'll have to call Mr. Blago's attorney. After eight A.M."

"Yeah, right, I got it," Catherine said. "After eight."

"That's correct. Will there be anything else?"

"Anything else? Doesn't that imply that there's been something to begin with?"

Paul chose not to dignify her question with a response. Probably for the best. She wouldn't have either, in his shoes. She was frustrated, but giving this poor sucker a hard time wouldn't make things any better. He already had the unenviable job of staying up late answering Emil Blago's door. Nothing she could do would make his life worse than that. "Thanks, Paul," she said. "I'll check in later."

"Do you know how to reach Mr. Blago's attorney?" he asked.

"I'm sure I can figure it out."

20

THERE WAS, CATHERINE FOUND, something about the Las Vegas Strip that she always found stimulating, no matter how many times she drove it, how many hours she spent bogged down in traffic, or how much she knew about the sometimes unsavory truth behind the lights and the glitter. Casinos—not these, but primitive early versions of them, mostly downtown on Fremont Street—had transformed a little watering hole in the middle of a vast and forbidding desert into an international tourist destination. Big casino hotels, the ones that now lined the Strip with reproductions of other destinations—Paris, Venice, New York, Egypt, ancient Rome, the emerald city of Oz, a volcano, a feudal castle—had swollen its fame and created more showrooms for big-name performers, and then still more sophisticated hotels without glitzy, artificial themes created an air of maturity for a city that was still mostly dedicated to allowing adults to live like teenagers,

without responsibility or rules. Legal or not, every
sort of activity took place in the city, every imagin-
able sexual liaison, every form of gambling, and
various other transactions involving weapons and
drugs and flesh.

A law enforcement officer in Las Vegas never had
much cause to be bored.

Catherine, who had been born in Las Vegas, and
then in a way reborn out of its seamier side when
she shifted from a career as an exotic dancer to one
in law enforcement, didn't romanticize the city she
lived in. But she couldn't help loving it just the
same.

And being a cop, even a CSI, had its perks. She
pulled into the valet area of the Palermo and
showed her badge to the first uniformed young man
who ran up to her. "Leave it where it is," she said. "I
won't be long." She dropped her keys into her
purse, to make sure it wasn't inadvertently moved.
She had been trying to get here for what seemed
like hours, but the sudden flood of information on
the Blagos and Victor Whendt had changed her priorities.

Inside, a hotel security officer Catherine had
known since her strip club days had arranged for
her to meet Melinda Spence's father in a private
conference room. The security man's name was
Glenn, and he'd harbored a longtime crush on
Catherine—just enough of one to give her power
over him. He wanted to stay for the meeting with
Mr. Spence, but Catherine dismissed him. "Round
up all the surveillance footage you have, starting at
the time Melinda had dinner with her family," she

instructed him. "I won't be here long, so get it ready for me to take away with me."

"You don't have—"

"A warrant? No, Glenn, I don't. But I don't need one. We're on the same side here. We all want to find the girl."

"I'll get it burned onto DVD for you, Catherine," he said. He opened the conference room door. "Mr. Spence, this is Supervisor Catherine Willows, with the Las Vegas Police Department Crime Lab. She's going to be looking for Melinda."

"Thanks, Glenn." Catherine closed the door behind her, to make sure Glenn didn't come in.

Mr. Spence stood up. He was a tall, lean African-American with red, worried eyes. "I hope you can be more helpful than the last detective I talked to," he said.

"Have a seat, Mr. Spence." She waited until he sat again, then sat across from him. The chairs were black leather, butter-soft and comfortable, and the conference table a modern steel and glass construction. "First, I want you to know how sorry I am that your daughter is missing. I know this must be terrible for you, and not at all what you were hoping for when you came to Las Vegas."

"That's for damn sure."

"Look, Mr. Spence, if you talked to a detective who didn't seem sympathetic, it's because Melinda hasn't been missing nearly long enough for an actual missing persons report to be filed. People go off the radar all the time in this city. They usually come back on their own after a few hours. Sometimes it even takes a few days, but they usually turn up. The number of distractions this city holds is impossible to count. I'm sure you've considered all the things she could be doing—she could be at a nightclub, a rave, gambling at some other casino. She might have met a man and had one of those whirlwind Las Vegas romances. She could be getting married by an Elvis impersonator as we speak. I know you don't want to think about these possibilities, but this city is a strange place and it has a powerful effect on some people. It causes people to relax their inhibitions . . . or forget they ever had any."

"We came to Las Vegas to see some shows, and because hotel prices are reasonable," Mr. Spence said. "And it's easy to get cheap flights from almost anywhere in the country. There are thirty-three of us here, ma'am, from seven different states. I can assure you that Melinda is no hardcore gambler and she is not the sort of girl who would run off with some man she hardly knows."

"Under ordinary circumstances, I'm sure that's true."

"Under *any* circumstances."

"I'm sure you want to believe that, Mr. Spence. And it's very possibly true. I'm just asking you to keep an open mind while we look for her."

"We didn't realize what an evil city this is, Ms. Willows. I don't know you, and I don't know if you like it here or not, but it is *truly* evil. Any place that profits so heartily from the degradation of human beings, exploiting their weaknesses, their addictions . . . well, I just don't know another word for it. Evil. When we find Melinda, we're leaving here and never coming back." He squeezed his hands into trembling fists on

A MURDER
WELL DONE.

WELL, BECAUSE FIRST OFF, I KIND OF ALREADY MADE MY LUNCH.

AND SECOND, I JUST THINK WE REALLY SHOULD EAT IN AS MUCH AS POSSIBLE.

the tabletop. "You've got to get my little girl back for me."

"Even though it's early, Mr. Spence, we're going to spare no effort. We'll be looking for her, using every resource at our disposal." That part wasn't strictly true. Las Vegas was the most heavily sur-veilled city in America, with cameras in every casino and on most major streets running 24/7. But to get access to all that footage, and to get the entire LVPD on the lookout for Melinda, the required time would have to pass. On her own initiative, Cather-ine could get the crime lab's resources on the job, and if they found evidence of foul play, then they could bring in the rest of the department.

The Palermo's security team had already checked their internal surveillance video for Melinda. They didn't want guests running to the cops, or cops spilling through the front doors and making a fuss. But they had other things on their plates, too, and how seriously they looked would depend on how seriously they took the Spence family's word that Melinda was so straight an arrow that Las Vegas couldn't possibly tempt her to stray.

Like all casino personnel, they had a vested inter-est in believing the opposite—that anyone could be tempted at any time.

"Well, I appreciate that, Ms. Willows. We all do."

"I have a daughter too, Mr. Spence. I know ex-actly how I would feel in your position, and I will make every effort to get Melinda back to you as soon as possible."

"Thank you, ma'am."

"If there's anything else you can tell me about

her—what sorts of things she is interested in, what games she plays when she does gamble, what she was wearing . . ."

"She's a twenty-four-year-old Christian girl from Hamilton, Ohio. She works in a bank. She goes to church on Sunday mornings and sings in the choir. She's never had a serious boyfriend, although she's dated a few nice, polite young men . . . When she came to dinner she was wearing a red silk blouse and black pants. I don't know what kind of shoes she had on, but if I had to guess, I'd say they were sensible."

"Okay, Mr. Spence." Catherine put her business card on the table. "If you think of anything else, or if someone hears from her, call me. I mean it, no matter what time it is. Even if it's good news. Especially if it's good news. If I find out anything at all, I'll call you here at the hotel."

"You've just got to find her, Ms. Willows." His eyes brimmed with liquid. She didn't want to see him cry. If something had happened to Melinda, he would be doing enough of that later. "Please."

"I'll do my best," Catherine said. That, she meant.

Greg Sanders stood in the lab's layout room cutting plastic. He had thought searching for fingerprints was the boring part of the job, but this? *This* was truly the boring part.

He was a smart guy. He had gone to school early, then to a private school because, even though enrolled younger than most of his classmates, public school hadn't proved challenging enough for him.

He had earned a free ride at Stanford, a full academic scholarship. Maybe he hadn't graduated at the very top of his class, but he'd been Phi Beta Kappa, and he could smell the top from where he was.

And here he was cutting plastic.

He had taken samples of all the irrigation tubing at the airport that seemed to match the tube that had been used to direct carbon monoxide into Jesse Dunwood's cockpit. Then he had rounded up a variety of cutting implements—clippers and shears and knives of every description, from toolboxes and hangars and sheds, even a Buck knife from a snap-fastened scabbard on the janitor's belt and a pocketknife from Patti Van Dyke's purse.

With those edged implements, he cut plastic.

The Strokes blared in the background, but he barely heard the music, so intent was he on his work.

He made circular cuts around some of the tubing with each one in turn, noting which tool he was using, what time it was, and what he was cutting. Then he took pictures of the tool and the cut plastic. Then he made another cut, with a different part of the blade, and repeated the notation process. Then he looked at the cut marks under a comparison microscope, next to the end of the tube that had actually been used in the crime.

At first glance, one cut in a plastic tube looked pretty much like the next. But under enough magnification, minute differences became apparent. Some edges sliced more cleanly through the plastic, others feathered it, some had imperfections in the blade that were apparent in the cut.

It had taken years—*years*—to attain the professional stature that would allow him to spend an hour cutting plastic in one of the most advanced crime labs in the world.

His parents would be so proud.

21

CATHERINE WAS FINALLY DRIVING back to the lab when Wendy called.

"Catherine, I got a hit off one of the dogs," she said.

"The dogs?" She wasn't sure she'd heard right, or if this was some new usage of the slang word *dawg* as it was used to refer to a person.

"The bones from the pit, at the Empire Casino construction site? One of them turned up in Canine CODIS."

"You're kidding." Canine CODIS was a database of DNA taken from dogs impounded during the investigation of criminal cases. A lot of them were fighting dogs, but by no means all. She had once dealt with a sweet-faced sixty-seven-year-old woman who had murdered the widower next door. The woman had nine Chihuahuas in the house, and they'd had to be impounded before the CSI crew could begin to process the house. She had worried about those trembling little things in the shelter along with pit bulls and Dobermans and the like, but several of them had been adopted almost immediately.

"Not kidding," Wendy said. "The dog was a blue heeler named Tiffany, owned by a Halden Robles of Henderson. Robles is a sheet metal worker, but currently unemployed. Tiffany was taken in when Robles was picked up on a series of smash-and-grabs, five years ago. He beat the rap and was on the street again in time to reclaim Tiffany."

"So you think he's our animal killer? If he had been away for longer, it would make more sense, given that time gap between the skeletal remains and the sheep put there recently."

"I don't know if he is, Catherine. It seems like a stretch that he would reclaim his dog and then kill her. But maybe there's some kind of connection between him and the killer. Robles lives in Henderson now, but when he was arrested he lived in Las Vegas, just about four miles from the Empire Casino site."

"Interesting," Catherine said. "So if he knows who killed his dog . . ."

"It's a long shot, I admit," Wendy said. "But when the dog turned up in the database, I thought you should know."

Catherine thanked her and detoured to Henderson, a side trip that took her well out of her way and would eat up valuable time. But knocking on someone's door in the middle of the night was often a good way to catch them off guard. Lying was harder to pull off convincingly when you were still mostly asleep.

Halden Robles lived in a tiny square adobe-walled house in a poor neighborhood. A waist-high chain-link fence surrounded a yard of patchy grass and bare earth. On the corner, a streetlamp beamed down on it, illuminating the place from above like one of those lights mounted on picture frames. *Still Life with Poverty,* Catherine thought. *American post-Gothic.*

She let herself in through the fence, looking for signs of dogs and not finding any. The house had no doorbell, so she knocked hard on the hollow wooden front door, which rattled in its frame. The stoop was simple poured concrete with no mat.

After a couple of minutes, a Hispanic man wearing faded jeans and an unbuttoned plaid shirt pulled the door open. He appeared to have just thrown the clothing on; even the top button on his jeans was undone. His black hair was matted, his face puffy. He had a thin mustache that dropped down past the corners of his mouth, and prominent eyebrows roofing large, liquid eyes. "Who the hell are you?"

"I'm Supervisor Catherine Willows, with the Las Vegas Police Department's crime lab," Catherine said, showing her badge.

He eyed it, then made a dismissive motion with his hands. The house was dark behind him, and reeked of stale cigarette smoke. "Man, you people get your hooks into someone once, you don't never let go, do you?"

"What do you mean?"

"I mean it ain't like I'm some kind of gang king-pin or anything, right? Why can't you guys just leave me alone? I made some bad decisions, years ago. I got arrested, but then I got off because some of the state's witnesses didn't bother to show up. Maybe they never existed, I don't know. I don't see how they could because I never did the things they charged me with. Since then, it's like every cop in the city is so pissed I didn't do time they just keep bothering me." He let his gaze wander up her body and rest on her face. "Never seen you around before, though."

"I spend more time with dead people than live ones," she said.

"Who got dead?"

"Tiffany, for one. If you're Halden Robles."

"I am. Who's Tiffany?"

"Your dog?"

"Oh." He grinned. "Come on, you're really here about a dog?"

"I am."

"That was like five years ago. Don't tell me you're actually investigating dog kidnappings now."

"No, Mr. Robles. Only when they might be associated with some other crime."

"You know how close people get to their dogs? That was me and Tiffany. She was like my kid. Or, I don't know, my sister, only without the mouth my sister's got on her. I loved that dog, man."

"I'm sorry for your loss." The words, so familiar to Catherine that they flowed from her mouth almost without conscious consideration, seemed odd in this context. Not quite right, but not quite wrong, either.

"Thanks. So what's this all about? The same person who snatched Tiffany take another dog?"

"Maybe several of them, Mr. Robles. Do you have any idea who took her?"

He pawed his open shirt aside and scratched his chest. "I lived in Las Vegas then. Way on the edge of town. Not like this place, the houses were farther apart. Neighbors weren't all up in each other's business all the time. Tiffany would bark her head off if anybody came around my house. I guess there were some strange people in the area." He chuckled. "They probably would have said the same thing about me."

"Any who still stand out in your memory?"

"There was this one guy who kept adding onto his house with sheets of corrugated steel or plywood or whatever he could find dumped someplace. He used to practice target shooting in his yard, painted a Confederate flag on one of his walls. He wrote letters to the newspapers about the dangers of illegal immigration—this is before it was sexy, you know? Drove this jacked-up truck he painted in a camouflage design. And he always slowed down when he went by my place, giving me the dick-eye, like maybe I was smuggling Mexicans in or something."

"Charming. You remember his name?"

Robles wrinkled his forehead. "No. Bill something . . . some plain name, I don't know."

"Did he ever specifically threaten you or the dog?"

"No. But if he could have shot me with his eyes, I'd have been dead a long time ago."

"Does anybody else come to mind?"

"There was a kid who used to deliver pizza who

always looked at Tiffany. He didn't want to play with her, just stared at her. Skinny white kid, always a little nervous, like he was maybe afraid of her. Little girl from down the road liked to play with the dog, but I didn't want her to because I wanted to keep Tiffany a little wild, you know? So she'd bark at intruders and whatnot. Most people left us alone, and that was the way I liked it."

"I don't suppose you remember either of their names?"

"The girl . . . her name was Maryluz something. I'm not so good with last names, I guess. Pizza kid . . . I don't know, it was a long time ago. Donnie, Dougie, something like that maybe. I'd tell you to check with the pizza place but they went out of business before I even moved away. Area's grown a lot since then, there's probably all kinds of chain places going in."

"Probably so," Catherine agreed. "Do you know for sure that somebody took the dog? She didn't just run away?"

"She wouldn't have done that. She used to sit in the yard for hours. No fence, nothing. She would stay there all day and all night if I wanted. No way she would have just taken off." He narrowed his eyes, looking at Catherine as if something had just occurred to him. "If you're here, does that mean you found her? Or you found her tags or something? She was legal, straight up."

"We found some . . . remains, I'm afraid. Some hairs that survived, probably because they were buried in a dry area, and we were able to identify Tiffany from that."

Robles shook his head. "Hairs? And you came out here for that?"

"Like I said, it's part of a bigger case. But I really can't talk about that." She handed Robles her card. "Thanks for talking to me, Mr. Robles. I'm sorry I bothered you at this hour, and very sorry about your dog, but I appreciate your cooperation."

"No problem," he said. "Some beautiful cop knocks on my door in the middle of the night, it's easier to take if she's not trying to jam me up over something."

"I imagine it is. Please call me right away if you think of anyone else who might have wanted to hurt Tiffany, Mr. Robles."

He flicked the corner of the business card. "I will, don't worry."

"Good night, then."

"'Night."

He didn't close his door. He stood there, looking at Catherine. Finally, she turned away and went back to her vehicle. Unless he had a sudden flash of memory, this wouldn't help her find Melinda Spence.

Suddenly, getting back to the lab took on greater urgency than ever.

"Greg?"

He almost dropped the plastic tubing, so startled was he by the officer's voice. "Yeah?"

"Mr. Rosen's in the interview room for you."

"Rosen?"

"Airport guy?"

Greg remembered. Riley had collected some long

red hairs in the material that she had vacuumed from the airplane cockpit—her speculation was that Jesse Dunwood had yanked out a hank of them while the nameless redhead was performing one of those acts that he liked having done to him while flying. There had been plenty of follicular bulbs still attached, from which Wendy had been able to get nuclear DNA, and from that she had identified the legitimate owner of those hairs as one Martina Rosen, the manager of an independent Las Vegas coffee shop. Greg had asked to have her husband, a financial analyst named Fred Rosen, brought in for questioning, since he, not his wife, had threatened Dunwood's life.

Now it looked as if he would be doing that questioning himself, since just about everyone else who could do it was off on some other case, and all he was doing was cutting plastic tubing.

He was thrilled to have a distraction from that chore, important as it might be. He picked up the growing Dunwood file, went into the interview room, opened the door, and saw a lean, curly-haired man in wire-rimmed glasses sitting behind the table. The man's shirtsleeves were pushed up over freckled, muscular forearms. He looked like a tennis player, with that stringy leanness that hours on the court brought.

"You're Fred Rosen?"

"That's right. Should I have my attorney here?"

"That's your call, Mr. Rosen." Greg sat down across from him and put the file on the table. "You haven't been arrested or charged with a crime, so I haven't read you a Miranda warning. But of course you're entitled to an attorney if you want one."

"Maybe you should tell me what this is all about," Rosen said. "And tshen I'll decide."

"That's fine. My name's Greg Sanders. I'm a level-three crime scene investigator with the Las Vegas Police Department's crime lab, which is where we are."

"I'm aware of that, Mr. Sanders. I'm not stupid."

"I'm sure you're not."

"I appreciate the introduction, but you haven't addressed my question. What am I doing here?"

Greg refused to let him lead the conversation. "Your wife is Martina Rosen?"

Rosen scowled. As he had declared, he wasn't stupid. He could see what Greg was doing, and he was smart enough to know he had to go along with it. But he was perfectly willing to show that he didn't like it. "That's right."

"She has long red hair?"

"I don't know if it's long. A little past her shoulders, I guess."

"Her DNA is in the CODIS database."

"If you say so." He glared at Greg for a moment, then peered at the mirror as if trying to see who was behind it. He sighed and knuckled his eyes under his glasses. "She was raped, all right? Ten, eleven years ago now. DNA samples were taken from her as evidence, so I imagine that's what's in the database."

"Probably so," Greg said. He already knew that, but he wanted to get Rosen talking about anything but Jesse Dunwood. A painful subject was even better, because if it tweaked Rosen's emotions, the truth would be easier to reach. "I'm sorry I had to bring that up. Is your wife at home now?"

"Of course. She's home in bed, like any sane person would be."

"And you pretty much always know where she is at any given time." Greg felt a little sleazy, going there. But if Rosen had killed Jesse Dunwood because of his wife's affair with the pilot, he had to find out, and he couldn't do that by dancing around the topic indefinitely.

"Of course I do. She's my wife."

"Some people lose track of their spouses from time to time. Some spouses don't like being on a short leash."

If Rosen had been a wild animal, Greg would have worried about being bitten. "I don't see how my marital life is any of your business. The fact that she was raped doesn't make her some kind of a tramp, you know."

"I understand that, Mr. Rosen. But in a homicide investigation, our job is to follow the facts. The fact is that your wife had an affair with a man named Jesse Dunwood, isn't it? A pilot? Didn't you assault him recently, at the Desert View Airport after he took her up for a night flight?"

"Okay, yeah. She's not the most faithful wife in the world. So what? I followed her one night, and I saw her come out of the plane with that creep and I decked him. End of story. If you already know all the answers, why do you bother asking questions?"

"I didn't say I know all the answers—but I know

enough to understand when you're being evasive. And I have to tell you, in your present circumstances, evasive isn't the way you want to come across."

Rosen shoved his hands deep into his pockets. "Wait . . . now you're talking about a murder? Maybe it *is* time to call my attorney."

"That's up to you."

"What is it going to take to convince you I had nothing to do with whatever this is all about?"

Since they didn't know precisely when Dunwood's plane had been sabotaged—only that he had last flown it four days before his final flight—it would be hard to pin down a specific time to ask Rosen about. The tube could have been planted any time during those four days. Greg could check under the man's nails for grease from the engine, but that could have been washed out over several days. Instead, he took a different tack. "What do you know about airplanes?"

"Fasten your seat belt, don't tamper with lavatory smoke detectors, in the unlikely event of a water landing your seat cushion can be used as a flotation device. Don't count on a meal anymore, you're lucky if the peanuts are free. And if there's a gremlin on the wing, don't shoot it from inside the plane. That's pretty much it."

Rosen's sense of humor was encouraging, showing that he wasn't too anxious. That could imply innocence. On the flip side, it could mean he was a conscienceless murderer. "Do you carry a knife of any kind?"

"I work in a bank, what do I need a knife for? I

mean, there's one of those dinky Swiss Army jobs on my key chain. Not much more than a letter opener, really. I do use the toothpick attachment sometimes."

"Do you mind if I take a look at it?"

Rosen fished a bunch of keys from his pocket and tossed them on the table with a clatter. "Knock yourself out."

Greg picked up the keys, isolated the little red knife, and opened its biggest blade, which was barely an inch and a half long. It would cut eighth-inch plastic tubing, though.

"I'll be right back," he said.

"Wait, you're taking my keys?" Rosen asked.

"I don't need the keys, just the knife. You want to take it off the ring?"

"No, go ahead and take it all." Rosen crossed his arms over his chest and dropped his chin. *Funny how a grown man can look like such a little boy sometimes,* Greg thought.

Greg carried the keys back to the layout room, where he had left his tubing samples and tools. He made a couple of cuts and took a picture of the knife. Then he took it back to the interview room, bringing with him the uniformed officer who had been waiting outside. Rosen was sitting where Greg had left him, still pouting.

"Thanks," Greg said, handing back the keys. "You can go now."

"I can go?"

"Yes. The officer will take you home."

"So we're done?"

Greg didn't think Fred Rosen had killed Jesse Dunwood. He could have been wrong, but the guy didn't strike him as a murderer. He was upset but not afraid; he seemed genuinely put out that he'd been hauled in, offended that he might be accused of such an act. If the knife cuts matched up to the actual tube, Greg would have to rethink his position, but for the moment he had no reason to hold Rosen. "We're done for now. Don't make any vacation plans just yet."

"I don't take vacations," Rosen said. "I work."

And that, my friend, Greg thought, *just might be one of the reasons your wife takes night flights with other men.*

22

"I'M SURPRISED THE SECURITY people at the Palermo didn't catch this," Archie Johnson said. He had summoned Catherine to his A/V lab, and she had hurried down to see what he'd turned up. He was running through the video footage from the Palermo's surveillance cameras that Glenn had burned for Catherine.

"Me too," she said. "I mean, it's not like they don't have good equipment."

"The best money can buy. And when you're talking casino surveillance, I mean a *lot* of money. Those guys have too much on the line to cut costs there, either in equipment or training. But there can be human error, same as anywhere else."

"We can't afford any human error tonight, Archie."

"That's why you've got me. Look, there's Melinda." He pointed out an attractive young woman on the screen. She was curvy, just this side of volup-

tuous. She wore, as her father had said, a silk top and
jeans. And sensible shoes, albeit leather ones with a
little bit of flair to them. She was walking out of the
Palermo's buffet restaurant with other members of
her family. Catherine recognized her father, hand-in-
hand with a woman who looked enough like Melinda
to be her mother. A time stamp in the lower-right corner of the screen said 19:42:11.

"Okay," Catherine said. "This must be the last
time her family saw her, when she left the restaurant. That's what her father said."

"Right. It took a lot of guesswork at first, but I've
managed to edit together a reel that shows where
she was when. I had to figure out where I thought
she might go as she moved from camera to camera,
and then widen my search if I didn't find her in one
camera's field of view. A couple of times she managed to get completely out of view, and then I had
to widen even more, but she always turned up
again. I used facial recognition to search for her
those times."

"You're right—that's nothing the Palermo
shouldn't have been able to do."

"Yeah, if they'd been willing to spend the time.
But here's where it gets trickier," Archie said. "She
played the quarter slots for a while, then went up to
her room. They don't have cameras on the guest
floors, though we can see her on the elevator, and
getting off on twelve. That's where her room is,
twelve-fourteen. The Spence family is spread out
over three floors: ten, eleven, and twelve. She
shares a room with one of her cousins."

Catherine watched the events Archie described

unfold on the video. The time stamp said 20:19:51 when she left the elevator. The screen went black for an instant, and then she got on a different elevator, wearing different clothes—a loose sweater, blue jeans, and sneakers. The time was 20:28:17.

"She changed clothes."

"A lot of people aren't used to how cold the air-conditioning is in the casinos," Archie said. "They wear something a little more revealing, and then realize they're freezing their . . . whatevers off, and they go change."

"That shouldn't cause facial recognition software to fail, though."

"It didn't. Here's where it failed." He fast-forwarded through Melinda's journey through the casino, back to the quarter slot machines, and a twenty-five-minute stretch of her playing there. Then she got up, crossed from the field of view of one camera, and emerged into that of another. But this camera only caught her from behind as she went into a casino bar, sat down facing the bartender, and ordered a drink.

"She never showed her face to the camera," Catherine observed.

"That's right. That's where my zone method beat out their FR. I was watching for her to enter another zone, and when she finally did, I was ready. If I'd been relying on the FR software, I still wouldn't have her."

"Which you could do because you're you, and you're not also watching for card cheats and scam artists and hookers and thieves."

"That's right." Archie hit fast forward again. "So

she sits in the bar, sipping her drink for about twenty minutes." He returned the footage to regular speed. "And then this guy shows up."

A skinny young white man came into the bar, eyed the clientele, and then picked the stool next to Melinda Spence. He said something to her, and she turned to greet him, offering almost enough of her face to the camera for the facial recognition software to pick her up. The man was about her age, maybe a couple of years younger. He wore a porkpie hat, dark glasses, a white T-shirt under a black blazer, and skinny black jeans. He kept his face away from the camera, maybe deliberately, and the hat and sunglasses helped.

"They stay there for a half hour," Archie said, fast-forwarding again. "But at twenty-four minutes . . ." He slowed the footage, slower than real time. "Okay, watch his hand."

The man must have said something funny. Melinda—on her third drink now—bent forward laughing. The man put one hand on the back of her head, forcing it even more forward, and at the same time swept his other hand over the top of her drink. With her head at the angle he held it, Melinda couldn't have seen him do it.

"He drugged her!" Catherine said.

"That's what it looks like. Rohypnol, GHB, keta-mine, we can't tell from here, but those are the date rape drugs of choice, right?"

Catherine was all too familiar with all of them, both as a CSI and as the concerned mother of a teenager who she hoped was still sleeping soundly in her bed. "Yeah, they're the usual suspects."

Again, Archie described what Catherine watched on the screen. "So a few minutes later, our girl is getting a little unsteady on her stool. They're still laughing, still having fun. By this time, I figure she thinks the booze is finally hitting her—or from what you told me, she might not be experienced enough with it to know that it hit her a long time ago, and now she's feeling the dope. And now look at this move."

The young man snatched off his porkpie hat, exposing lank dark hair and a sallow complexion. He jammed the hat onto Melinda's head. Then he got off his own stool and helped her from hers. He looked down, toward her feet, toward the floor, as much as possible—shielding his own face from the camera, and making sure that she did the same. The hat blocked the camera's view even more, so that even though she had to turn to leave the bar, it only caught the lower third of her face.

"Ordinarily, modern FR software uses 3-D modeling to capture faces," Archie explained. "It doesn't need the full-face image the old 2-D software did. But it has to have some nodal points to go on, and what we can see here, the length of the jaw and shape of the mouth, just isn't enough. If he would take off those dark glasses, or even look up at the camera, we might be able to get a read on him. And we already know who Melinda is, but with the hat on and her face toward the floor, the Palermo's software couldn't find her."

As they left the bar, the footage showed the bartender scooping up their glasses, dumping them into soapy water, and wiping their place at the bar with a damp bar rag. Another couple took the stools almost immediately. "So much for fingerprints," Catherine said. "They're gone. Not that we'd have been able to isolate his. There must be hundreds of prints on those stools at any given time." Sometimes there was a fine line between building an airtight case and wasting precious time, and with the number of prints they would find on those stools and the difficulty of matching them all to their owners, checking the bar and surrounding seats would be a pointless effort.

"And you couldn't even locate her at this point with gait recognition software," Archie pointed out, "because she hasn't walked like this since she arrived in Las Vegas."

Melinda swayed on her feet, unsteady even in those flat, sensible shoes. The young man put an arm across her back, helping her, but also steering her so that she never faced directly into the security cameras.

"Man, this guy is taking no chances. Do we know who he is?"

Archie tapped a couple of keys and a close-up of his face appeared, his gaze downcast. "I did get one pretty decent shot of his face," he said. "But it's not matching to anything in our system. Apparently he's never been in trouble, either with us or at the Palermo."

"Great. At least we have that, though. Copy that image, and a couple of those shots of them leaving the bar together, and get them over to Sam Vega. I'm going to call this an abduction, based on what we've seen. Where do they go from here?"

Archie punched the keys again. A new camera's footage came onto the screen, this one mounted in a parking garage outside the casino. "Garage," he said. "Watch that Camry on the right side of the screen."

The young man reached into his pocket, and an instant later the Camry's rear lights flashed. "Electronic locks," Catherine said.

"That's right." Melinda was almost unconscious by this point, moving forward slowly and only with the young man's help. He put her in the Toyota's passenger seat and closed her door. She immediately slumped against the window. The man got in behind the wheel, backed the car from its parking space, and headed toward an EXIT sign.

"That's it?" Catherine asked. "No shots of the plate?"

"He was parked in a good spot, for his purposes," Archie said. "If he'd been farther from the camera, we'd have the plate. As it is, he made the turn just before the plate came into view. And it's a free lot, so there's not even a parking ticket to check, or a camera on the way out."

"What year is that Camry?"

"2002," Archie said.

"And how many 2002 Camrys do you figure there are in Las Vegas right now?"

"Assuming it's even got Nevada plates? A couple thousand, easy."

"Right. I need something to go on, Archie. I need to know who that guy is. He took Melinda Spence."

"Yeah, it looks like it. If I can find anything else in the footage the Palermo gave us, I'll let you know."

"You do that," she said. It seemed as if Mr. Spence's worst fears about Las Vegas had been realized, or were in the process of being, and Catherine didn't want to let that happen. "You let me know right away."

Catherine headed back to her own office. She had never kept particularly conventional working hours. For most of her adult life, day had been her night, and the hours of darkness her day. Her mother had held to a similar schedule.

But regardless of when she woke or slept, there were common threads. Midnight was the witching hour, and the dark night of the soul came between three and four in the morning. For inexplicable reasons, even though it was part of her working day, everything had greater import at that hour, more tragic resonance. Seeing Melinda drugged and taken away gave concrete life to her fears, eliminating the possibility that the young woman was just having too much fun to call her family. Melinda's fate weighed more heavily on her now than it had fifteen minutes before. Adding to it was the knowledge that the same thing could happen to almost any woman in Las Vegas. Even Lindsey.

With that certainty—the acute awareness that no one was truly safe, no one's daughter immune from harm—weighing on her shoulders like barbells left there by accident, she turned her attention back to the task at hand.

Melinda Spence had to be found, and fast. Catherine would accept no other outcome.

23

WENDY WAS GLAD THAT her dog DNA idea had borne fruit, even if it had ultimately been a dead end. She believed it was important to play all the angles, not to let her tasks become so routine that she couldn't come up with new ways to utilize the data she developed in her lab.

Another idea had been nagging at her, though, as she worked on the last of the hairs from the burial pit. These hairs had provided one potential lead, and might still offer more. The likelihood grew slimmer with every one she analyzed that offered no positive results, however, and she wasn't optimistic.

But that ewe that had been brought in . . . she was still relatively fresh. And to get her into the pit, the killer would have had to move her, most likely by hand. Maybe he wore gloves . . . but maybe not.

She took some of the last bits of hair follicle and put them in a chloroform and phenol mixture, which would separate the DNA from other material found in the cell nucleus, and headed for the morgue.

"Duane Allman was a far better guitarist than Eddie Van Halen," Doc Robbins was saying when she passed through the doors. "Not that Van Halen is bad. A little showy, but not bad. But Allman's lilting notes could carry as much emotion as a poem, a soulful voice, and Van Halen could never approach that sort of meaning."

"I guess," David Phillips answered. He was sitting on a stool near the sheep's rear end, while Doc Robbins removed what looked like its liver. "But Eddie just . . . he just rocks, you know? And sometimes that's what you want, a guitarist who can drive a song from beginning to—Oh, hi, Wendy."

"Sorry to interrupt," Wendy said. "And has anybody mentioned Albert Lee, if you're talking great guitarists?"

"Already stipulated to," Doc Robbins said. "What brings you to our little fiefdom, Wendy?"

She nodded toward the table. "The little lost lamb. Can I see her for a minute?"

"Help yourself."

"You ever notice sheep in nursery rhymes never have names?" David asked. "Little Bo Peep lost her sheep—but she didn't lose Susie and Chuckie and Daisy, just a bunch of nameless sheep. And 'Baa, Baa, Black Sheep' is named after the noise the sheep makes, not the sheep's name." He hesitated a moment. "Or if that is its name, it's a lame one. Have you ever heard of a dog named Bark Bark Dog?"

Wendy eyed him briefly, then turned back to the ewe. "This is a little unusual, isn't it?"

"Having a sheep on my table?" Doc Robbins said. "Yes. Perhaps not quite scrapbook material, but certainly not an everyday occurrence. I concur with Greg's inclination—it does look to me like the possible work of a would-be serial killer—so it behooves us to find out if it was really the slit throat that killed her, or something else. I'd hate to have the PD out looking for a cutthroat when they should really be looking for a poisoner."

"Makes sense." She walked around the animal a couple of times, trying to ascertain where someone might grip her to carry or drag her. Probably drag, she guessed, although a person could hoist the animal up if necessary. She would try lifting it herself, but she didn't want to risk wiping away exactly what she was searching for. Finally she decided the most reasonable spot would be just behind the front legs—conveniently for her, a place where the wool didn't cover the skin. She pulled the right front leg out of the way and swabbed the fleshy area. "And what happens when you're done with her? It's not like she'll be embalmed and buried or anything, right?"

"We'll turn her over to the city's animal control officers for disposal. I'm not a big fan of embalming under any circumstances, in fact."

Wendy replaced the swab in its protective vial, hoping she had picked up some skin cells that hadn't belonged to the ewe. She would find out upstairs. "Why not?"

Doc Robbins leaned on his crutches and fixed

her with a steady gaze. "Embalming is done for the benefit of the survivors, not for the dead. It's been promoted as a permanent solution, but in reality it's far from permanent. It keeps the body looking vaguely lifelike long enough for a funeral, and then for a little while after. But there's absolutely no purpose for it, once the body's in the ground. And taking up precious space, at that. Cremation makes far more sense in most cases. Embalming corpses and sticking them in fancy brass caskets is stupid, when it would be far more practical to encourage the bodies to decompose quickly, to return essential nutrients to the earth. If I had my way, burials wouldn't involve caskets at all—we'd just wrap the bodies in some easily biodegradable fabric, bury them, and plant a tree."

"Sounds good to me."

"Did you know that embalming fluid is a relatively recent invention?" Doc Robbins continued, on a roll now. "It became commonplace during the Civil War. Any liquid works—the point is just to replace the blood with something that will decompose more slowly. For years the liquid of choice was arsenic, which was cheap and widely available. Old cemeteries can be picturesque, but so much arsenic has leached into the soil in some that they can also be hazardous. To anyone not yet dead, that is."

"I'll, umm, keep that in mind. When I'm doing my planning."

The medical examiner had turned his attention back to the sheep's insides, but he eyed her over the top of his glasses. "See that you do."

"Thanks for the swab," she said. "I've got to get going."

"Touch DNA?" Doc Robbins asked.

"Excuse me?"

"You're looking for touch DNA—DNA traces left behind when a person touches another person or object."

"That's right," she said. "It's a relatively new technique, but I'm trying to get better at it, and figured this might be a case where it would come in handy." She would use polymerase chain reaction and short tandem repeat on the extremely small specimen she expected to have, to amplify the sample, making enough copies of the cells so that she would be able to analyze the DNA.

"So you're saying that if someone just touches some object, he might leave DNA on it," David said.

"That's the theory. We leave a little something behind everywhere we go."

"No more searching for drops of blood or saliva or flecks of skin or tiny strands of hair?"

"Those things still help, don't get me wrong. But they might not be as crucial as they once were, once touch DNA becomes more commonplace."

"Weird."

"Anyway, thanks," Wendy said again. She really wanted to get busy processing the swab, to see what she might have picked up.

"Good luck," Doc Robbins muttered.

"Let me know if you think of a nursery rhyme sheep with a name," David called as she was leaving.

"I will, absolutely," she said. She let the door swing shut.

I am completely surrounded by nerds, she thought on her way back to her lab. *Like I'm an island in a sea of them. And global warming is raising the sea levels. . . .*

In science, as in most aspects of life, patience often pays off.

Greg had thought he would go crazy before he finished comparing edged tools to the marks left on the irrigation tube. Even his interrogation of Fred Rosen only offered a short break, and Rosen's knife hadn't come close to being the right tool.

Finally, he found a match.

It was a pair of pruning shears that he had taken from a gardening shed at the airport. The marks he made with them on identical black tubing were a precise fit—the same tool had definitely cut both tubes. It wasn't what a professional landscaper would use to cut irrigation tubing, he was sure, although it was a tool to which that landscaper would have access.

His next concern was who had handled the shears. If the same fingerprint turned up there as on the muffler, canopy, cockpit, or tube, then he would have a solid suspect. There had been no landscaper on duty, so he hadn't yet fingerprinted any, but he did have a list of airport employees and could send an officer out to collect those prints.

Mandy was busy with other things, so Greg checked the shears for fingerprints himself, fuming them in a small cyanoacrylate fuming chamber, which made two friction ridge impressions stand out distinctly under ultraviolet light. He added a little powder for contrast, photographed them, and lifted them with low-tack tape. Finally, he downloaded the images from the camera and ran them through the Automated Fingerprint Identification System, or AFIS.

A short while later, he had his answer. Or part of it, anyway. One of the fingerprints had come from someone who wasn't in the system.

But the other belonged to the night janitor at the airport, Benny Kracsinski.

He realized there could be a perfectly legitimate reason for Benny to use the landscaper's clippers from time to time. Greg had no way of knowing how much overlap there was between the two jobs. Ordinarily a janitor worked inside and a gardener or landscaper worked outside, but he supposed it was possible that the janitor had needed to prune an indoor plant, or wanted to cut back one that had grown too close to a window he had to wash. Any number of other scenarios presented themselves.

Still . . . since it was the only print he had that definitively linked an airport employee with a tool used in the commission of a homicide, he had to dig deeper.

Benny's prints were in AFIS, he learned, because they had been taken when Benny had joined the Air Force, years before. That was strange in itself— Greg wouldn't have taken Benny for a veteran. He had assumed that Benny's disability had been long term, maybe from birth, but apparently that wasn't the case.

He delved into what he could find online and in law enforcement databases about Benny Kracsinski, and the picture filled in a little more. *Time to bring Catherine into the loop,* he decided. *We just might have a murderer here.*

24

WHEN HER CELL PHONE rang, Catherine snatched it up, hoping it was Jim Brass with some sort of explanation for his presence in Deke Freeson's motel room. It was already halfway to her ear when she recognized the tone assigned only to Lindsey. She smiled. This late, Lindsey had to be calling back to tell her that the earlier emotional crisis had been resolved. The storms of youth blew furious but passed quickly. "Lindsey? What are you doing up? It's a—"

"It's July, Mom, there's no school tomorrow. And anyway, it's Friday night."

"Okay, I know that, but still—"

"Jeez, do you want to talk to me or not? Because sometimes you say I don't communicate enough and then when I try—"

"Fine, I'm sorry. What is it?"

There was a long silence, as if Lindsey was reconsidering her phone call. "It's about Sondra," she said finally.

"Sondra."

"You know, Sondra. My friend."

Catherine's turn to reconsider. She wanted Lindsey to be able to come to her with any problem—never wanted her daughter to feel that her troubles were unimportant, or that she would be turned away. But how had Sondra's problems become hers? "I know. Is this still about her and what's his name, Jayden? I tried to call you earlier, by the way. I thought you were in bed."

"I'm still out."

"Because?"

"Because Gemma is, like, freaking out over it."

Now she had inherited Gemma's problem, too. Was this how it worked these days? She didn't think she had ever dumped all of her friends' emotional issues on her own mother. She had given her grief in plenty of other ways, but not that one. "Okay . . ."

"I mean, when I called you we had just left the club. But then Gemma wouldn't get in the car. She waited around in the parking lot until Sondra came out with that guy she was with, and then attacked her. Like, physically."

"Was there a fight?"

"I don't know if you could call it that. We pulled them apart pretty fast. I think Gemma got in a punch or two, and Sondra scratched her face a little. It wasn't like anybody called the cops or anything."

That's good, Catherine thought, *because the last thing I need tonight is to bail you out of jail.* "Then what happened?" she asked.

"Then I tried to talk to Sondra about it, but she

didn't want to talk. She took off with that guy. She was acting like a stranger, like I don't even know her. And so I came over to Gemma's place and I've been trying to calm her down. She got pretty wasted."

"Are you okay, Lindsey?" That was the only part of this Catherine found truly important.

"I'm okay. I just . . . I don't know. Why do people act like that?"

"Like what?"

"Like either of them. It's like two of my best friends have been possessed by aliens or something."

Catherine couldn't resist. "Do aliens possess people? I always thought that was more of a demonic thing."

"Whatever, Mom. You know what I mean."

"I know, honey. I wish I could answer you. People are just—sometimes it's like we're all wearing masks. We show the world the image of us that we want others to see. Or that we think they want to see. Looking inside—getting under the mask to the real person beneath—that's the hard part, because they have to be willing to let us in. If someone wants to keep the mask in place, it's almost impossible to see under it."

"You're not making any sense, Mom."

"I'm not?"

"You're talking about masks and stuff. That's crazy. I'm just talking about Gemma and Sondra."

"It's a metaphor, Lindsey."

"I know that! But . . . you really think I don't know my best friends?"

"You tell me. You're the one who said they're acting like strangers."

"Well, yeah I guess."

"Did you ever expect to see these things happen to them? To have to pull Gemma and Sondra apart? Over some guy?"

"Of course not."

"Then maybe you don't know them as well as you thought. That's all I'm saying, Lindsey. People show one face to the world, but that doesn't necessarily represent who they really are. It might take a lifetime to truly know someone, if you ever do."

"Maybe you don't really know your friends, Mom, but I don't have that problem. We're like family."

"I'm your real family," Catherine reminded her. "I'm just saying—"

"Saying what, Mother? That I don't know what I'm talking about? That's how it usually goes, right? You've been through every possible experience, and I don't know the first thing about the world."

Pulling out the big gun of daughter/mother arguments: the "Mother" word. Once it had been considered a sign of respect. Now it signified sarcastic dismissal at best, and often outright antagonism.

"That's not it at all, Lindsey—" she began.

Lindsey cut her off again. "Mom, Gemma's puking. I gotta go."

"Take care, Lindsey. Get her to bed, then go home!"

The phone clicked midway through her final sentence. Lindsey was gone. Catherine pictured her holding Gemma's long blond hair as she knelt over the bowl. Not an image she had ever had of her daughter before.

But then, the things she had been trying to say applied to mothers and daughters as well as to friends. There had been a time, years really, when she had known Lindsey. Or believed she did, anyway. Then the teenage years had struck with the force of a hurricane, erasing that knowledge and trust like floodwaters did names scrawled in beach sand.

Now? Not quite strangers, not quite friends. They loved each other, she was sure of that.

She wasn't sure of much else, though. Not much at all.

Her life seemed to be coming untethered around her. Sara and Warrick were gone. Gil was away from the lab, and in his less guarded moments, she thought she sensed an increasing distance there, as if he was working toward a departure as well. Lindsey would one day be an adult, and while that wouldn't mean Catherine was no longer her mother, it would change their relationship. A child and an adult were two different people, she believed—there was continuity there, but Lindsey would have her own interests, her own life, and Catherine would be less a part of it than she had been for all these years.

Then there was Jim Brass, seemingly mixed up in a murder. She wanted to find him, grab him by the collar, and make him tell her what he was up to. She couldn't control the people she loved, but the more they seemed intent on straying away from her, the more she found herself wanting to do just that.

She wasn't the sort of person who liked to dwell on self-analysis, but if she were she might put it down to abandonment issues, because of her father's absence from her childhood. Not wanting to be left again, her first reaction was to grab hold, to refuse others permission to move away from her gravitational orbit.

That, no doubt, was an unhealthy response. Unhealthy and unhelpful.

Which didn't mean it wasn't real. It was just something she would have to deal with, on her own terms, on her own time.

She put her phone away, and looked up to see Greg standing in the doorway.

"You there?" he asked.

"I seem to be."

"You looked a little lost in space for a minute there."

"It's . . . it's nothing. What's going on, Greg?"

"What's going on is Benny Kracsinski."

"Who?"

"The night janitor at Desert View Airport."

"Oh," Catherine said. "The Dunwood case, right? You think he's your guy?"

"I'd bet on it," Greg said. "He handled the garden shears used to cut the tube that was jammed into the muffler. Everyone at that airport hates everyone else, as far as I can tell, even though they all claim to get along, but he's the only one I can positively connect to the murder weapon."

"The first part sounds familiar. How many workplaces are any different? Present company excluded, of course. I think a lot of people get along with their coworkers, but a lot of them would just as soon never see them again when they go home at the end of the day."

"Probably so," Greg said. "Here's the clincher to me. Benny and Jesse Dunwood were in flight training together at Lackland Air Force Base in Texas. They knew each other almost twenty years ago, which Benny never mentioned, to me or Grayson Williams, when he was being interviewed. He didn't even say anything about being in the service, much less knowing the victim decades ago."

"That's definitely suspicious."

"But wait," Greg said, imitating an infomercial spokesman. "There's more! Turns out they even hung out together off duty. At least, they did until one night when they went out to a couple of bars in San Antonio. On the way back, Benny was driving, Jesse riding shotgun, and there were a couple of other flyboys in the backseat. Benny, according to the newspaper accounts I found online, was sober— designated driver—but the others weren't. The drunk ones were arguing about the radio, Jesse cranking it up and another guy reaching up from the back to turn it down, and Jesse bumped Benny's arm just enough to send the car skidding into the path of an oncoming truck. Benny tried to correct course, but the truck rammed into his car, front left. Jesse and the guys in the backseat sustained minor injuries, but Benny was crippled for life. Obviously his flying career was over. He got an honorable discharge."

"And that sounds like motive," Catherine said. "Revenge best served cold, and all that."

"I think it's even more complicated than that," Greg said. "Think about it. Benny's career is shot. I don't know what kinds of jobs he held in the meantime, but probably nothing terribly lucrative or glamorous, considering he wound up a night janitor at a little airport in Las Vegas. Meanwhile, Jesse Dunwood has an honorable Air Force career as a fighter pilot. That was the future Benny dreamed of. After that, Jesse goes into business for himself, makes a lot of money, goes night flying over Las Vegas with a succession of beautiful women. Maybe—and this might be the worst part, the hardest sting—he doesn't even recognize Benny Kracsinski. If he had ever acknowledged the relationship publicly, the others would have told us about it. But as far as anybody there knew, Benny and Jesse only knew each other from the airport."

"That's definitely enough to bring him in for questioning, Greg. Good job. Do you want to be there?"

"Is there anything going on with the Melinda Spence disappearance?"

"We're working it," Catherine told him. "But there's nothing concrete yet."

"Okay, then," Greg said. "I guess I'll go to the airport."

Greg had barely left Catherine's office when Wendy came in. The revolving door again. *It's a miracle Gil ever gets into the field.*

"I've got something," Wendy said. She was practically bouncing with excitement, or as close to bouncing as Wendy ever got at work.

"Something on what?"

"Something on that sheep. Or off it, rather."

"Excuse me?"

"Touch DNA. I swabbed the sheep's . . . not arm-pits, but whatever you want to call them, and got some microscopic epithelials. The last person who handled her without gloves on was a man named Dawson Upson."

"That's good to know," Catherine said, her heart beginning to race. Halden Robles had identified the pizza delivery kid who was interested in his dog as Donnie or Dougie, she remembered. "Tell me more. Who is Dawson Upson?"

"He's a twenty-two-year-old Caucasian male. He's a lifelong Las Vegas resident, except for the last four years when he was going to college back in Boston. He graduated in June, though, and he's back in town, living with his mother, Vera Upson. He's not currently employed. His major was history, so there probably aren't a lot of jobs in Vegas suited to him. And get this—Mom's house is less than two miles from the Empire Casino construction site."

"Are you trying out for detective, Wendy?"

"I guess I got a little carried away. Touch DNA is still pretty experimental, so when I actually got a result I took it a couple of steps further."

"There's nothing wrong with taking initiative."

"I'm glad you feel that way." Wendy proffered a photo printed from the LVPD's database. "This is his driver's license picture."

Catherine took the sheet of paper and alarm bells started ringing in her head.

Dawson Upson was the guy who had drugged Melinda Spence and taken her out of the Palermo.

"Okay, I have to call Sam Vega," she said. She felt a surge of almost maternal pride at Wendy's discovery. Wendy was pretty, with a good body; in this city, a few wrong decisions might have pushed her down Catherine's original path instead of her current one. Wendy had even acted in a low-budget horror movie once, so a career on one sort of stage or another hadn't been out of the question. Catherine was glad she had chosen forensic science instead, because she showed a lot of promise. "How did Upson's DNA happen to be in the system?"

"It was evidence in a domestic violence case. His father beat him and his mother. The father claimed Dawson hurt himself falling down a flight of stairs, but investigators found his blood on a fireplace poker. The father killed himself rather than go to prison."

"That's definitely rough on the kid," Catherine said. She was sympathetic toward victims of abuse—but only to a point. "It's no excuse for turning into a murderer, but it's hard anyway. Thanks, Wendy." She reached for the phone to call Sam.

"There is one more thing, Catherine."

"What is it?"

Wendy hitched herself up, seeming to grow a couple of inches taller. *Pride,* Catherine thought. She was glad to see it. "I did a quick scan through the newspaper archives of Boston papers, from while Upson was in school there. During that time, six young women were abducted in the area. Some of them were released right away, unhurt, but a couple were tortured with knives and razor blades before being released. None of them were killed, and no suspect was ever apprehended. The last incident was in April, and nothing matching that pattern has turned up since then."

"Because he was studying for finals?"

"That's possible. And then he came back to Las Vegas."

"And now he has Melinda Spence. Great work, Wendy. I'm going to have this guy picked up fast."

25

NICK AND RILEY WERE on their way back to the lab when Catherine called. They were both still steamed about having to let Victor Whendt go, but they couldn't come up with a legitimate reason to hold him. Riley reminded herself that she was a CSI, not a detective. She wasn't supposed to play hunches. She found evidence and followed its trail.

Catherine had called Nick, but he was driving and Catherine wanted to relay a street address. He handed the phone to Riley.

"I need you to make a detour," Catherine said.

"Where to?"

"We've identified a suspect in the Melinda Spence disappearance."

A thrill coursed through Riley's body. That was the case that had started with the discovery of the animal burial pit. Saving Melinda's life was of primary importance, but if in the doing of it they could also bring in whoever had killed those poor animals, so much the better. "Who is it?" she asked.

"A man named Dawson Upson—I guess not much more than a boy, really. He lives with his mom a couple of miles from the Empire Casino site. He just came back from four years of college in Boston—"

"Which would explain the time gap in the animal corpses!" Riley interrupted. "Sorry."

"That's right," Catherine said. "He may have abducted and tortured some women in Boston. And he's a physical match for the person we have on video taking Melinda out of the Palermo. I have a feeling this is our guy."

"Good. Where do you want us to go?"

Catherine read off an address, which Riley wrote down in a notebook she kept in her pocket. Low tech, but it worked. "Vega's on his way, and so is backup," Catherine told her. "But I don't want to waste a second. You're not too far from Dawson Upson's house. And chances are he doesn't take his victims there, since his mother lives there, too. I need you to get over there now. If he's there, we need him in handcuffs. If he's not, process his room. Work the whole house if you need to. There's a warrant in the works, and it'll get there soon. If there's any clue as to where Upson would have taken Melinda, I want it found."

"We're on it, Catherine," Riley said. She filled Nick in, then brought up a route correction on the vehicle's GPS unit. He put his foot down and the SUV shot through the dark Nevada night toward the northeast side.

Established neighborhoods fell away behind them as they entered new development territory, surrounding the Empire Casino construction site. A few of the developments had been here for ten or twenty years, but they had been built with plenty of open desert between them. Now most of that desert had been filled in by more houses, constructed with a sameness that Riley found depressing. Watching out the window, she saw what seemed like an endless progression of signs advertising new housing projects and one brown stucco wall after another after another—some of them tan, occasionally an olive or a dun, but all within the same general palette and built in similar styles.

Every now and then they passed patches of undisturbed desert, or at least desert that appeared, to her relative newcomer's eye, to be pristine. Small forests of creosote bushes shot past the window, stands of cottonwoods and mesquites and other trees she couldn't identify but had admired elsewhere in daylight, sparse and scrubby, with profuse blooms somewhere between pink and magenta. Occasionally the headlights swept over shaggy yuccas or barbed chollas. "It's a long way from here to the Strip," she said.

"Not too bad when there's no traffic."

"I meant metaphorically. Out here you still feel like you're in the desert. On the Strip, you could be anywhere. I mean, nowhere but Las Vegas—but Las Vegas could be set down in the middle of Tokyo or New York or on the moon. It's something apart from its surroundings."

"I guess," Nick said. "To me it's all Vegas. Desert

and heat and lights and noise and greed—it's all one and the same. Vegas is as different as can be from where I grew up in Dallas, but I guess it's kind of worked its way under my skin. You can't remove any one element, because then it wouldn't be the same place anymore."

"But as all the desert gets eaten up by new construction, doesn't that throw it out of balance anyway?"

"Yeah, it might. The one constant here is change, though, so if there wasn't continual growth it still wouldn't be the same."

"I guess," Riley said. "Okay, left turn up here."

Nick slowed the SUV and turned left into one of the older developments, meaning it had probably been there since the 1980s. Hidden spotlights beamed toward the fronds of mature palm trees, set into a patch of thick green grass that could only exist in the desert thanks to an abundance of cheap water. From everything she had heard about Las Vegas's future, that kind of thing was on its way out. Citizens could already be fined for watering a lawn during the day, or for hosing off a driveway.

From the other direction, multiple headlights split the night. "Here comes the cavalry," Nick said.

The approaching vehicles turned into the development. Nick pulled over and let them pass, two squad cars and one unmarked, racing toward the Upson house. They followed taillights the rest of the way, and by the time they had gathered their field kits, officers in assault gear had fanned out around the house. Sam Vega and a couple of officers approached the front door, all clad in Kevlar vests. The

Upson house, a single-story ranch, had a xeriscaped yard, raw dirt and rocks with some native plants scattered sparsely across it. Better for the environment than a lawn, plus housing a single mother with her teenage son away at college, it would be easier to maintain. The windows were dark, the house silent.

Riley and Nick stood back to let the police do their thing. Vega watched one of the uniforms pound on the front door. "LVPD!" the cop shouted. "Open up!"

A light flicked on at the end of the house. Moments later, a woman came to the door, clutching a cotton robe at her chest. She was in her mid-forties, Riley guessed, with short red hair that had spiked off everywhere while she slept. Her eyes were puffy. "What is it?" she demanded. "What's going on?"

"Las Vegas Police Department, ma'am," Vega said, stepping forward and displaying his badge. "Are you Vera Upson? Dawson Upson's mother?"

"Yes, that's right. Yes, I am. What—"

"Is your son home?"

"Of course. I mean . . . I assume he is. He should be."

Assuming, Riley thought. *Never a good idea, especially when your son might be a monster.* "Do you mind if we check?" Vega asked. His manner was calming, which considering she could see heavily armed police officers surrounding her house, must have been intended to put her at as much ease as was possible.

"I . . . I have trouble sleeping. I took a pill. He was still up when I went to bed, but it's late now, so—"

"We'll just have a look, ma'am," Vega said. "It's very important."

"Do you have a . . . what's it called? A warrant?"

"Do you have something to hide?" Vega asked. "There's a warrant on the way, but we'd like to be allowed inside. A young woman's life might be in danger."

"I don't . . . what are you talking about? I don't understand what you're saying."

"I'm asking you to step back from the doorway and let us in, Mrs. Upson. If you cooperate, it'll be better all around."

"But, a woman's life? Do I need a lawyer?"

"Honestly?" Vega said. "It might not be a bad idea. Now if you don't mind . . ."

"Fine!" Mrs. Upson waved them in. "Go ahead. He's probably sound asleep in his room. You know how boys are."

"We'll find out," Vega said. "Which one's his room?"

She pointed down the hall. "Third door," she said. She was awake now. She looked shell-shocked.

As soon as she moved out of the doorway, cops flooded into her house. Riley and Nick waited outside. Banging doors and shouts of "Clear!" rang from the house.

A few minutes later, Sam Vega emerged, shaking his head. Vera Upson trailed him out the door. "The kid's not here," Vega said.

"I . . . I just don't know where he could be. He's not some wild thing, not like some other boys."

"Do you take pills to sleep every night?" Vega asked her.

"Like I told you, I have trouble sleeping."

"Do you have any idea where he goes at night while you're unconscious? What he does?"

"Apparently not," Mrs. Upson said. There was a hint of indignation in her voice. "I don't think I like your tone."

"I apologize, ma'am," Vega said. "We're just trying to find someone. It's very important."

"This woman you mentioned? I'm sure she's not here."

"It doesn't appear that she is. Does Dawson have someplace that he likes to go? When he's not here?"

"I'm sure I don't know every place he goes. The library, the mall. He goes to a lot of movies. He goes hiking in the desert."

"Where in the desert?"

"I haven't the slightest idea."

"Sam, we're going to get started in his room," Nick said.

"Yeah, go for it. If I get anything else, I'll let you know."

He and Riley went into the house. At least one of the Upsons was a smoker, as the odor of old smoke enveloped them at the door. Police officers milled about, not needed now that it was clear Dawson and his victim weren't on the premises.

Every door in the house had been left open. Riley and Nick entered the room Mrs. Upson had identified as her son's. Riley was slightly staggered by the appearance of his room, the walls painted black, the cream carpeting stained from spills and caked with dirt, wastebasket overflowing, every surface covered in streaked dust except for a computer on a desk and a small flat-screen TV mounted on one wall between horror movie posters. An ashtray, thick with ashes and butts, sat next to the computer.

She went back into the hall. Sam was just sitting Mrs. Upson down in the living room.

"One more thing, Mrs. Upson," Riley said. "Do you go into Dawson's room often?"

"Dawson is a young man. He needs his privacy. I give it to him."

"That's what I thought. Thank you, ma'am. We'll let you know when we're done here."

"What was that about?" Nick asked when Riley returned.

"She never comes in here or she would know what her son was really like," Riley said. "Look at this place." She pointed out the movie posters on the walls: *Murder 9, Corpse with My Face, A Taste for Blood, Can I Lick the Spoon?, I Was Satan's Bitch,* and more of the same.

"He's got a thing for slasher flicks," Nick said. "Bloodier the better, it looks like. That doesn't make him a killer."

Riley had already moved toward his bookshelf, which she had found was sometimes the easiest way to get a glimpse of someone's personality.

"It's not just fictional slashers he's into," she said. "He has true crime books here about John Wayne Gacy, Ed Gein, Jeffrey Dahmer, Richard Ramirez, Gary Ridgway, even Albert DeSalvo."

"The Boston Strangler?" Nick asked.

"Maybe the Strangler was a role model for him. Catherine said he went to college in Boston."

"And that's where he made the leap from abducting animals to people."

"Abducting, cutting, torturing—we've got to find this guy, Nick. We have to find him now."

Nick opened a couple of desk drawers. In the second, he found a cigar box. When he pulled it out, it appeared to have rags in it. He unfolded them, revealing three straight razors and a hunting knife. "Blades are dirty," he said. "I'm going to try a little luminol on these . . ."

"We'll find blood," Riley agreed. "He's got to have more than those, though. He wouldn't have taken Melinda Spence someplace with no weapons."

"He used guns on those animals too, right?"

"He's a shooter and a slasher. Greg's theory was that he was trying to figure out which one he was more comfortable with."

"Okay, let's get organized," Nick said. "We need to divide the room and see what's what. And it wouldn't hurt to call Catherine, let her know what we've found so far."

"I hope that warrant gets here soon," Riley said. "If Mrs. Upson decides to rescind her invitation . . ."

"Vega will just have to make sure she doesn't. I'm gonna call Cath from outside, so Mrs. Upson can't hear."

Nick went out, leaving Riley alone in the presumed monster's lair. There were touches—a team photo of the New England Patriots, a stuffed Teddy bear on the bed—that made Dawson Upson seem like a normal kid. The kid his mother believed him to be.

But Riley suspected he hadn't been normal for a long time. And not really a kid, either.

She just hoped they could figure out where he was. And fast.

In case Melinda Spence was about to become his first human kill.

26

O<small>UTSIDE, THE SUN HAD</small> just crested the eastern hills. It would be glinting off the still waters of Lake Mead and igniting the red peaks of Valley of Fire State Park. The lights of Las Vegas would dim and many of them—but not all—would be turned off until sunset. The day shift would come on duty soon.

They would have their hands full. If Vegas never slept, neither did its criminal element. Catherine's crew had to keep working their ongoing cases. You could go home if you were working on cases involving dead people and you had done absolutely everything you could for that shift. But you couldn't walk away from two missing women. It would mean overtime for the crew. She didn't care.

Finding Melinda Spence and Antoinette O'Brady was what mattered.

Sleep? Career considerations?

Those could wait.

At least she had been able to break away from

the lab again, if only for a short while. She had received a call from Nick about their disappointing but hardly surprising discovery at the Upson house, and another from LVPD headquarters letting her know that cops on patrol had spotted the Chevy Malibu registered to Deke Freeson, parked outside a gas station on Eastern Avenue, well south of McCarran.

The next call, from Melinda's father, had come while she was en route to see Freeson's car for herself. "I'm sorry to bother you, ma'am," he said. "I'm just checking to see if you have any new information on Melinda."

She didn't want to tell him about Upson yet, didn't want to build up his hopes in case that angle didn't pan out. "We're following up on some solid leads," she said after a moment's pause. "We hope to have something more definitive to tell you very soon now."

"That would be wonderful. I'm glad there's progress being made. We're praying for Melinda and for you."

He was bizarrely calm. If she had been in his position, if she was a civilian and Lindsey was missing, Catherine was sure she would behave like a lot of other parents she had dealt with over the years—demanding, insistent, possibly insulting, and almost certainly unreasonable. She would want answers when there weren't any to be given. Mr. Spence, on the other hand, seemed to accept that she was doing what she could, and that the Las Vegas Police Department wasn't comprised of barely functional and probably crooked morons who would make the Keystone Kops look like models of efficiency.

Maybe his calmness could be attributed to his faith. Or maybe he simply accepted that bad things happened in life, along with the good ones. *I should take a lesson*, she thought; parents and their children didn't automatically turn into antagonists, either during the teen years or at the onset of adulthood, and relationships could apparently deepen with time. Even if some, or much, of that time was spent apart.

Catherine had barely finished with that call when one came through from Lindsey. She glanced at the position of the sun over the horizon.

"I hope you're just waking up," she said.

"I haven't been to bed yet, Mom. I've been dealing with Gemma."

"You've been up all night? Lindsey, are you okay? Is she?"

"I'm a little sleepy, I guess. But sometimes friends come first, right?"

"I suppose. You can't take care of anyone else if you don't take care of yourself, though."

"Like I don't know that."

"I'm just saying, Lindsey."

"Well, don't treat me like a child, Mother. I do know a few things."

"I'm aware of that, Lindsey."

"Good."

"Did you ever get a chance to talk to Sondra about the whole situation?"

"I called her. We talked."

"And?"

"You know what you said about people wearing masks? Not really showing you their true selves?"

"Yes."

"She told me to mind my own business. She said she knows what's best for her, and she's breaking up with Jayden."

"That's her prerogative."

"I know, Mom. It's just . . . I never would have expected her to take that attitude with me."

"You can't ever get inside someone else's brain, honey. You can only go by what they show you." She didn't add how aptly that summed up her job: studying evidence to determine intangibles like motivation and intent.

"Well, she sure had me fooled."

"It might not be that so much," Catherine offered. "She's young. Maybe she wasn't hiding anything from you, but she doesn't really know her own mind yet."

"Yeah, maybe. I guess. It didn't seem like that, though. It just seemed like she turned into this heinous bitch, out of nowhere."

"That can happen too, Lindsey. It's less common . . . but when you're dealing with human beings, just about anything is possible."

"I guess."

"You should go on home, get some sleep."

"Okay, Mom."

"I'm pulling some extra hours today, but with any luck I'll be out of here before too much longer. I'll buy you dinner."

"That sounds good. See you later!"

Lindsey hung up. Catherine was pleased with the way the conversation had gone, overall. The tension of their previous talk had been overcome or forgotten. Lindsey was apparently willing to accept that her mother was not a complete tool, maybe even that she knew a thing or two. Catherine had to accept that Lindsey had her own life and made her own decisions, at least about many things. She knew that would only continue, that she would make more and more of them on her own, that the gap between them might become a canyon.

On the other hand, bridges could always be built, even across the widest of chasms. She didn't have to lose Lindsey—she had only to maintain the right kind of ties. Trusting her, as Mr. Spence had apparently learned to trust his daughter Melinda, was probably a good first step.

A few minutes later, Catherine pulled up at the Mi-T-Gas. A female officer, slender and honey-blond, in her mid-twenties, stood on the side of the building next to a blue Malibu with a dented rear fender and a broken taillight. "I'm Supervisor Willows of the crime lab," Catherine said as she approached.

"I was told to expect you," the cop said. "I'm Liz Tavrin."

"I'm Catherine. Where's your partner, Liz?"

"Dave's looking around the neighborhood to see if he can find anyone who saw the driver."

"Tell me what happened."

The cop pointed to the taillight. "I saw the busted light as I was driving past the station. That's a violation, so we figured we'd have to write a fix-it ticket. But when I stopped my vehicle, my partner Dave remembered the BOLO for a blue Malibu. We checked on the tag number, and this was the car.

We called it in, then went into the gas station to see if the missing woman was inside."

"And?"

"No dice. There's no convenience store or anything at this location—just a couple of service bays and some outdoor vending machines. Restrooms are accessed from outside and left unlocked if there's anyone here. There's a cashier and a single mechanic on duty, but neither one saw the car pull up or anyone get out."

"There a security video?"

"They only have one camera, on the pumps. She didn't get gas."

"What did she do, then?"

"I don't know. She's not here, and I was told to watch the car."

"Okay," Catherine said. "Thanks." She eyed the car's position, badly parked on the side of the building nearest the restrooms. Intentionally out of sight of anyone inside, she supposed. Overnight there had probably only been one attendant on duty, if that—the pumps took credit cards and could function 24/7 with no human supervision.

Logic suggested that Antoinette had stopped for the restroom. Catherine walked past the car, looking inside it as she did. Some fast food wrappers, a days-old newspaper, and an empty plastic water bottle were all she could see inside. None of it pointed to Antoinette O'Brady—the stuff could have been hers but just as easily could have been left there by Deke. She could find out who had handled it, given time.

But time was what Antoinette might be running out of.

The keys weren't dangling from the ignition, which told her Antoinette had not left the car for good. She had meant to come back to it and wanted to know it would be there. Of course, if she had started to come back and seen a uniformed cop standing there, that might have scared her away. Depending on what she was mixed up in . . . Catherine wished once again that Brass had responded to her phone and radio calls.

Tugging on a pair of latex gloves, she went into the women's room. The waste bin was full to overflowing, the floor dirty and strewn with toilet paper, paper towels, and sanitary napkin wrappers. If they left the restrooms open overnight, then probably there was an attendant on duty inside, but that attendant hadn't bothered to come out and clean them in some time. Rust stains streaked the white porcelain of the sink, and the mirror had been splashed with water. Every wall had graffiti on it, a sort of ongoing conversation between utter strangers.

Catherine glanced in the toilet, which was always a fairly high-risk activity in a place like this. It had been flushed since its last use, and while she wouldn't call it clean, no obvious clues stared her in the face.

She tried to re-create Antoinette's mental state. She had been running from someone who was trying to kill her. She, not Deke, was probably the real target of the shooter in the motel—otherwise, would Deke have worried about shielding her with his body? Would she have escaped out the bathroom window and taken his car? The fact that she was Emil Blago's wife only complicated things further.

So Antoinette would have been scared, maybe desperate, even close to frantic. She had no wallet, no ID, maybe no money on her at all. She had whatever she'd been wearing when the attack had come, but her clothing, and she, were covered in blood. Hours had passed, during which things had not started looking any brighter for her situation.

And she had to pee. Who wouldn't?

It was the covered-in-blood part that spurred Catherine. In Antoinette's place, she would want to clean off as best she could. That meant the sink. And the waste bin.

She pulled the lid off and set it on the floor. Used paper towels and other trash cascaded to the floor. Antoinette would have shoved her trash deep inside, though, to make sure it stayed hidden from casual view.

Catherine reached in, pushing through layer after layer of waste paper until her hand touched a particularly wet clump.

Jackpot. The paper towels she pulled out were soaked and pink with blood. Wendy Simms could match the blood to Deke Freeson's in no time, Catherine guessed. But she didn't need the lab work at the moment—she was convinced it meant Antoinette had come in here to clean up. Perhaps with the sun coming up, she had begun to feel vulnerable.

She wasn't here now, however, and she had left her wheels behind. If she had another ride, she might have left the keys behind. So maybe she hadn't gone far.

Catherine left the paper towels on top of the trash, intending to come back and collect them shortly. First she wanted a look at the neighborhood.

Eastern was a busy street, with traffic day and night. If Antoinette had crossed it on foot or walked down its length, she would have been an easy target. Not something Catherine would risk, in her position—not with someone chasing her. Even if she had lost her immediate pursuer, she wouldn't want to show herself that way.

She turned away from the street and then saw it.

Set back from the avenue, behind a wide parking lot, was a Select Stop Mart twenty-four-hour discount department store. That's where Catherine would go if she were in Antoinette's shoes. She would need new clothes. Maybe she was carrying a credit card or some cash. Maybe as part of whatever escape plan they had arranged, Deke had left those in his glove compartment for her.

And perhaps he had left a gun.

"Did your partner go into that store?" she asked Officer Tavrin.

"He might have."

"Radio him."

Tavrin tried to raise him on her radio, but he didn't answer. She squinted into the morning sun, shaking her head. "I don't know what's wrong."

"I'm going to call for backup," Catherine told the uniformed officer. "And then you and I are going shopping."

* * *

"Officer Morston?"

"That's right."

"This is CSI Greg Sanders. You're still at the airport, right?"

"Yeah."

Greg was silent for a moment as he darted between two trucks that hadn't quite made room for him, despite the flashing lights announcing the urgency of his mission. This was why it was better to have two people in the vehicle, one to drive while the other handled details like communication with the outside world. There hadn't been anyone else available at the lab to join him, but he would meet other cops at the airport.

"Listen, Officer Morston, I need you to do something for me."

"Okay."

"Make sure that janitor, Benny Kracsinski, is still there."

"That's the crippled guy?"

"Let's go with 'differently abled.'"

"Whatever."

"Find him and don't let him go anywhere."

"Should I arrest him?"

"Only if he tries to leave. I'm almost there, and there are some other officers meeting me."

"Got it. Anything else?"

"That's it. I'll see you soon. And thanks."

Greg had nothing against rookie cops. He wasn't even certain that Morston was a rookie. But he was either new on the job or he'd been in trouble for something—in any event, he could be spared for a night to nursemaid an empty airplane, so he couldn't be that important.

Which meant Greg didn't trust him to handle the arrest of his murder suspect by himself. He hadn't even been around to keep people away while the plane was processed. Greg had spent hours doing that himself and cutting plastic tubes. He didn't want to let Benny possibly walk on a technicality after all his effort. He wanted to make sure any potential arrest was by the book, start to finish.

With the roadway finally clear ahead of him, he jammed his foot down on the accelerator and raced through the dawn's first light.

27

NICK AND RILEY DIDN'T worry about fingerprints. The room was full of them; they could see them in the dust. Most undoubtedly belonged to Dawson Upson. They had found no indication that he brought Melinda Spence, or anyone else, into the house. And at this point they weren't trying to identify anyone—they were trying to find people. That changed their search parameters. Nick rifled the desk and closet, looking for a map, a photo, a sketch, anything that might tell them where he took animals to kill them.

"This guy's got to keep souvenirs," Nick said. "He's a textbook case."

"Maybe he's not that far along yet," Riley replied. "He obviously doesn't think much of animals. Could be he wouldn't think to take souvenirs until he's had a human victim. Just keep looking." She was on her knees, shining a flashlight under his bed, illuminating cobwebs and dust bunnies almost big enough to conceal corpses. "Then again, maybe he's one of the smart ones. It always strikes me as insane that people intentionally keep evidence of their crimes around."

"But then it's insane to go around murdering people, too. I don't think this one's too smart."

"Well, we're here, so he's not as smart as he might be. Then again he's not here, so maybe he's no dummy after all."

Riley turned around. Nothing under the bed but dust. If she flipped the mattress she might find some porn magazines—at least traditionally that was where she thought people kept them. Porn often figured into the psyches of serial killers, as part of the whole process of objectifying human beings. But Upson was obviously computer literate, so maybe he didn't bother with magazines.

Her light fell on a sneaker. It looked huge, but then guys' shoes usually did to Riley. She sometimes wondered if it was evolution or global warming or something, but most young men these days seemed to wear size eleven or twelve shoes, while her father had worn an eight and a half. She didn't see the evolutionary advantage of clown feet, but maybe there was some aspect of it she was overlooking.

Its mate was behind it, along with some other casual shoes, in a nook across from the bed, between the desk and a bookcase. They were piled up in no particular order. She visualized Upson sitting on the edge of the bed, prying the first shoe off with his other foot and kicking it off into the pile, then doing the same with the next one. She used her light to scan the space between the bed and the pile of shoes, hoping for some sort of soil or other trace evidence that might signify Upson's whereabouts. The carpet was dirty but nothing in particular stood out.

She moved the shoes out of the nook, setting them neatly beside the desk, and ran her light across the carpet there.

On the carpet, as if it had fallen from a shoe's treads, was a tiny pink something. Riley took forceps from her kit and picked it up, bringing it into the light. It was a flower petal, or part of one, that had been folded and crushed in the grooves of a shoe or boot's tread.

"Nick, help me out with this," she said. "I haven't been in town long enough to know every flower in Las Vegas."

"No human on earth has," Nick said. "The natives aren't that hard to learn, but if there's any plant under the sun that hasn't been imported or grown here in some greenhouse or nursery, I don't know what it would be. Some arctic lichens, maybe."

"I don't know much about Upson, but I doubt if he's the kind of guy who hangs out around greenhouses." She showed him the bit of flower petal.

"That one's easy," he said with a smile. "I thought you were gonna test me."

"What is it?"

"Desert willow."

"I think it fell out of one of his shoes."

"That doesn't help us much. Those suckers are everywhere."

"Except the desert isn't everywhere, Nick. Not anymore. While you were driving over here, I was watching out the windows. There are a lot more housing developments in this area than there is open desert."

"That's true."

"Is this a kind of scraggly-looking tree with a ton of blossoms?"

"Pretty much, yeah."

"I thought so. I saw a bunch of them, about midway between the Empire Casino site and here."

"But like I said, these aren't rare."

"Maybe not. But everything's getting rarer except grass and palm trees that don't belong here. And we know where he lives, and where he dumps his prey, so if there are desert willows between the two, I think it's worth a look."

"Yeah, you could be right, Riley."

"You see anything better? Find his souvenirs? Maybe a map with 'X marks the spot' written on it?"

Nick shrugged. "Nothing yet. But there's got to be something."

"Maybe this is it. Maybe this flower is our best shot. We could vacuum up the soil in the carpet and send it to the trace lab for analysis, but by the time we get any results, Melinda Spence could be dead."

"Okay, you're right. We're drawing a blank here. Unless Sam's gotten something better out of Mrs. Upson, let's go for a hike in the desert."

28

GREG DIDN'T SEE Officer Morston anywhere. He parked outside the hangar in which Jesse Dunwood's plane was stored, which was the last place he had seen the cop. In the morning light, the airport lost what little glamour it had owned the night before, when blue runway lights had glowed through the darkness and the illuminated tower had floated above the field like a glowing mirage. Today it just looked dusty, dingy and functional—not at all romantic. No wonder Dunwood took his dates flying at night.

Where the hell was Morston? If he had gone to sleep in the past five minutes, or had taken another break, he would lose his badge. Greg would make sure of it. He didn't want to lose Benny Kracsinski now. He thought with what he had on the guy, he could squeeze a confession out of him. But not if he'd managed to slip away from Officer Morston.

He got out of the Yukon and went into the shadowy hangar. It was empty, silent. "Officer Morston!" Greg called. His voice seemed to reverberate off the corrugated steel walls and bounce back at him. "Are you in here?"

He was about to walk away when he heard a low groan. "Who's there?" Greg demanded.

Another groan, followed by the awkward scuff of shoes on pavement, came from behind the airplane.

Greg drew his duty weapon.

He didn't even like carrying a gun, much less the possibility of having to use it. But alone here, not knowing who was in the shadows behind that plane, he would use it if he had to. "Come on out," he said. "Let me see your hands."

Slowly, Officer Morston staggered into view. He was holding one hand out before him, and had the other clapped to the back of his head. His collar was red, soaked with blood. "It's . . . it's me. Sanders?"

"Officer Morston? What happened?"

The cop looked at Greg with bleary, haunted eyes. "I don't . . . I'm not sure. I was on the phone with you, and I thought I heard something in here. I came in to look. The lights were out, but . . . I heard a noise behind the plane. I went back there, and . . . then I . . . I guess someone hit me. Hell of a blow on the back of my skull."

"How long ago?"

"Just a few minutes. I think I . . . blacked out for a little while, but not for long."

"Do you know where Benny is?"

"No . . . no clue. He's probably the . . . the bastard who hit me."

"He might be. Do you need a doctor?"

Officer Morston tried to stand upright, but he swayed on his feet and reached out to the airplane for support. Greg hurried to his side. "Sit down," he said. "I'm going out to see if I can find him. I'll call the paramedics for you."

Greg made the 911 call as he stalked the airport grounds. Sirens wailed in the near distance. His backup, no doubt, on the way. He would be glad to see them, but he hadn't known when he made the call that medical assistance would be required.

The sun was higher in the sky now, gleaming down on the runway and blasting off the east-facing windows of the office building. He didn't see Benny Kracsinski anywhere. The morning was quiet, the only noise except for the approaching sirens coming from a small plane revving up as it started across the tarmac from another hangar. It was white with red striping, and its wings ran across the top of the fuselage instead of coming out from underneath it. Greg thought it was a Cessna, but he really didn't pay a lot of attention to the private aircraft industry. His theory was that it was good to have a wide base of knowledge, and even better to know how to look things up when he had to. Airplanes fell into the latter category.

The clatter of running footsteps caught his attention. They came from the direction of the office building. He looked that way, shielded his eyes against the glare coming off the windows, and saw Patti Van Dyke sprinting toward him. Her eyes were huge.

"That's Benny!" she cried. "Stop him!"

"What? Where?" Greg asked.

"In the one-fifty! He can't fly that airplane—he's not licensed! It isn't safe!"

Greg looked at the white plane with red stripes, picking up speed as it rolled down the runway. "Benny's in there?"

"Yes!" Patti reached him and latched on to his arm. Her face was blotched red from effort, and tears glimmered in her eyes. "He can't fly a plane, not unless it's been specially configured for him!"

Greg jerked his arm free of her grip and ran for the department Yukon. He couldn't outrun a taxiing airplane, but if he could outdrive it and block the runway, perhaps he could still stop it. He yanked the door open, slid into the seat, started the big SUV, and slammed it into gear.

Earlier he had marveled at driving on an airport tarmac, however lowly an airport it was. Now he was chasing a runaway plane over the pavement, surprised that it wasn't smoother. The speedometer needle crept up as he floored the accelerator, powering through the smell of exhaust coming from the plane. *ROP or LOP?* Greg wondered with a grim chuckle. He was gaining on the plane. Its wings bobbed as it bounced over the runway's bumps, its flaps making tentative up and down motions. Greg didn't know how long it had been since Benny had flown, so maybe he was trying to get used to the controls before taking off.

Which gave Greg some small hope of success.

He knew that blocking the runway could turn out to be suicidal, if Benny failed to stop or veer away in time. He just didn't feel like he had a lot of choice. He was nowhere near a good enough shot to take out a tire, or to hit Benny through the plane's small windows. And even if he did that, what would stop the plane from swerving into him anyway? His best bet was to count on Benny's survival instincts, on his realization that even a long stretch in prison would be preferable to dying in a fiery runway collision.

He started to pass the plane. Glancing over for as long as he dared, Greg saw Benny in the pilot's seat, his bent spine hunching him over the wheel. Benny was staring straight ahead, with a determined set to his jaw and a ferocious gleam in his eyes. He looked utterly intent on his goal, as if nothing would dissuade him from this mad escape plan.

For an instant, Greg's hope wavered.

He wanted to stop this guy. This killer. Wanted to be able to prove in court that he had found the motive, and discovered the evidence that put the murder weapon in his hands. It wasn't just that he had spent all that time cutting plastic—it was what he had chosen this career for. He wanted to use science as a tool for solving crimes, because solving crimes meant putting bad people away, honoring their victims, and protecting those who might otherwise have been next.

But did he want it enough to risk dying for it?

Greg had unconsciously let up on the gas, just the slightest bit. Realizing his mistake, he pressed down again. *Of course I do,* he thought. *I risk death every time I go out into the field. Hasn't stopped me yet.* The SUV lunged forward. His ears were full of the roar of engines, his Yukon's and the airplane's, battling for supremacy on the narrow runway.

Greg gained ground, starting to pass the plane again. He was running out of runway, so he was going to have to make his move fast. He edged past the plane's nose and kept going, pulling ahead. Then he saw the plane in his rearview, falling back. Was Benny giving up? Slowing down? Greg squeezed a little more speed from the SUV, then braked and cranked the wheel at the same time.

The Yukon fishtailed, skidding across the runway in a cloud of smoke and the stink of burnt rubber. The engine died. The abrupt stop jolted Greg, and when he caught his balance again, he looked out toward the airplane.

It came on fast. Benny hadn't slowed or stopped; Greg had simply outraced him.

And now Benny was going to ram him.

Greg pawed at the door handle. He had to get out, now—there wasn't time to start the engine again.

He just managed to get the door open when the airplane's wheels left the ground.

Greg threw himself to the tarmac and covered his head with his hands, anticipating the worst.

The airplane lifted off the runway, gaining altitude. It didn't veer from its course. Greg's last glimpse of Benny before the plane's nose blocked his view showed a man utterly intent on his flying, as if he didn't even understand what a close call he'd had. Greg glanced up to see the plane zoom over him, raising a fog of dust and debris, its landing gear barely clearing the Yukon's roof.

He stood up in the airplane's draft, wind whipping his hair and clothes.

Benny urged the plane higher, continuing the steep path that had carried him over the SUV. Greg watched him go. Twenty feet high. Thirty. Climbing fast. He figured he would have to call the FAA, to make sure that wherever Benny touched down he was arrested on the spot. Fifty feet.

At sixty or thereabouts, Benny tried to level the plane out. He had shot up at such a steep angle that it seemed to Greg as if it would arc over backward, perform a somersault in midair.

But he didn't have room for any fancy aerobatics—he wasn't high enough yet.

Seventy-five feet, and still climbing fast.

And then the engine noise changed abruptly.

Greg had been hearing its roar for so long that the sudden shift was as startling as a slap in the face.

He didn't know a lot about flying, but he knew what a stall was. Push the airplane up too steep a curve and you stall. Stunt flyers did it for kicks.

Only when they had plenty of room and time to pull out of it, though.

Benny had no room, no time.

The plane shuddered violently and dropped, tail first. Started to flip over. Benny worked the flaps.

Nothing helped. The plane hit the ground with a bang, crunching and folding like wet cardboard. Greg braced for an explosion that didn't come.

The plane deconstructed right in front of him, wings shearing off, fuselage compacting. The smell of gasoline was thick in the air, so an explosion might still be coming.

He had to get Benny out before it did.

Greg ran toward the airplane. Coming up behind him, he heard sirens, engines. His backup, airport safety personnel, maybe those paramedics he had called. He couldn't spare the time to look back. A bloody hand poked out through a broken window, weak. Chunks of glass embedded in its flesh sparkled in the morning sun.

Benny Kracsinski was still alive.

With greater urgency, Greg dashed forward. His foot caught a wet patch of grass, slipped, and he went sprawling. Caught himself on hands and knees and pushed up again, his forward motion barely halted. He realized he had cut his left hand on a shard of twisted metal. Blood wet his palm. He took another step—

—and then the plane blew.

One instant it was still recognizable in its basic essence, and the next it was a fireball, ballooning out toward Greg, hurling a wall of knife-edged debris and a concussive blast that slammed into him like a pro linebacker, pinwheeling him backward. Heat swept over him, pinning him to the grass.

Grass that reeked of gasoline.

Greg rolled, scrambled. Flame ran toward him along a dozen paths, like self-generating roadways cutting through open country.

He ran, slipped, steadied, and ran faster.

Ahead of him vague forms gathered, their details blurred by the red film that had settled over his eyes. Cymbals clashed in his ears, drowning out all sound.

Heat snaked up his left leg. He screamed—

—and cold foam struck him, arctic slush chilling him to the core, but it cut the heat—

—and pain consumed him, swallowing him whole, and as he dropped willingly into its giant maw, the world went black.

29

"THIS IS CSI Supervisor Willows, calling for backup."

"What's your location, Supervisor Willows?"

Catherine watched the front of the store from the street next to her SUV. All was still. Sunlight glinted off the big windows, blinding her to anything that might have been going on inside. "Select Stop Mart, on Eastern Avenue."

"I already have a unit on the way to that location," the dispatcher reported.

Catherine glanced up and down the street. Traffic was light, with no black-and-whites in view. "I don't see any on approach. There is one car here already." She read off the identification numbers on the back of Liz Tavrin's car. "Why is another en route?"

"It wasn't an emergency call, but there's a unit en route. They're ten or fifteen minutes out."

Catherine tried to rein back her frustration. "*Why,* dispatch? Who called?"

"Store security is what I show. A security guard caught a shoplifter. He's detaining for arrest."

A shoplifter? Maybe someone with no cash, wearing bloody clothes? "Does it say what the suspect was after? Was it women's clothing?"

"I don't have that information, I'm sorry."

"Well, see if they can get here faster. I'm going in."

"I have to advise you to wait for the unit, Supervisor."

"I have a uniformed officer on the scene already." Catherine looked at Liz Tavrin. She hoped the lady knew her job. "And her partner might be inside the building. Just get that unit here as fast as you can."

Catherine was about to click off the radio when another thought occurred to her. "One more thing," she said. "Did this call go out over the air?"

"I didn't know who was in the vicinity, so, yes, it was broadcast as a general bulletin. About thirty-five minutes ago."

"Thanks."

Catherine didn't know a lot about Emil Blago, but according to his reputation he was an old school mobster, or wanted to be. Even a crime boss had to have goals, she supposed. Old school usually meant having police on the payroll. She still got a hard lump in her throat thinking about the murder of her friend Warrick Brown at the hands of a dirty undersheriff who had worked for gangster Lou Gedda. She liked to think better of her fellow officers of the law, but somehow when no one was looking, Las Vegas had turned into a very big city, complete with big city problems.

One of those problems had always been an over-abundance of corrupt cops.

So, if Blago—or one of his gangland enemies—was after Antoinette, then broadcasting her whereabouts, however obliquely, might have been a bad idea. No telling who might have been listening in.

Catherine had to hope that no one else had put together the pieces that she had—that Antoinette, badly in need of fresh clothes and with no money to pay for them, might have resorted to stealing from a store she probably wouldn't have been caught dead shopping in.

Catherine smiled at that. You didn't have to be a CSI for long to see people caught dead in a lot of unexpected situations. There was a certain cleverness to Antoinette's choice of stores, which Catherine supposed also applied to the choice of the Rancho Center Motel—both were places a man like Emil Blago would not expect to find his wife.

"Come on," she said to Tavrin. "We're going in."

"In where?"

Catherine ticked her head toward the store. "Select Stop Mart. Have you ever been in there?"

"I've been in some of their locations, but not that one."

"That's too bad." She'd been hoping the cop knew the layout. Chances were good that they would go in, find the security guard who had detained Antoinette in a locked back room somewhere, and that would be that. Easy. Maybe Tavrin's partner was already taking custody, and the store's heavy walls and shelving had interfered with his radio. Then again, it might not even be Antoinette.

They might walk in and find a terrified sixteen-year-old kid.

You couldn't count on easy when you were dealing with people like Blago. Catherine wished she knew more about what had gone on in that motel room. Had Antoinette been the target, or Deke? Was Antoinette still being pursued? As a witness, or as the original object of the hunt? Who wanted her dead, if the latter was the case?

And where did Jim Brass fit in? That remained the biggest question mark about the whole affair.

She and Tavrin trekked across the parking lot, ridiculously vast and mostly deserted at this early hour.

Two of the few cars parked outside, both drawn up to the front of the store instead of back in the rows of painted slots, looked familiar.

The first was a black Dodge sedan she recognized as the unmarked unit driven by Jim Brass.

The other was a patrol car that she remembered was the one Officers Wolfson and Tuva drove. Now she knew the shoplifter was Antoinette, and there would be nothing easy about what was to come.

She tried to swallow back her anxiety. She was a scientist, not a cop. But her duties included both—she had sworn to uphold and enforce the law in addition to investigating crimes, and if her usual tools included fingerprint brushes and test tubes instead of guns, she had to be competent with the latter in addition to the former.

Today it might well be guns.

"Draw your weapon," Catherine said. Her tone was quiet but forceful. It was hard to get the mixture right—she wanted to sound calm, but any time you told someone to take out a firearm, you were also warning them that there might be shooting.

The weight of her Glock 9mm should have been comforting, but instead it felt like she carried ten pounds of trouble.

"What's going on in there?" the officer asked her.

"I'm not sure, but I have a feeling we're walking into the middle of an unpleasant situation. I think we should try to clear the store and hope all the people with guns are somewhere in the back. No guarantees, though."

"Should we wait for backup?"

"We can't. Your partner might be in there. I know there's a friend of mine in there, and maybe a woman in danger. You don't have to go in, but I'd appreciate the assist."

"All due respect, Supervisor, but you bet your ass I'm coming."

"Good."

Before they could reach the sidewalk outside the door, the shooting began.

Catherine heard the familiar crack and echo of gunfire, followed immediately by shrieks from within the store. The front double doors, glass and steel, burst open and people came running out. Store employees in matching canary yellow polo shirts and black pants were accompanied by a scattering of others, presumably customers. A young mother held on to the hands of two toddlers, trying to hurry them out of the way. A hulking bald guy with long whiskers wearing a leather vest, torn T-shirt, ragged jeans, and heavy black boots—Catherine guessed he belonged with the Harley parked a couple of spaces from the front of the lot—stormed through the doors with a frightened look on his face. An elderly Asian couple, clutching each other by the arm, somehow managed to walk with what seemed to be a casual gait but at a rapid pace.

Catherine broke into a run as soon as she heard the shots, holding her badge out in one hand and her weapon by her side in the other. Liz Tavrin came behind her. Catherine picked one of the store employees, a thirty-something African-American woman who struck her as anxious but not panicked, and approached her.

"LVPD!" she called. She moved right in front of the woman, so her badge would be seen, and stopped, blocking her way. "What's going on inside?"

"I don't know," the woman said, halting suddenly. "Someone's shooting in there!"

Shoppers and store staff streamed past them. The woman was obviously ready to move on, but Catherine grabbed her arm. "Did you see any police officers inside?"

"Two or three went in. Not all together, but separately. That's when the shooting started, when they went toward the back."

"Okay," Catherine said. "Thank you. You'd better move on away from the windows."

The woman nodded and hurried away. Catherine looked toward the doors again, but they had gone still. She couldn't see any movement from inside.

"You still want to go in?" Liz asked.

Clichés warred in Catherine's head. *Discretion is the better part of valor. Fortune favors the brave.*

Hell with it. Brass is in there, and Tavrin's partner. Maybe Antoinette O'Brady. Caution dictated waiting for backup, but when lives were on the line, sometimes cops had to take chances.

"What do you think?" she asked.

"What are we standing around for, then?"

I think I like this lady, Catherine thought. She gave Tavrin a grin and started for the doors.

She approached the big plate-glass windows from the side, not wanting to present an easy target in case someone was inside drawing a bead on the doorway. Hanging her badge on her belt, she pressed one hand against the glass to cut the glare and peered into the store.

She saw no movement at all. Lights burned in fixtures hanging from the high ceiling, and others glowed at cash register stations, indicating which lanes were open. Those were probably the first employees who had exited, though, since they had been so close to the doors when the shots rang out.

Just as it struck Catherine that there had been no other shots, she heard two in quick succession. Muzzle flashes flared near the back of the store, briefly illuminating the far wall. There was no indication of backup on the way, but Catherine had to get inside just the same. She hurried to the door, moving at a crouch in hopes that the cash registers would block her from the view of anyone inside. Liz Tavrin followed suit.

At the door, Catherine paused for the briefest

instant, swallowing hard. Time to get it done. She raised her weapon, supported it with her free hand, and swung inside. Liz moved almost simultaneously, covering the lower half of their field of view while Catherine took the upper, tracking across the store, point to point. The faintest scent of disinfectant hung in the air; the floors had probably been mopped during the night.

"Las Vegas Police Department!" Catherine shouted. "I need everyone in here to put down their weapons and move slowly toward the front, hands on your heads!"

A shot rang out. Catherine and Liz both ducked, and one of the big windows took the bullet, cracking but not shattering.

"This is your last warning!" Catherine called. "You're shooting at a police officer!"

"Catherine?" A familiar voice.

"Jim?"

"They don't care, Cath! They *are* police officers!" Brass's voice came from the left rear of the store, but she couldn't pin it down more than that. She couldn't ask him for his location because he might be hiding from someone.

Not just someone, she was certain. Officers Wolfson and Tuva.

She beckoned to Tavrin and the two of them hurried at a crouch to the nearest register lane. The heavy counter and machinery would help block any rounds from deeper in the store. But they couldn't stay there for long. They had to keep moving, find out what was really going on.

Like Tavrin, Catherine had been inside other

Select Stop Mart locations. As far as she could tell from here, this one was laid out in a similar fashion to the others. Off to the right of the cashier lanes were sections of cleaning supplies, then pets, cosmetics, and health and first-aid supplies. Groceries started after that, wrapping around the corner. Across a wide aisle from those were cards and gifts, then linens, kitchenware, and small appliances. Directly across from the registers were women's clothing and a small glass jewelry counter. Women's clothes blended into children's wear, then men's, with shoes at the very back. Going left from the registers took one into office and school supplies and crafts, then around the corner into housewares, home improvement, and home furnishings. Beyond those, along the back wall, came toys, electronics, CDs and DVDs, and books.

"How many are there, Jim?" Catherine called.

He wouldn't answer if doing so would put him in danger.

"Three," he said.

A shot sounded, then a ricochet. Something smashed, back in Jim's corner.

"Jim?"

"Fine," he called.

Something had been nagging at her, and she had just figured out what. Where was Antoinette? If the suspects had her, they would be using her as a hostage, trying to lure Jim into the open. If Brass had her, he would be trying to get her out of the store. As it was, it seemed like everyone had claimed a protected area and was essentially trapped there.

"Backup will be here any second!" she called. She hoped, anyway. But the bad guys didn't have to know that part.

"A bus?"

"Someone hurt?" Was that why Antoinette wasn't a factor?

"Cop got shot in back. And a security guard."

"Dave?" Tavrin asked.

Oh, no, Catherine thought. Tavrin tensed up, her eyes saucering. Catherine knew what she would do possibly before she did. "Tavrin, don't!"

She was too late. Tavrin darted out from the protection of the cash register and darted toward the back of the store, weapon out to fire, as if she could get off a decent shot at a full sprint. "Dave!" she screamed.

Her voice echoed through the empty space. Her boots thundered on the linoleum floor.

The gunshots that cut her down were louder still.

Catherine watched for muzzle flashes, light blooming in the store's center right, and she squeezed off two shots in that direction. Brass did the same.

A spray of blood burst from Liz Tavrin's left shoulder. The round caught her in midstride, spinning her so the blood arced around her as she fell.

Catherine ducked back behind the register and used her radio to call for paramedics. Dispatch assured her that backup was less than five minutes out, and that multiple units were responding. Not wanting them to sound off and give her position away, she switched off her radio and her cell phone.

Once that was taken care of, she had to get Tompkins out of the line of fire. Then she had to reach Brass, needed to find out what the score was. Catherine felt like she was stumbling in the darkness. Dangerous enough under ordinary circumstances, far worse when bullets were flying.

You're a scientist, Willows, she reminded herself. *You're not a street cop. Wait for backup.*

The world outside had gone silent, though. No sirens wailed in the distance. It was as if the store had been cut off from everything, untethered from the earth and floating alone in the vacuum of space.

No, she couldn't wait. With Tavrin down, Catherine and Brass were on their own.

30

"Liz," Catherine called, remembering Officer Tavrin's first name. "Can you move?"

The downed cop groaned and shifted position on the floor. She pressed her right hand against the wound on her shoulder. "Not much," she said.

"I'm coming," Catherine promised. "Jim, give me cover!"

She started toward the fallen officer. Jim waited until she had covered about half the distance, then fired three shots in the direction from which the last muzzle flashes had come, spaced well apart. They kept the bad guys, who she still believed were Officers Wolfson and Tuva, pinned down long enough for her to get to Tavrin. Moving her might be rough on the officer, but it would be better than getting shot again.

She looped an arm around Tavrin's shoulders and hoisted her up. The officer shrieked in pain and tears sprang from her eyes as Catherine half-dragged her, aided by the slick linoleum, back to relative safety between two of the cashier stands. "Stay put," she urged. "Help's on the way."

Tavrin grabbed her hand and squeezed. "Thanks," she whispered between clenched teeth.

Catherine nodded once, then abandoned her there. She went back around to the front of the register stands and moved at a low crouch as far left as she could. From there she headed for the far wall, racing past aisles of pens and markers and envelopes, paper and poster boards and scrapbooking supplies. At the corner she passed through housewares and into home improvement. So far, no one had shot at her.

Spotting a lightweight hammer, she yanked it off the shelf and went to the end of the aisle. It was a good weight, and she wouldn't have minded having something like it at home. For the moment, though, she had a different use in mind. She cocked her arm back and Frisbee'd it through the air. It spun and spun (the rubberized handle throwing its arc off, curling it left and down sooner than she had hoped). It crashed into a shelf somewhere amidst the kids' clothing and hit the ground with a raucous clatter. Shots came from somewhere off to the right—but not as far back as before, Catherine believed—tearing toward the sound.

So the bad guys were on the move. Good to know.

She was too.

Ducking back to the far aisle, she continued toward the rear of the store. In the furniture section, tall bookcases and heavy desks offered cover. She used it to move closer to the store's center. Catherine was pretty sure Jim was somewhere in the men's clothing, sheltered by shelving units thick with denim jeans and cotton T-shirts. In winter he would have had more protection, with the fleece and hoodies and heavy coats out. No one bought winter clothes in Las Vegas in the summer, not with temperatures hovering in the triple digits. Maybe the occasional adventure tourist preparing for an Antarctic jaunt did, but those people didn't shop at Select Stop Mart.

Lowering to her hands and knees, she sighted across the floor and saw a shoe that seemed out of place. When she found the sock and dress pants connected to it, she knew it was Brass. She crept forward, making sure there were plenty of racks or shelving structures between her and the far side of menswear. "Jim," she whispered. "Behind you."

He twisted, looking back over his shoulder. He didn't quite smile, but acknowledged her with the arch of an eyebrow and a finger raised to his lips. She went closer, stopping behind a circular rack of dress pants. "Where's Antoinette?"

"She was in custody," he said at a low whisper. "But they got here before me. They were taking her out when I showed up. The store security guard tried to play hero and they shot him. Then that other cop barreled in and they got him, too. Antoinette broke free during the shooting and I haven't seen her since."

Catherine scanned her memory, but she hadn't seen Antoinette leaving the store after the first gunshots she'd heard. She had stared long and hard at the woman's picture during the night, and she had known Antoinette might be in the store, so she had studied each face coming out.

"I think she's still in here," said Catherine, "unless she went out the back."

"No. We all started out in back. She took off into the front. We followed, and here we are."

"Backup should be here any second," Catherine said.

"I don't hear any yet."

"I don't either," she admitted.

She was about to ask if he had a plan when a voice sounded. She recognized Wolfson's high-pitched tone. "I see you, Mrs. Blago! Hold it right there!"

"Damn it!" Brass said. He burst from his hiding place and ran toward the voice, toward the rear wall.

Instead of following, Catherine stayed low and dashed toward the front, cutting across to the center at the same time. She stopped in the boys' department, breathing hard, her back against a solid blond oak cube holding shirt-and-tie combinations wrapped in plastic.

From there, peering under the miniature suits, she could see Antoinette O'Brady, frozen close to a swinging door that led into the back area. Wolfson was close to her and moving in, his gun pointed at her head. Brass closed in too, but Wolfson had the advantage. Wolfson stopped with the barrel of his weapon just inches from Antoinette's head.

"Just put that piece on the ground, Captain,"

Wolfson said. "And maybe everybody'll come out of this alive."

"Look," Brass said. "You know how it works. This place will be surrounded inside of two minutes. Then things get complicated. Nobody's going to let you walk away, but if you hurt me or Mrs. Blago, then things get that much worse."

"Don't listen to him!" another voice called. It didn't sound like Tuva, and Catherine didn't recognize it. "There's already a dead security guard and two shot cops. How much worse can it get?"

"Yeah, well, if you had hit her in the first place we wouldn't be here," Wolfson said.

"If you're going to kill us anyway," Jim said, "then I got nothing to lose, do I?"

Catherine didn't like the way the conversation was headed. She decided to bring an end to it while she could.

Brass had not shot at Wolfson while he was standing behind tall, voluptuous Antoinette. Catherine didn't have much of a shot either—she would have to thread it under the boys' suits and between a couple of CD racks. But Antoinette wasn't directly in her line of fire. And Brass was right—these guys were in too deep to let anybody out alive. They had to close it down before backup came, which meant life spans were measured in seconds.

She planted her bottom on the floor, feet spread for balance, and braced her right hand with her left. Took a deep breath and let it out again. Squeezed the trigger.

Her weapon thundered and spat smoke and

flame, and Wolfson's leg exploded just above the knee. Blood splashed onto the floor. Wolfson swore, fired a wild round that spanged off a steel support post, and buckled, clutching at the wound. Gunsmoke stung Catherine's nose and eyes.

She rolled away from her position even as Wolfson fell. Someone unloaded two shots where she had just been, and a third chewed into the wood of the shirt-and-tie cube. She risked another glance and saw Tuva standing near Wolfson, staring her way. He saw Catherine and raised his gun. She ducked back just before he fired, and she felt the cube shudder under the impact of his shot.

"Get me out of here, you no-neck bastard!" Wolfson said.

"I gotta find them first," Tuva said. "I know where that CSI is, but I lost the captain and Mrs. Blago."

Wolfson swore. Catherine moved away from the cube, ducking around a tall unit that held boys' jeans on one side and little girls' T-shirts and casual tops on the other. Movie, TV, and cartoon characters smiled down at her.

From there, she caught a glimpse of Brass and Antoinette. He had her arm clutched in his left hand, his weapon in his right, and he was backing her toward the front of the store. Brass knew where Wolfson and Tuva were. But he had said there were three of them, and so far she had only seen the two dirty cops. Which meant there was another player somewhere—the one whose voice she didn't know.

Tuva made his move. He charged out of cover with a gun in each hand—probably he had taken

Wolfson's—firing wildly. Brass squeezed off a couple of shots and the big man cried out and went down hard, upending a rack of underwear and socks.

"Come on, Antoinette," Brass said, pulling her along faster. He made it sound more like a growl than an invitation. Catherine dashed to their side. "There's another one somewhere, right?"

"Somewhere," Brass said.

"Vic's still in here, I think," Antoinette said.

"Vic Whendt?"

Brass cocked his head toward Catherine and flashed her a quick grin. "I always knew you were good."

"Hey, it's what I do."

"That was some nice shooting, too, Catherine. It's almost like you do this for a living."

"This is a little outside my usual ballpark. But I'm always up for a change of pace." In truth, she was shaken, her stomach like bunched fists. She knew this morning would take some time to get over. And they were far from done.

Catherine recognized the danger they were still in. They had to make it out the front door, which meant crossing the open space between the merchandise and the cashier stands, and then past those to the doorway. She slanted her head toward the door, and Brass nodded his assent.

He put one arm over Antoinette's shoulders. Antoinette's head was tilted forward, gaze on the floor, like she was afraid to meet Catherine's eyes. Her body language was submissive, beaten. She wore a low-cut white knit top and tight dark pants more appropriate for a woman half her age, and the coloring that Catherine had taken for a pattern at first glance, she now realized, was Deke Freeson's dried blood. "I want to get her out of here," said Brass.

"It'd be easier if we knew where Whendt was."

"Yeah."

"Victor Whendt!" she shouted. "Your friends are done. It's time to give it up!"

He didn't respond. As far as she could tell, he had left the store.

But she didn't honestly believe he had. If they got away, then he would be hunted down. If he could finish the three of them, he would have earned Blago's gratitude and he would be rewarded. He could count on a secure retirement, out of the state or out of the country.

There was little downside for Whendt in staying inside the store long enough to kill the three of them.

"So much for that," Brass said. "He didn't bite."

Before stepping out into the open space, Catherine tried to scope out Whendt's best shot at them. If he was in one of the aisles, he could swing out at any moment and open fire. But there were three of them, and he would be vulnerable in those first instants before he got his weapon into position, then again after his first shot gave away his location. She thought Whendt would have himself situated someplace from which he could fire as soon as they were in range. At the far end of the store were glass-fronted coolers full of beer, soda, and dairy products. She didn't think he would be hiding in one of those—not for long, anyway—but if he was, she would never spot him from here. Light from the hanging overhead fixtures glinted off the glass doors, making them opaque from this distance.

Her job was to see things others couldn't. Usually those things were tiny, even microscopic. It was the seeing that was important, though, and the recognition, upon seeing, of what was out of place. A speck of blood, a sliver of skin, the faint parallel tracks of a fingerprint, a hint of soil on the edge of a shard of broken glass. She was good at it, because she had an organized mind that could comprehend patterns. When the pattern was disrupted, she had her target.

Catherine tried to apply the same skills to this situation. She was looking at the macro picture rather than the micro, but the principle was the same. If Whendt was out there, watching for them to step from shelter, possibly already drawing a bead on her head as she hunted for him, his presence would break the pattern of orderly shelves and neat rows.

When the first shots had been fired, people had dropped merchandise in their haste to flee. There hadn't been many people in the store, but Catherine had already seen towels on the floor, a shattered bottle of juice, a spray of colorful greeting cards.

Now she spotted an end cap display of dog food, big fifty-pound bags of it on the bottom shelf, smaller ones above. A couple of the big bags had slid partially onto the floor, and some of the small ones had been piled on top of the large ones remaining in place.

That didn't make sense. If someone had been starting to lift a big bag into a shopping cart when the shooting started, where was the cart? And if they dropped that big bag so that it, and maybe another one, had slid partway off the shelf, they wouldn't have taken the time to stack small bags on the displaced ones.

And they wouldn't have arranged those small bags in such a way that there was a small gap between them and the back of the shelf.

Catherine ducked back behind the rack that shielded them. "Pet food," she said quietly. "He's hiding behind some bags of dog food, maybe eighteen inches off the floor. He's got a weapon aimed this way. If we step out, he'll open fire."

"You got that CSI X-ray vision," Brass said.

"I try."

"Stay here," he told Antoinette. He moved to the edge of the shelf, peered around the edge, and showed just enough of his weapon to get off a shot. He fired. Dog food sprayed onto the floor with a sound like a swift, sudden cloudburst.

"Okay, Whendt!" he called. "Hide-and-seek's over, and you lose. Now throw your weapon out here and show your hands. Do it now!"

In the long silence that followed, Catherine heard sirens approaching. *At last.* Then a .45 automatic skidded out from behind the dog food, spinning across the slick floor. Vic Whendt came out next, hands in the air.

"Put 'em behind your head," Brass ordered. "Get on your knees."

Whendt obeyed. Brass took handcuffs from his pocket and clipped them over Whendt's wrists, holding his weapon on the big man the whole time.

Antoinette waited with Catherine, finally meeting her gaze. There was moisture in her brown eyes and her lower lip quivered a little, but she squared her shoulders and held her chin up. Not proud, but trying for it. She knew the worst was over, for the moment. She also knew people had died because of her. No matter what had happened between her and Blago, that wouldn't be easy to deal with.

"You okay?" Catherine asked.

"No. Not for a long time," she said. "But I will be, I think. You know Jim, I take it."

"Yeah, for years."

"He's one of the good ones, isn't he?"

"One of the best," Catherine said. "They don't come much better."

31

CATHERINE AND BRASS held their badges high and walked through the phalanx of cops approaching the store. Brass turned Victor Whendt over to some of the uniformed officers, then put Antoinette into his unmarked car. Catherine explained that there were still two wounded cops inside, as well as a security guard who was either badly wounded or dead, along with two wounded suspects who were also cops. The police charged into the place, clearing each section, then allowed the paramedics in.

While she waited for Brass, Catherine turned her radio and cell back on. Messages had piled up. Greg Sanders was being checked out by paramedics, having suffered light burns and some bruising and lacerations, but he would be fine. Jesse Dunwood's killer, on the other hand, had not pulled through. Benny Kracsinski's end had come about in the same place as Dunwood's: in an airplane at the Desert View Airport.

Dunwood's death had been more peaceful. Small comfort, but some comfort just the same.

Elsewhere, Nick and Riley were chasing a lead on Dawson Upson. Sam Vega and the LVPD backed them up. Catherine had been informed, but there was little she could do to help at the moment. Anyway, she still needed to talk to Brass.

When Antoinette was in his sedan with the doors closed, Brass sauntered over to where Catherine waited, wearing a hangdog expression. "I guess I owe you an explanation."

"I guess you do," she agreed. "And it better be good. I don't mind saying you had me pretty worried."

He took her elbow and steered her away from where any of the police swarming the area now would be likely to overhear. "I don't know how good it is, but it's the best I've got."

"Is it the truth?"

"Absolutely."

Catherine folded her arms over her chest and gave him the same face she showed Lindsey when she came home three hours late. He noted it and turned away. "I had to do one of those press conferences a few weeks ago, with the mayor. You know, when that toddler was found in a packing crate and we were trying to get an ID on her."

"I remember," Catherine said. "Inez Balboa." It had been the worst kind of case.

"Right. Awful thing. Anyway, a couple nights later, I was leaving work, and this woman walked up to me. Blond, nice body, you know. My age. Dressed to show off. She looked vaguely familiar and I wondered if I'd arrested her once. But as soon as she spoke, I remembered who she was."

"Antoinette Blago."

"Except that I knew her as Antoinette O'Brady, most of a lifetime ago."

"You went to high school together."

He gave Catherine an appreciative glance. "I should have known you'd figure that out."

"You should have. Like you said, Jim, we're good at what we do. We know you were in the motel room where Deke Freeson was killed."

"I'm not surprised. Anyway, she had seen me on TV, at that press conference, and recognized me right off. We dated, back in the day. Pretty hot and heavy for a while there, during my senior year. It turned out that she had a taste for bad boys, and I mean *real* bad. I wasn't enough trouble for her and she dumped me hard. When she came up to me that night, I thought she was coming on to me too, if you get my drift."

"I get it."

They started walking across the parking lot, toward Catherine's SUV, still parked down by the gas station near Deke's car and Liz Tavrin's squad car. Brass's shoulders were hunched, his hands buried deep in his pants pockets. His shirt and suit were wrinkled, but he had no doubt worn them all day and all night, so she wasn't surprised. "I figured maybe she wanted to make it up to me, but it didn't take long to realize that a roll in the hay for old time's sake wasn't what she had in mind."

"That surprises me. Sometimes for old time's sake is the best reason there is."

He shrugged. "Guess I'm still not bad enough for her. Her latest bad boy, as it turns out, is Emil Blago. You know who he is, right?"

"Who doesn't?"

"He's just about as bad a boy as they get."

"So I've heard."

"She's been married to him for twenty-four years now. That's about twenty-three and a half years too long, to hear Antoinette tell it."

"Why did she stay, then?"

Brass moved his shoulders. "Why does any woman stay in a bad situation? Who knows? She had all the material things she could want. Blago was too fond of booze and dope and he screwed around on her, but he told her he loved her, gave her expensive gifts, nice trips, big parties, lavish presents. But she was always surrounded by crime, fear, and violence . . . some of it directed at her. She was afraid to stay and even more afraid to go.

"A couple of years ago they moved to Vegas. He called it a fresh start. In some ways it was, she said, but not in every way. The other women became even more numerous and in her face. He had stopped using drugs and drinking so much, but it didn't take long before he started up again. When he used, he got mean. She figured if they were really making a fresh start, then the best way for her to start over was to get out. But she wasn't sure how to get away clean. He had always kept her in the dark where business was concerned, so she didn't know enough details about his criminal activities to turn state's evidence and get into a witness protection program. Besides, she knew he had people on the police force and, for all she knew, in the district attorney's office and the FBI. She was stuck, with nowhere to go."

"Until she saw you on TV and recognized her former main squeeze."

"Exactly. She said she knew I would never end up on Blago's payroll. I was too much of a good guy. I thought she was gaslighting me, playing me like she did all the boys back in high school."

"She was right, though. You are a good guy. Some things don't change, I guess."

"I guess." Hands in his pockets, Brass kicked a pebble, and for an instant Catherine could imagine him as he might have been in his younger days. She understood why Antoinette might have fallen for him in the first place. "Anyway, my first inclination was to tell her to get lost. She hurt me a lot, way back when, and that had never seemed to bother her. Tell you the truth, I was glad we lost track of each other when I went to Vietnam. I didn't sit around pining for her, I can tell you that. Well . . . maybe a little. For a while. But then I'd remind myself how she tore my heart out, and I'd feel better."

"She was an attractive girl," Catherine said. "She's still good-looking."

"I never said she wasn't, just that I wasn't interested in getting mixed up in her life again. She went around looking for trouble, and whenever it got too deep, she looked for someone to get her out of it. That was always her MO, and I was tired of being the dumb guy who got tangled up in it."

"So what happened?"

"She took me to her place and took off her blouse."

Catherine had started to be proud of him for resisting temptation. This new admission surprised her. "And that's all it took?"

"She showed me her back," Brass said. "She asked Blago for a divorce once, a few years ago. They were in the kitchen. I guess she was searing some steaks in a frying pan. His response was to dump the steaks on the floor and press the bottom of the hot pan against her back."

Catherine winced. "Prince of a guy."

"When she showed it to me, she was weeping. Real tears, not the crocodile kind I had gone there expecting. She went into incredible detail. I could smell the steaks cooling on the tile floor and that special, sharp stink of burning flesh and feel the sizzle of hot grease dripping down the back of her legs."

A shiver sliced through Catherine's body.

"Long story slightly shorter, I told her I would help her," Brass said.

"Of course you did."

Brass looked a little embarrassed. It wasn't something Catherine had seen many times over the years she had known him. "He warned her that if she even brought up the subject again, he would kill her. Flat out."

"She should have had him arrested then."

"It would have been suicide. He wouldn't have stayed away for long, and his people would have known who to blame. They wouldn't have let that slide."

"That's probably true."

"I tried to get her to open up about what she had on him. She told me a few things, but mostly small-time stuff she had picked up here and there. She was right—she didn't know enough to guarantee him a long prison term or herself protective custody. And even if I tried to build a case out of what she did know, as long as I was in the dark about who he has inside the LVPD, I couldn't be sure that she'd be safe. I came to the conclusion that she needed a way out of the marriage that would prevent Blago from looking for her—or at least from finding her."

They reached the Yukon. Catherine leaned against the side that faced into the sun. A light, warm breeze had picked up and she let it waft across her face, bringing the smells of exhaust and fast food and city living with it. "You were stepping into a world of trouble, getting mixed up in something like that."

"Tell me about it."

"You could have reached out."

"To you or Gil, sure. A couple of others. But I thought I could handle it alone. Maybe that was a mistake." He shrugged again. "I got her a new ID in her old name, because I wanted to make sure she'd remember it and be able to respond to it in a pinch. Got her a fake credit card, laid some groundwork. I wanted to move her out of the house first, and then once I knew she was safe, I'd worry about how to discourage Blago. When the day came, I parked her in a cheap motel because I knew that would be the last place Blago would expect her to go. She didn't even like them when she was a kid, and since then she's developed champagne tastes, you might say. I had hired Freeson to keep an eye on her, and made the handoff at the hotel."

His voice caught. Catherine glanced over, but he had turned his face away from her. "I didn't mean for him to get hurt. I thought it would just be a babysitting job. Figured he might get laid, given Antoinette's past habits, but nothing more dangerous than that. You should have seen her face when she walked into that room. She's had money for a long time now, and she pretty much forgot dumps like that existed. It should have been the perfect setup. Just in case, we had a backup plan—Freeson's car parked behind the room, keys under the seat, a piece in the glove. But we weren't supposed to need it."

"Best-laid plans . . ."

"That's right. Once they were safely stashed, I went out to make some travel arrangements. She couldn't go back to Newark, but I have some friends in Montana I thought might be able to take her in for a while. I wasn't gone more than a couple of hours. I still don't know what happened—someone at the motel must have recognized her, I guess. Lot of scumbags hang around that place, which I should have counted on. Somebody made a call, hoping to earn brownie points with Blago."

"And Blago sent Victor Whendt after her. No more fooling around—this time he wanted her dead."

"Just as he threatened. God bless him, Freeson tried, from what I hear."

"He did try," Catherine assured him. "He took a round and returned fire, and then the second round took the back of his skull off and painted the ceiling. But he bought Antoinette time to get out through the bathroom window."

"That was the idea. Glad it worked, except for the price Deke paid."

"He knew the score going in."

"That doesn't make it okay."

"I know, Jim. I'm just saying. We found your fingerprints in the room, and DNA. We knew you, Antoinette, and Whendt had been there. Plenty of other people, too. We just couldn't tell in what order you were there."

"I knew you would figure out I'd been there. At the time I didn't think it would become a crime scene."

"You should have come to me, Jim."

This time he met her gaze, his eyes steady. "I know. It hurt to not return your calls. It wasn't that I didn't trust you. I just couldn't be sure who else might get their hands on whatever you came up with. And I don't trust everyone on the day shift or swing shift as much as I do you. I wanted to know how the investigation was going—once I even called Hodges."

Catherine let out a sharp laugh. "Hodges? He must have been thrilled."

"I think so, yeah. He didn't know much."

"Good. I'd hate to have to suspend him for talking to a suspect."

"He's all right. He may be a kiss-ass, but he's all right."

"I know he is."

"What I wanted was to find Antoinette before

Blago did. Then I could stick with my original plan. Hide her someplace else, lean on Blago, convince him to let her go. I spent all night trying to track her, but I haven't known her for more than thirty years. I couldn't predict her movements well enough. All I knew was that she was on the run."

"She didn't call you?"

"She couldn't know whether or not I had set her up at the motel. By that point, she was as scared of me as she was of everyone else."

"I don't blame her. Think how *alone* she must have felt. Watching Deke get shot, then running all over town with his blood on her. Not knowing if there was anyone she could trust."

Brass moved his big head solemnly. He projected solidity, gravitas. But under the growls and the grins, there was a guy who sincerely cared about victims and who wanted to make people's pain go away. "I had the police radio on all night, just in case. I heard the shoplifting squawk and wondered if it was her. I even started heading this way. But when the guard who had caught her called the cops, she panicked and made him call me, too."

"Because she still trusted you more than she trusted strangers."

"I guess so. He told me he'd picked her up and was holding her for arrest, so I raced over. Apparently I got here a little too late."

"Later than Whendt, anyway. And those cops, Wolfson and Tuva."

"It's a good thing you were around, Catherine. You and that uniform, what's her name."

"Tavrin. Liz Tavrin. They had just spotted Deke's

car, so they were close by. Tavrin was told to wait for me, so she didn't answer the call, and her partner was trying to see where Antoinette might have gone. Maybe he thought, like you, that she might have been the shoplifter."

"Anyway," Brass continued, "far as I can tell, by the time he got here, Wolfson and Tuva were about to take custody of Antoinette. He made a fuss, and they shot him and the security guard who had caught her. I was just walking through the store, on my way to the back, when that happened. Then Whendt showed up and I showed up, got off one shot, and Antoinette ran for it. That's about when you came in."

"We were just outside when the first shots were fired, trying to get the lay of the land."

"It could have been pretty hairy in there. I appreciate the help."

"I think you've left Antoinette alone long enough," Catherine said. She didn't want him to get mushy. "I think you should get a couple of cops you do trust to take her off your hands for a while."

"So I can do what?" he asked.

"So you and *I*," she said, emphasizing the last part, "can go see Emil Blago."

32

NICK AND RILEY MOVED through a wide, shallow desert wash, trying to cover a lot of ground at a fast pace with a minimum of noise. The sun had risen high enough to throw long shadows and to offer the barest hint of the heat the day would bring. For the moment, they moved between pockets of warm and cool, passing from sunlight to shadow and back again.

Tracks from an astonishing variety of creatures pocked the wash's floor. Nick had spotted the marks of birds large and small, lizards, snakes, rabbits, rodents, dogs or coyotes, and something he believed was a bobcat. What he hadn't found were the tracks of a man and a woman traveling together, or any vehicle tracks less than several days old.

Riley had convinced him that her theory was correct. Dawson Upson knew his burial pit was compromised, but since he had never killed there, he should still feel safe at his original killing ground.

And because Melinda Spence—if their operating theory was correct—would be his first actual human kill, he would want that extra edge of psychological security.

On the way over Riley had called in a report, and even now a helicopter flew over the desert searching for Upson. But there was a lot of open desert around Las Vegas—if not much of it left in this neighborhood, as Riley had pointed out—and Upson had his Camry, so there was no guarantee that he did his killing anywhere near his dumping ground.

It was the best shot they had, though. The two of them concentrated on the ground search of this area while the helicopter covered wider swaths of territory and search parties fanned out in other zones. Nick was pleased at how quickly and efficiently a plan had been made and carried out.

"I wish it had stayed dark a little while longer," Riley said. They went from the shade of a patch of blossom-filled desert willows into a bright stretch of sunlight, where no shrubs grew taller than knee-high. They hurried across the open space at a crouch.

"You and everybody else in the city," Nick said. "It's gonna be a hot one."

"No, I mean, when Upson didn't know we were looking for him, the dark gave us an advantage. Especially if he needed light to do his . . . work."

"Nice word for it," Nick said sarcastically. "Work."

"You know what I mean."

"I know. And you're right. We're out in the wide-open spaces now. Depending on where he is, he could see us coming a mile away."

Another thought struck Nick. He must have made a face without realizing it. "What?" Riley asked.

"Nothing."

"It's something. You're pretty transparent, Nick."

He supposed he was, at that. Deceit had never been his strong suit. He liked for people to be straightforward with him, and he offered them the same courtesy. "I was just thinking, I hope he hasn't set himself some sort of arbitrary deadline."

"What . . . like sunrise?"

"Yeah, like that."

They picked up their pace even more.

A hundred yards on, an old dirt road bisected the wash before curving off between two nearly identical rises with steep, rock-strewn slopes. They were the first of a series of hills that grew ever taller as they marched into the distance. Nearing the road, Nick saw something promising in the way the sun lay on the dirt. "Come on," he said, breaking into a jog.

Riley kept pace with him. Soon they were at the road, examining tire tracks that cut straight across the wash and disappeared between the hills in one direction, off toward civilization the other way. "You think they're fresh?" she asked.

Nick squatted and broke the edge off one of the treadmarks. "I think so, but it's hard to tell out here," he said. "There hasn't been any rain in weeks, and not much wind. Tracks can last a long time in the desert. I can show you places where there are still tracks left over from pioneer wagons."

"That is a long time," Riley said, impressed. "But

these are pretty deep. And there aren't any bird tracks or anything else on top of them."

"Yeah, you're right. I'm thinking they're pretty recent."

She stood tall, hands on hips, swiveling at the waist. "Which way do you think they're headed?"

Nick pointed toward flat desert. "That way goes toward the main road." He jerked a thumb the other way, over his shoulder. "This way's into the wilderness. So I'd say we go this way."

"That works for me."

They followed the arc of the road, which really wasn't much more than a place where someone had driven across the desert and then other vehicles had followed in the first one's tracks. It was gouged deep on the sides and rose a bit in the center, where thorny mesquites and stunted shrubs grew. Nick judged that a vehicle wouldn't necessarily need high clearance or four-wheel drive to negotiate it, but both features would make the journey more comfortable.

Inside the canyon cutting between the two low hills, the sun had not yet penetrated and the air remained cool. The roadway cut up through a couple of terraces as it climbed out of the canyon, growing rockier and more precarious almost by the yard.

Around another bend, an empty silver Toyota Camry was pulled off the road on a relatively flat, shady spot. A tall mesquite partially shielded it from the air, and it was parked close to the base of the hill.

"I guess you called it, Nick."

Riley kept her voice low, barely audible three feet

away. Nick answered in the same manner. *"You* called it, Riley. We might still be at his house looking for clues if you hadn't insisted on coming out here."

"We haven't found him yet," she reminded him.

"We're closer than we were a few minutes ago, though." He scanned the landscape, looking for any sign of Upson or Melinda Spence. On this side of the hills the desert was wilder, with more rises and gullies, thicker growths of yucca and mesquite and cholla, and even more desert willows than on the low side. The hills came closer together, marching toward higher ones in the near distance.

"I've got some footprints," Riley said. She had circled around the car, about eight feet away from it, where the dirt was softer than on the packed road. "Scuff marks, too."

Nick hurried to her side. Sure enough, two people had left footprints leading away from the car. A male in sneakers, and a woman in smooth-soled shoes with squared-off toes. Every few steps, at least at the beginning, she had apparently offered at least token resistance and he had dragged her along. Digging her heels in had cut deeper furrows in the earth. The tracks led into a canyon wedged between two steeper, taller mounds.

"Let's go over the hill," Riley whispered.

"Over it?"

"If he's in there, he might be watching for someone coming along his trail. Going up and over, we might be able to catch him by surprise, if he's in there, or spot him if he's not. We'll get the jump on him."

"Literally," Nick said with a quick grin. "Okay, I'm game."

They started up the southern slope of the hill. At first the short ascent was gradual, but nearer the top they found themselves leaning forward, grabbing embedded rocks and well-rooted plants for hand-holds. Breaking leaves and stems, combined with the warming rays of the rising sun, sent waves of spicy aroma wafting around them.

As they reached the peak, they stayed low to keep stray shadows from giving away their position. The far side dropped sharply into the canyon. Nick was glad they had climbed the side they did, since the other side would have posed a far greater challenge. There were a few plants to hold on to—most thorny or barbed, as desert flora usually was—but otherwise the slope was covered in small, loose stones, with a few larger flat ones scattered about, until it reached a sheer cliff.

Dawson Upson paced in the shade, in a clear, flat stretch near the foot of the opposite hill. Skinny and anxious, he had dumped the blazer he wore in the surveillance video, and his porkpie hat was no-where to be seen. Melinda Spence was bound with rope and duct tape, lying on her side near a low shelf that marked the beginning of the rise on the canyon's other side. She was conscious, wriggling and writhing but not really fighting hard against her bonds. Her cheeks and forehead had been cut. Fine red lines traced against her brown flesh and fresh drops dampened the soil beside her.

A stainless-steel razor blade knife glinted in Upson's fist, the kind you cut open packages with.

Nick was surprised—he had expected Upson to use more exotic tools. He muttered as he walked, more to himself than to Melinda. Nick only caught snatches of what he said: " . . . cut you. Cut you up. Gonna make you bleed, make you bleed and beg and cry and bleed . . ."

Abruptly, he spun around and dropped to his knees beside Melinda, between her and the rock shelf. She whimpered as he brought the blade close to her face again. "Shut up just shut your mouth!" he cried, brandishing the blade before her terrified eyes. He sounded like he might cry. He had been screwing up his courage all this time, Nick realized. All the animals he had killed, the women he had abducted . . . they were just setting the stage for this moment. Now that it had arrived, he was facing the fact that murdering a human being wasn't like those others at all.

Still, he couldn't be allowed to make another cut.

Nick drew his service pistol, steadied his aim with his left hand, and shouted: "Las Vegas Police! Put the knife down and step away from her!"

Startled, Upson let the knife fly from his hand. He stared up the hill at Riley and Nick. His mouth fell open and he started to raise his hands.

But a smile that Nick didn't like spread across his face, and as his hands elevated past his waist, he snaked one arm behind his back. When he brought it back out, he had a black steely pistol in his hand, pointed at Melinda's head.

"Don't be stupid, Upson," Riley said. "Put the gun down before you hurt someone."

Nick believed he could drop Upson with one

shot. But Upson was still partially shielded by Melinda's trussed-up body, so if he missed, a stray round or a ricochet off the rocks could injure the person he was trying so hard to save.

"You put yours down," Upson said. "I *will* kill her if you don't. A shot to the skull isn't exactly what I had in mind when I started all this, but it'll have to do. I'll live with it, anyway." A nervous giggle burst from his lips. He wiped saliva from his chin with the back of his left hand, struggling to bring his laughter under control. "Even though she won't."

"You won't live for long," Riley warned.

"Please. You won't kill me. You're all about the law. You'll want me to stand trial, and all that happy nonsense. Justice, you call it. But me . . . I've been waiting a long time for this. A very, very long time. One way or another, today I will kill a human being. I'm beyond anything your justice can dish out."

"If the prospect of dying doesn't bother you, then I might as well shoot," Riley said. "I mean, you're calling the play, right?"

He's not going to shoot, Nick told himself. Yes, he had shot some of the animals found in the pit. But those were early ones. All the later ones had been killed with a blade. He had tried both methods, and he still carried a gun, but only as backup. He hadn't used one on the women in Boston, according to the reports. A gun was meant primarily for distances, and it was the proximity of Upson's victims that excited him, the feeling of the creature dying in his hands. Maybe he even thrilled to the warm, wet splash of blood on his slender fingers.

Shooting would wipe away the things that appealed to him about killing. It wasn't simply the final result he was after, it was the process. Killing someone with a gun was easy enough, but he hadn't done it yet.

Nick believed he wouldn't shoot. But could he take that chance? Or should he and Riley shoot first, hoping they didn't accidentally hit Melinda?

It was Melinda who provided the answer for him.

33

BOUND AS SHE WAS, Melinda still had some freedom of movement. In an effort that must have taken unimaginable courage, bound and gagged and with the madman who had abducted her pointing a gun at her head, she kicked out with her duct-taped legs. The impact didn't hurt Upson, but it knocked him off balance. He threw both arms out to steady himself. The instant the gun barrel veered away from Melinda's head, Nick made his move.

He took a couple of skidding steps on the rock-strewn slope and jumped, aiming for the low shelf right behind Melinda. Upson saw him coming, whipped the gun around, and squeezed off a single panicked shot. The round took a bite of the cliff face behind Nick, spraying dust and rock chips.

Then Nick crashed into him, hard, bringing his arm down solidly against Upson's wrist. Upson cried out and the pistol flew from his hand. Nick, still off balance, got a grip on Upson's T-shirt and fell back-

ward, pulling the thin young man with him. The
two of them rolled over Melinda and Nick landed
on his back on the hard canyon floor. Upson's bony
knee dug into Nick's chest and sharp rocks stabbed
into his kidneys.

With the breath squeezed out of him, Nick lost
his purchase on Upson's shirt. The young man
pushed off Nick's solar plexus, gained his footing,
and broke into a sprint. Nick scrambled to his feet as
Riley reached the bottom of the hill, having taken a
considerably more sensible route to the bottom.

"Make sure she's okay," Nick told Riley. He took
off after Upson, his calves still smarting from the jolt
they had taken upon landing.

Upson was lithe and fast. His long legs scissored,
eating up desert ground and carrying him away in a
hurry. Nick raced behind him. He kept thinking he
was making up ground, but every plant he encoun-
tered seemed determined to slow him down, tearing
and clawing at his pants and shoes. Upson led him
deeper into the canyon, across a narrow valley, and
toward higher, steeper hills on the far side. Nick
didn't know if Upson was familiar with this area, or
if they had left his comfort zone behind, but he
showed no signs of uncertainty.

On the flatter ground of the valley, Nick was able
to pour on more speed. Upson's breathing became
increasingly ragged. Nick was starting to feel the
same way, as if his lungs might burst, leaving him
shredded, popped balloons in his chest. But he kept
the pressure on, kept gaining. Dirt that Upson
kicked up pattered against Nick's legs. Finally,

Upson stumbled as he descended a few inches into a wash and Nick took advantage of the moment, launching himself into the air. The instant of flight and the collision with Upson's running legs brought back fleeting memories of Nick's high school football days in Texas, where high school football was a major event. He remembered roaring crowds, anxious parents, lissome cheerleaders shaking pompoms with abandon, and city officials, teachers, administrators, and what seemed like every kid in the city packing the stands.

Then he and Upson went down in a tangle of kicking legs and flailing arms, flying dust and rocks with keen edges. Nick held on to Upson's legs and clambered to his knees. Upson writhed and twisted, managing to turn around and release a series of punches to Nick's stomach, ribs, and chest. At the same time he kicked like a wild burro. Nick tried to apply downward pressure to keep him put. But when he reached for the handcuffs on his belt, Upson kicked him in the solar plexus, his hiking-booted foot feeling like a cannonball to the gut, and squirmed right out of his grasp.

Nick sucked in the pain, dropped the cuffs, and lunged after him.

Upson wasn't backing away, though. He pulled a knife from someplace, either a switchblade or a gravity knife, and lashed out with it. The sharp blade ripped through Nick's shirt, and a moment later a sharp sting burned into him. Blood soaked the torn edges of fabric, a thin line at first, but spreading quickly. Nick fought through the sudden distraction, but he lost his hold on Upson once again. The world took a crazy tilt, and someone started to draw a curtain across the sun.

Upson shot to his feet and started running again.

He only made it inches before his high forehead collided with the barrel of Riley's gun. He staggered and fell to his knees. The gash that her gun barrel opened up bled ferociously.

Nick grabbed Upson and turned him facedown in the dirt. He wrestled Upson's hands behind his back. When he leaned over to retrieve his cuffs, the world threatened to spin out of control, but he blinked and righted it again. He snapped the handcuffs over Upson's scrawny wrists.

Riley extended a hand and helped Nick to his feet, and Nick, still holding on to the chain linking the cuffs, brought Upson along. Since Upson couldn't reach the wound in his head to mop away the blood, it flooded into his eyes.

Nick couldn't bring himself to be too concerned. He looked at Riley. "I thought you were staying with Melinda."

"And let you have all the fun? You said to make sure she was okay, and considering what she's been through, she seems to be. Anyway, she's not going anywhere, and there's no way I was letting this creep get away from us."

"What were you gonna do, shoot him?" Greg had told Nick how angry she'd been about finding those animal skeletons, and he'd seen glimpses of that while searching Upson's room and the desert with her.

"If absolutely necessary, yes. But I was hoping he

would see the weapon and stop. Who knew he would dash headlong into it?"

"Hey, I'm bleeding here!" Upson complained. "It stings my eyes!"

"And we're supposed to feel sorry for you?" Riley asked. "After what you've done?"

Nick turned him around and started marching him back toward Melinda and the vehicles. "What I've done? I haven't done anything," Upson complained. "I tied a girl up and scratched her a little. Big deal."

"It is a big deal," Nick said. "A very big deal. Which you'll find out at your sentencing, if you don't clue in before that."

"And we know about the rest of it," Riley added. "We found the animals you killed and buried. We know about the abducted women in Boston. We know you drugged Melinda's drink at the Palermo."

Upson blinked blood from his eyes and stared at her. "You . . . you can't know . . . How could you . . ."

"If I were you, Dawson Upson," Nick interrupted, wanting to make sure this case went to trial with no complications, "I would keep my mouth shut until I had a lawyer present. You ever hear of the Miranda warning? Because you're about to become very familiar with it. You have the right to remain silent . . ."

34

AN ANGRY BUZZ, like giant wasps defending a hive, emanated from the Clark County Raceway. Crowds of people flocked from the parking lot into the stands. Inside, at ground level, the noise was almost unbearable, as race cars ran practice laps, pit crews used pneumatic tools, and people shouted at one another just to be heard over the general din. Heat waves rising off the black pavement of the track shimmered the air, lending it a thick, liquid quality that partially obscured the cars on the far straight-away. The air was tinged with oil and racing fuel, burnt rubber and tobacco and spilled beer. No won-der Victor Whendt's wife, with her sensitive nose, didn't like it here.

Catherine wasn't crazy about it, either. But Desert Palm Hospital had already released Greg, and Nick and Riley had brought in Dawson Upson and re-turned Melinda Spence to her grateful family, so it was going to take a lot more than some stinky air and unpleasantly loud noise to ruin her mood.

Emil Blago stood on the tarmac just outside his team's pit area. He was a short, heavyset man, with silver-streaked black hair that curled around his collar and receded from the top of his head at the same time, as if it had always been the same length but was shifting down under the pull of gravity. Sun blasted down on his scalp, where a deep tan didn't hide the age spots. He wore a white tracksuit with red and green stripes, white sneakers, and wraparound shades, and he stood with his feet spread apart, his hands clasped behind his back, like he expected a gust of wind to try to knock him over. His attention was riveted on the cars speeding past him.

Catherine Willows and Jim Brass badged their way onto the track. As they made for Blago, a couple of bruisers blocked them, big guys who could have worn refrigerator cartons for coats, and who looked about as intellectually proficient as the cardboard that made up those cartons.

"Where you going?" one of them asked. The smaller of the two, he wasn't much taller than a mature oak tree, and probably weighed marginally less. He had lost most of his teeth along the road of life, and many of those remaining were clad in gold.

"To see Blago," Brass said. "Not that it's any of your business."

"Nobody bothers Mr. Blago on the track."

"And anything that happens here is our business," the bigger one said.

"I'm not nobody," Brass said. He showed his

badge. Catherine did the same. "And I will bother him. You can watch me if you want. From a distance."

"No," the bigger guy said. Trying to keep both of his shoulders in view at the same time was like trying to watch a tennis game. He had more teeth than his smaller friend, but adolescent acne had left his cheeks patchworked with black scars. Catherine wasn't sure which thug was less pleasing to the eye. *Sometimes life gives us hard choices,* she thought.

"Yes," Brass countered. "You see these badges? They're like all-access passes. We go anywhere we want, and people who try to interfere with us only go one place."

"He means prison," Catherine said, because it didn't look like the two men understood and she didn't want them to strain themselves trying to figure it out. She was pretty sure neither one was the attorney that Paul the estate manager had mentioned.

"Maybe you can see Mr. Blago after the race. He don't like to be disturbed before, while he's concentrating."

"We'll see him now, thanks," Brass said. He offered one of the least sincere smiles Catherine had ever seen and put away his badge. As he did, he flapped his jacket back and showed his gun. "I don't think he's driving today, anyway." He started toward Blago.

The smaller giant reached a meaty paw toward Brass's chest. Brass put up a warning hand, blocking him. "You're going to want to think long and hard before you lay a hand on me," he said. "Because if you touch me, I'll consider it assault. And once you're in the system—I'm guessing not for the first time—then we'll turn over every rock you ever stepped on and we'll see what else we can find out about you. My guess is you'll be back on the street by the time you're ninety, so maybe you're not too worried about it. Ninety's the new eighty, from what I hear."

The huge hand hovered for another moment, then fell away. Brass smiled again, this time almost seeming to mean it.

The giants stepped aside. As Brass and Catherine passed between them, Catherine thought she knew how the followers of Moses felt walking on the floor of the just-parted Red Sea.

"Mr. Blago!" Brass shouted.

Blago turned around. The wraparounds were pitch-black, but those parts of his face Catherine could see were without expression except for the slightest jutting of his lower lip. He didn't speak.

"I'm Captain Jim Brass, Las Vegas Police Department," Brass said. "This is CSI Supervisor Catherine Willows. We need a minute of your time."

"I don't even know why you bother with a badge," Blago said. "An infant would know you were a cop with a single glance. A blind infant, at that. You *smell* like a cop." He eyed Catherine; she could feel the laser beam of his eyes even through the shades. "You, not so much." He returned his attention to Brass. Catherine already wanted a steaming shower, in spite of the day's increasing warmth. "Me, I'm always happy to meet law enforcement officers of any sort," Blago continued. "What can I do for you folks?"

"I need to talk to you about Antoinette," Brass said.

"My wife? Have you met her? She's lovely."

"I know. I *have* met her."

Blago's lips parted and a wedge of pink tongue swept across them. "I got it. So you're the guy."

"Which guy is that?"

"The one who got away."

"That's not exactly how I'd put it."

"It's how she makes it sound. You'd be amazed how it makes a guy feel to hear his wife constantly saying, 'If I had only stayed with James, things would be so different.'"

"That doesn't sound much like the Antoinette I knew."

"Maybe." Blago did the tongue thing again. "But you knew her a long time ago, right? People change."

"I've heard that. I don't see much evidence of it in my line of work. Once a scumbag, always a scumbag, that's my experience."

A couple of race cars, one red and one black, roared up the straightaway toward them, and Blago raised his voice. "I feel like we're getting kind of personal here!"

"We definitely are," Brass replied. "And we're going to get more so!"

"Maybe we should go into my office."

The cars disappeared around the first turn, and the noise level dropped again. "I think we're fine right here," Brass said.

"Have it your way. Why don't you tell me what you want?"

"Right to the point," Brass replied. "I like that. Here's the thing. Antoinette's leaving you. She's already gone. You will never see her again."

"Should I be calling my lawyer?" Blago asked. "Alienation of affection or something like that. I can sue you for that, right? In civil court? All I have to do is show that you moved back into her life with your badge and scooped her right into the sack."

"I'm not sleeping with her, Blago. That's not what this is about."

Blago grinned. "I thought you knew Antoinette, but maybe not. If it's not about sex, then what the hell is it about?"

Brass moved closer to him, so their heads were inches apart, and lowered his voice. Blago had to strain to hear. "It's about frying pans. It's about decades of abuse and suffering. It's about a troubled but decent woman finding herself married to a dirtbag loser with a defective cerebral cortex and no moral compass."

Blago licked his lips again, and when he spoke, spittle flecked his chin. "You're calling me a loser, Mr. Can't-Wait-for-My-Pension? Remember, I got some rights here. The law is pretty clear about someone coming between a husband and wife—"

Brass raised a hand to Blago's collar, then dropped it again without actually making contact. Catherine could read the tension in his spine, the set of his chin, the edge in his voice. "No. You don't get to claim the protection of the law. You forfeited that right, Blago. The only thing you need to know about all this is that you'll be getting divorce papers from her lawyer. He won't be a Las Vegas lawyer, he'll be from some other city, but that won't be where she is. You'll sign those papers right away, giving her whatever she asks for, which I assure you won't be unreasonable. You will never appear in court together. And you will never go looking for her. That's a key thing here. You will not search for her, or send anyone else to look for her."

"I don't know who you think you are, Brass, but I got friends who can—"

"I don't want to hear about your friends. I don't care if you know judges and senators. You probably do. So what? None of that matters here, because we're talking personally, not professionally. Just two guys ironing out a difficult situation."

The cars had started up the straightaway again, and Brass raised his voice to be heard over their deafening approach. "Those cars go pretty fast! I bet it would hurt a lot to be hit by a car going that fast!"

Blago tore his sunglasses from his head. His eyes were small and squinty. Catherine was reminded of a cartoon mole emerging from his burrow. "Are you threatening me?" he asked as the din faded.

"Not at all, Mr. Blago. If I wanted to threaten you, you wouldn't have to ask. Here's how that would go: It would be something like me describing how if you ever bothered Antoinette in any way, yourself or through any intermediaries, I would hear about it, and then I'd see that your legs were tied to one car heading south and your arms to another car heading north, and we'd get to see which parts were glued on better." Brass gave one of his special grins, the ones Catherine expected small fish might see on a shark's face right before becoming breakfast. "Now *that* would be a threat."

"Hey, you're a cop!" Blago sputtered. "You're a cop too, lady. You're standing right here! He can't just threaten a citizen like that! Aren't you gonna arrest him?"

Catherine shook her head and poked one of her ears with a finger. "Those cars are awfully loud," she said. "I can't hear a thing you boys are saying."

Blago put the shades back on, crossed his arms over his chest, and turned to look at the racetrack. "I got a busy day," he said. "You got no more official business, you need to get off the track."

"We're going," Brass said. "You just remember our little talk. And by the way . . . I'm going to be keeping an eye on you from now on. So you'd better behave yourself—one slip and you'll find out how it feels to live in a cage."

Blago didn't look at him. He said something but it was lost in the whine of a pneumatic lug wrench from the nearby pits. Catherine didn't imagine it could be very interesting anyway.

Brass was quiet until they reached his car. Once they were settled inside it, seat belts fastened, he looked over at her. "Thanks, Catherine."

"Are you kidding? I wouldn't have missed it. Do you think it'll work? You think he won't go looking for her?"

Brass shrugged. "Who knows? If I understood

how the mind of a guy like that operated, I'd have to give myself a lobotomy just to get to sleep at night. I hope he won't, but there aren't any guarantees. Especially when you're dealing with head cases."

"But you think scaring him is the best way to go?"

"Well, I can't afford to buy him, and I don't think there are many things his kind responds to. Fear and money are two of the old standbys, though."

"That's true."

"Anyway, I appreciate you coming along. Backing me up"—he let that hang in the air for a moment, then added—"and volunteering. I felt like it would be presumptuous to ask you. It's the kind of thing I might have asked Gil to do, but . . ."

"But I'm a woman. The tender sex."

Brass didn't say anything.

"Presume away, Jim. We might have different equipment, but Gil and I are alike in a lot of ways. Maybe he's rubbed off on me."

"What is it you CSIs are always talking about?" Brass asked. "Locard's exchange principle?"

"Any contact between a person and another person, place, or object leaves behind traces," she summarized.

"That's right. I think maybe it works with people, too. Gil has left traces on all of us."

So have you, she thought. *So has everyone I've worked with—Warrick, Sara, Nick, Greg, and the rest of them. They've all left more than traces, but Gil Grissom has left the most.* "Big traces," she said simply. "And lack of patience for guys like Emil Blago is one of them.

Anyway, he left me in charge, so that makes it my business." She didn't add that she was glad Brass was still part of her extended crime lab family. She'd had her doubts about him during the night, and probably she shouldn't have. She hadn't had much choice, though. She had to listen to the stories the evidence spun for her. As she had told Lindsey, you couldn't know what was in someone's heart, you could only go by the facts available to you.

The facts had pointed to Brass's involvement in a murder. Now they didn't.

Now they pointed to a soft spot inside a hard man—a spot that would prompt him to put himself on the line for someone who had hurt him, decades before. Someone who had become a stranger to him, but who had once meant something.

So how could Catherine not be there when he needed her?

She was only pleased that he had given her the chance.

"One more thing," she said. The raceway was dropping away behind them. The sun was high in the sky, throwing shadows that were compact and dark. "Wolfson and Tuva, those two cops from Select Stop Mart? They should be the first ones you interrogate when you try to build a case against Blago."

"Who says I'm building a case against Blago?"

"I'm just saying . . . I have a feeling they'll be easier to roll over than Vic Whendt. They're not so tough, and Whendt knows he'll go down for murder one, but they're only accessories. By now they know they're going to do time, so they'll probably beg to tell what they know."

"Well, if he's got people inside the department, we have to root them out," Brass said. "Stands to reason."

"Stands to reason, Jim."

"Wolfson and Tuva, you say?"

"Lee Wolfson and Garland Tuva. That's right."

Brass showed his shark's smile one more time. "I'm already looking forward to my first conversation with them. Hey, you want to be in on it?"

"Jim," Catherine said, "I thought you'd never ask."

About the Author

JEFF MARIOTTE is the award-winning author of more than thirty novels, including *Missing White Girl, River Runs Red*, and *Cold Black Hearts* (all as Jeffrey J. Mariotte); horror epic *The Slab;* teen horror quartet *Witch Season; CSI: Miami—Right to Die;* and more, as well as dozens of comic books. He's a co-owner of specialty bookstore Mysterious Galaxy in San Diego, and lives in southeastern Arizona on the Flying M Ranch.

For more information, please visit www.jeffmariotte .com.